BECK

Book 3 in the Corp Security Series
A novel by Harper Sloan

Beck

Harper Sloan

Cover and Interior Designed by MGBookCovers
Cover Photo by Michael Stokes Photography
Editing by Katie Mac

ISBN 13: 978-1494735920
ISBN 10: 149473592X

Disclaimer:

This book is not suitable for younger readers. There is strong language, adult situations, and some violence.

To contact Harper:
Email: authorharpersloan@gmail.com
Facebook:
www.facebook.com/harpersloanbooks
Goodreads:
www.goodreads.com/harper_sloan
Twitter: @harpersloan
Instagram: @harper_sloan
Pinterest: www.pinterest.com/harpersloan

BECK PLAYLIST

Follow on Spotify

Sam Grow- Shot of Crown
Sam Grow- Fall to Me
Miguel- Adorn
Creed- With Arms Wide Open
The Lumineers- Stubborn Love
Bonnie Raitt- I Can't Make You Love Me
Justin Timberlake- Drink You Away
The CO- Keep it Together
John Newman- Love Me Again
Avicii- Addicted to You
Halestorm- Beautiful With You
Jason Mraz- I Won't Give Up
Papa Roach- Last Resort
Johnny Cash- Hurt
Seether- Broken
A Great Big World- Say Something
Ciara- Love Sex Magic
System of a Down- Toxicity
Saving Abel- Addicted
Little Mix- Cannonball
Bruno Mars- Gorilla

Dedication:

To Danielle Calcote.

For keeping me sane and laughing at my insane! Even if your taste in sweaters is questionable… I still consider myself blessed to have you as a friend, beta, and right-hand!

PROLOGUE

"Denise, you need to stop this nonsense. A girl your age needs to show some maturity and stop being so needy. You are perfectly capable of keeping yourself occupied. This is a big night for your father; you could try and be a little supportive." She turns her perfectly painted face back to the mirror, applying more of her make-up. I have always wondered how she is able to get all that make-up on when her face never really moves. Her weekly appointments at the spa take care of the wrinkles that I've never been able to find.

"But Mother, tonight's my chorus recital at school," I whisper meekly. Even at thirteen, I know I should stand up for myself, but I just can't seem to do that with my mother, the ice queen. "How am I supposed to get there?"

Before I can react, her hand cracks against my cheek. "Don't be such an ungrateful brat, Denise. Some children can only dream of living the life we have given you. I don't want to hear another word from you tonight. Go on up to your room."

Blinking back the wetness that rushes to my eyes, I back up slowly, keeping my eyes trained on my mother. I don't realize I have been holding my breath until I bump into the hard, unforgiving body standing behind me.

"What have you done now, Denise?" My father's deep baritone rumbles through the room. A cold ribbon of fear snakes down my back. I brace myself for his anger as I turn to face him.

"I'm sorry, Father. I just wanted to ask Mother about my chorus recital. I'm supposed to be at the school in an hour." I don't dare break eye contact with my father. No one would dare. He demands your full attention and respect. I will give him my attention, but before I started middle school, I learned he didn't deserve my respect.

"You stupid little girl. I've told you, extracurricular activities should be things that can further your career. Things like *chorus* aren't going to take you on the path to greatness. First thing Monday, I want you to speak with your teachers about dropping that."

My insides seize, because I knew better than to even mention the recital, and I still did it. I should just fake a sickness Monday at school. For the last year, I've been successful in keeping my 'fun time' hidden from my parents. They don't care what I am doing. They don't want me, so they've never even noticed.

"Am I understood, Denise?" His tone has a sharper edge to it, and I know this is not a point to drag my feet on.

"Yes, Sir," I reply. "May I be excused?" I just want to get away. Away from their room, them, and this life that they say I should be grateful to have. Who would be grateful for this? Two parents that don't want you. All the money in the world, but no happiness? I would rather be living in the slums.

Walking as quickly as possible, I make fast work of the maze of hallways and enter my room. Only when the door closes do I let out my breath and allow my body to relax. Ever since I've been old enough to know the difference, I've known that my parents don't like me. No, they don't just 'not like' me... They hate me. I am the accident that should have been terminated, or so they remind me often enough. I don't even think my mother cares either way. She just wants the life my father has given her, regardless of the fact that even her own daughter knows he is sleeping with the hired help.

And my father? My father is the reason that I know you can never trust a boy. Never allow one into your heart. They only care about one thing and one thing only. Themselves. Every man in my life has let me down. My grandfather died before he was successful in taking me away from my parents. My father is as evil as they come. And just today, my boyfriend, Toby, said he wanted to go out with Malinda 'I have bigger boobs than my eighteen-year-old sister' Monroe.

There will never be a boy in the world that can make me forget that the only person I can count on is me. I can't wait to get away from this place. The day I turn eighteen, I am running as fast as I can. I've made sure that I get good grades, and will have my pick of schools to choose from. Because the first day I leave this hell, I am going to be a new person. I am going to be happy. I am going to be loved. And, I am going to find people to share my life with that want to be around me.

But I will never, ever, trust a boy.

PART ONE
Meetings
&
Beginnings

CHAPTER 1
Dee

There has never been a moment in my life when I've felt well and truly loved. Accepted and wanted. My parents hadn't wanted me. I'm the accident that should have been 'taken care of', the disgraceful child whose silence they bought. After all, when you have as much money as my father, why should you actually show emotion or feelings?

My father, Davison Bennett Roberts, III, is a third generation banker. His father's father opened up the local branch, and the rest was, as they say, history. I don't remember my father ever really 'liking' me. Hell, I don't even really remember him liking my mother, either. He worked and worked, and when he finished he worked some more. When he wasn't at the bank, he was in his office at home. And when he wasn't consumed with whatever it was that he did, he was off screwing the hot little secretary, or teller, or college co-ed slut.

Always absent from my life.

Always reminding me, sometimes without his words, how un-important I was.

He was the first strike against mankind, in my eyes.

All the resentment that I held towards men, and my reluctance to start a relationship now, could all be traced back to the man who called himself my father.

The worst part, though... with all his busyness, and lack of care, he still made time to bring the wrath of Davison Roberts, III down on me at every opportunity. My 4.0 grade point average was never going to be good enough to please him. The extracurricular educational clubs that I was allowed to join were never going to help me amount to anything. Plain and simple, *I* was just never going to be enough.

He didn't want me, but he still wanted to sling his holier than thou attitude and self-righteousness my way. I'm not sure, even to this day, what he was attempting to teach me. He made it clear from early on that he would never allow a woman to run his company, so I was convinced he just liked to beat me down.

Literally.

He didn't take his hands to me often, but when he did, it wasn't pretty. And that was strike two against mankind.

Growing up, I didn't have many people that I would consider real friends. I had plenty of playmates who were the children of my father's associates. Those were the sort of children that my parents had allowed me to befriend. Those friends didn't want me because of me, but because of who my father was and how much money he had. You know, the kind of kids that walked around in their designer clothing, their backs so straight you knew that they had to have a rod shoved so far up their assholes that there was no way that they would be anything but fake.

As I got older, I was once again reminded that people only saw what they could gain by being around me to get closer to my father. Boys never wanted to date 'me'; they wanted to date my family's money and connections. The closer I got to graduating high school, the more painfully obvious it became that the boys I dated would never really like me. They were only there to hopefully gain something towards their future careers by being with me.

The only people that mattered to them were... themselves.

And there you have strike three.

I could only trust myself. I made a promise to myself that when I was old enough, I was going to get out of here and finally, be me. No one was going to tell me whom I could have as friends. Men wouldn't know who my father was so they would love me as me, and not as the daughter of Davison Bennett Roberts III. I would find people who loved me... for me.

And I was never going to need a man.

I am Denise Ann Roberts. Strong, proud, and independent. A loyal friend, godmother, and I radiate fucking happiness so that people will never see how lonely I really am.

Funny thing about these masks that people put on. I look like the happiest woman in the world. I look like I have everything that I want out of life. That everything is perfect. And that is exactly what I want people to see. But, inside? Inside, I'm dying. I'm not happy. I have amazing friends, and I know that they love me, but I am completely alone. Just like I have been my whole life, and the best part, the big kicker in my ass... I only have myself to blame.

Why? Because I have pushed the one man that I love away from me, and I keep pushing, even when he keeps coming back for more. I've found the one man out of millions that might be able to prove me wrong. That might be able to love me back unconditionally and never change.

And every single day that I have to pretend to be okay, to be happy, it's slowly killing me.

Three Years Earlier

Two long years and finally, finally, Izzy is living. Her beautiful smile is plastered all over her face, and that twinkle is back in her eyes. Nothing but worry has consumed me since that day she called me to come get her from Brandon. To come save her.

I had slowly watched her leave me. No, not in the sense that she wasn't my friend, but she was stolen from me. I watched her become the me that I used to be. A shell of my former self, afraid to move because of the people that tugged the strings to my life.

The last couple of days haven't been pretty. Between that bastard ex-husband sending Izzy a twisted package, and her almost shutting down, I've been so worried that she would revert back into the depression that she has been slowly waking up from.

When she opened that package and I saw the panic and fear take over, I didn't know what to do or how to help. The first thing I did was call Greg, the best 'big brother' that a girl could ever dream for. He's been right there with me, every step of the way, making sure that Izzy's okay and that we're both safe. Whatever Greg did earlier seems to be the wakeup call that she needed. Or maybe it's just the reminder he gave her that she wasn't allowed to check out.

Whatever the reason, here we are at Club Carnal, celebrating my best friend's thirtieth birthday and the anniversary of what is arguably the worst date in her life.

Even with all the unknown and lingering fear in her life, my girl is happy, and we are living life tonight. And, enjoying every damn second as if it is our last.

****

Damn I'm horny.

I've been eyeing the hot bartender for the last fifteen minutes. I had decided earlier on today that I would finally end this damn dry spell tonight, and he seems like a decent choice for a quick, one-night stand. Lord knows, I need a little action tonight or my vagina might just run off and join the circus. I snort at the thought and gear up to hopefully secure my orgasm for the night, one that doesn't require batteries.

Right when I get ready to open my mouth and invite him for a night of fun, I hear the most delicious voice come from behind me. A deep, southern drawl that can be heard over the pounding beat of the music, wraps around me like a warm blanket of sin, and my poor neglected vagina perks right up and says 'hey... me, pick me'!

I quickly close my mouth, and shift on my stool so that I can turn and face him. Oh. My. God. He has got to be the most attractive man I have ever seen. He looks like a walking ad for pure, raw sex. The kind of sex that stays with you for days, even months afterwards because it was *that* good. It looks as if someone has taken every panty-melting feature you could dream up, and stuck them on his legs. And damn, what legs those are.

He towers over Izzy, which really isn't that hard to do, but he towers over me, too, and *that* is hard. It's difficult to tell from my perch on the bar stool, but I'm guessing he's got at least six inches on my five-foot-eight. My fingers itch to run themselves through his messy brown hair. Like a movie reel, I can almost see it playing out, him between my thighs as I pull him closer to my center, holding on to his hair, and riding the wave. I have to clench my legs together at the thought of his thick lips licking and sucking against my core.

I quickly shake myself out of my lust-induced fog, hoping that no one noticed that I almost came on the spot just from looking at this stranger. I would've gotten away with it, but when I shift on my seat, and my throbbing clit rubs against my dress, his eyes snap my way, and I blurt the first thing that comes to my mind.

"Who in the hot hunk of sex are you?" I might have been mortified if it hadn't been for the warm smile that instantly took his face from ruggedly handsome to drop dead, pussy quivering sexy.

He walks around Izzy, who is looking at me with a big drunken smile, and steps right into my space.

"Hunk of sex?" he repeats. His dark brown eyes alight with mischief, and if I'm not mistaken, the same amount of interest that mine are projecting.

"Ah, yeah. I assume that you know how hot you are, so you're either fishing for compliments, or just trying to make me look ridiculous. Either way, you're still hot." I smile, hoping for a flirty come and get me look, but with the amount of alcohol that I've consumed tonight, I might just look like a blubbering fool.

He laughs, his eyes crinkling slightly at the corners. "I know what I look like, and if it works for you, then I'm all for it, Babe. I'm Beck."

He sticks his hand out to shake mine, and the second I place mine in his, I feel like my whole arm is on fire. This isn't just tingles or awareness. This is full-blown explosion of our bodies recognizing each other. Almost as if we were meant to collide in this place. My whole being becomes a livewire of electricity.

"D-Dee," I sputter, feeling my cheeks flame when he smiles down at me. "I'm Dee."

I shake my head, trying to clear the images of this man taking me hard against the bar. When I catch movement to my left, I turn my head and get one hell of a buzz killing shock. I can't even move my eyes when I look on in disbelief. It's a tragic, train wreck happening right before my eyes, and there isn't anything I can do about it. My whole body goes stiff, and I might have even whimpered. Beck's hand, still engulfing my much smaller one, tightens slightly, but enough to make me wake the hell up. Lord knows, my mind is foggy enough tonight, but when I meet the eyes of our newest arrival, I swear that my heart stops.

This is going to be bad. Really bad.

My common sense kicks in about two seconds too late. Izzy turns her beautiful, 'living life to the fullest' smile my way, and I know she can tell something is wrong. She looks confused for a second, and before I can call out a warning for the huge cluster fuck that is about to slam right into her, she turns, and all I can do is watch it play out like a damn horror movie from hell.

"What the hell?" I feel Beck say against my back. His hands grip my hips when I sway slightly.

No, no… There is no way this is happening. I would give anything to be able to stop this from happening, but I know there isn't a thing I can do. This is happening, and all I can do is wait to pick up the pieces when she falls.

It happens so quickly. She turns with her smile still in place, with only a little confusion, and when she sees what I've seen I watch as her legs give out, and her body falls limply into Greg's arms. And for the second time in as many days, all I feel is fear. That same fear that I'm starting to worry will never leave me.

I go to move off my stool to get to Izzy, but halt in my tracks when I hear his voice. "Are you fucking kidding me? Isabelle is your goddamn Iz?" The newcomer, who I instantly recognized as Izzy's old high school sweetheart, growls out in a tone that makes every hair on my body stand on end.

"Oh God," I squeak.

"Holy shit," Beck rumbles against my back.

"Yeah, holy shit about covers it."

Greg doesn't even pause. He wraps Izzy protectively in his strong arms and starts working his way through the crowd towards the back hall. Beck breaks me from my stunned immobility when he grabs my hand and pulls me after them. I can feel the others behind us, but I can only focus on the huge man barreling after Greg and Izzy, and making sure that I get where I need to be.

What a mess. As my legs race to keep up with Beck's much longer ones, the only thing on my mind is how Izzy's going to bounce back from seeing the man she never stopped loving again, the man she's thought was dead for over a decade.

****

We've been standing in the narrow hallway outside the owner's office for a while now. Not too long, but enough that Axel, Izzy's ex, is pacing like a caged animal. When his patience snaps, and he starts yelling through the door, I know I have to do something. Stepping in front of a feral beast probably isn't very smart, but if he has to physically plow over me, at least I will offer some kind of speed bump.

At this point, I can safely say that my earlier thought that this would be a mess was a great understatement. I know there isn't much that I can do if Axel wants to get past me, but right now, the only thing on my mind is keeping him away from Izzy so she doesn't have another episode. I can't let her sink back into that pit of depression that she was in for such a long time. There have been times when I really doubted my ability to keep her sane. Hell, I doubted my ability to keep *me* sane.

Right here, and right now, I have to put my best friend hat on and do whatever I need to do for Izzy. I spare Beck a brief glance before looking back up into the fire sparking, emerald green eyes of Axel Reid.

"Move the fuck out of my way, Woman. I will *not* tell you a-fuckin-gain." The cold fury lacing his words causes me to flinch, but I stand my ground. "I will get back there. Do you fucking hear me, Isabelle? I will be talking to you!" He screams loudly over my head so that his voice can do what I won't let him physically do... reach Izzy.

"You need to stop. I don't mean shut up and sit down. I mean shut up and go the hell on. If Izzy ever wants to speak to you, which I seriously doubt she will after your immature little tantrum, then she will call. But this, this shit that you are so inclined to throw in her face is going to stop. Right. Fucking. Now." I'm pretty proud of myself when I deliver all of that without my voice shaking with the fear still surrounding me.

When his eyes, already so full of anger and hate, turn towards me, I know it's not going to be pretty. I can almost taste the madness coming off of him. Right before he can get a word in, Beck hooks me around the hip and pushes me behind him. "No." One word, but one with so much meaning, only a fool wouldn't recognize the warning. This man, who doesn't even know me, just stuck up and picked sides against someone close enough to be his family.

That doesn't happen to me.

Never, not once, has a man ever been anything but a narcissistic ass towards me. I stopped expecting anything more than some tit staring, and if I'm lucky, an orgasm years ago. But with that simple move, Beck might become the first man to make me question my decision about getting attached.

It doesn't take long for things to get a little crazy. Even I'm not comfortable with all the testosterone waves pulsing off each of these men. All I want to do is grab Izzy and get back home to our safe little nest.

Beck stands his ground for a few minutes, nods his head, and takes a step back next to me, effectively making my wall of resistance against Axel one body longer. Not once does he remove his arm from my waist. I'm too busy trying to figure out my body's reaction to this man, so I don't notice when Axel's anger hits a breaking point.

"FUCK!" he roars. Literally roars. Goosebumps break out across my body, and each hair stands on end. He is nothing short of terrifying. "Get out of my goddamn way, Woman!"

Axel's last outburst must have been the straw that broke the camel's back. Before Axel can even continue his tirade, a spitting mad Greg pulls open the door supporting my back. One look at his face, and I know that he's reached his breaking point, too. Honestly, I figured he would bust out the door the second that Axel screamed for 'Isabelle'. After I right myself from losing the door that I had been leaning against, Beck and I calmly move to the side to get out of his way. I'm trying to keep my shit together, but inside, I'm anything but calm.

A million questions are running through my mind. Who has Izzy? Is she okay? Does she need me? Did I do the right thing keeping Axel away from her? *Where is she?*

I zone out with my worry when they start their pissing contest. I know Greg has Izzy's best interest at heart, but part of me wonders if we're doing the right thing by keeping these two apart. Something in my gut is telling me that things aren't what they seem.

I know I'm not the poster child for relationships, or hell, even a supporter of them, but there is something to be said about getting some closure. I just want her to be happy, however she gets there, and by whatever she needs to do to achieve it.

When I hear the door slam shut, I focus my eyes back on the tall man standing before me. Shoulders hunched, hand rubbing the back of his neck, and now with the fury dimming slightly, you can feel the waves of confusion pulsating off of him. I feel the arm around my hips tighten slightly, and I look up into Beck's concerned, chocolate brown eyes.

"Are you okay?" he whispers in my ear.

"Not really, but it's not me I'm worried about."

"Let me see your phone." I don't even question him. I pull my phone out of my back pocket and hand it to him. His large hand enveloping my iPhone makes it look like a tiny Lego. His long fingers hold me in a trance as he unlocks my phone and moves them across the screen in a slow dance that has my skin prickling with awareness. I jump slightly when I hear another phone ringing. He hands me back my phone, and with a twisted smile, and a gleam in his eyes, pulls his out of his front pocket.

"Will you call me when you get home? Let me know you're okay, and that everything else is okay?"

I just nod my head, my heart pounding so violently in my chest, and my mind screaming at me over and over to run. There are times in my life when I want so desperately to let my steel-enforced walls down. To let a man in. To believe that they won't hurt me. But then, I remember all the pain in the past, and all the pain *they* have ever caused me, and those walls just get thicker and thicker.

"You think maybe you can give me the words?" His smile grows when I nod again.

"Uh… yeah. I'll let you know." Because really, what else can I say here? If anything else, maybe in a few weeks when things calm down with Iz he could be a welcomed distraction. A way to relax and remind myself to enjoy life a little more.

The spell is broken when Axel takes a few steps back, and then drops to the floor in front of the closed door. As if even knowing she is in there is keeping him rooted to this very hallway. The handsome, blond man that arrived with them just shakes his head a few times and leans back as if settling in for a long stay. Beck mimics his move and sighs deeply. Of course, these men know something bigger than us is happening here. They just silently wait to help whichever side needs it.

I can't keep my eyes off of Axel. He sits there on the floor with his head resting against the wall, eyes closed, but body so tightly wound that there isn't a possibility he is relaxed. I want to hate him. I want to think he is this heartless bastard that just up and left Izzy and ignored her letters. I want to blame him for the series of events that followed. The ones that have had her thinking he has been dead and gone for the last decade plus. I want nothing more than to walk up to this man and kick him in the nuts for all that it's worth.

But… but something is holding me back from automatically condemning him to hell. Maybe it's the presence of these strong men silently offering what I think is support, or the fact that when he realized who Izzy was, the first thing that flashed in those green eyes of his was shock, and if I'm not mistaken... love.

Whatever is happening here is larger than any of us realize. So with the knowledge that I'm just going to have to watch it play out like the rest of them, I go to settle in for a long wait. Just when I'm about to get comfortable against the wall, the door clicks open, and out walks the other man who arrived with the group. I think Greg called him Locke. Every single fiber of this man is laced with a strong warning. He appears unapproachable or at least that's just the vibe he wants to project. His eyes, so dark they appear black, take in the crowded hallway but zoom in on Axel when he stands from his position on the floor.

Bottom line, that man scares the ever living shit out of me.

"What the fuck are you glaring at, Locke?" Axel growls, stepping a little closer to the big, scary dude.

"I'm looking right at you, Motherfucker. It shouldn't take a big leap of 'clue the fuck in' for you to realize I'm looking right at your dumb, fucking ass." His deep baritone snarls out the words. Eyes hard as coal, his large frame is puffed up and ready for a fight. I back up slightly, just from his strong presence. Even though his words are spoken in a low tone, the sheer power behind them has every instinct in my body telling me to run from the predator.

Obviously, Axel doesn't seem to have the same issues concerning this man as I do. He walks, calm as you please, right into Locke's space. "What the hell? Is there a reason you seem to think I pissed all over your shit?"

I watch them having their heated debate. Each time Axel opens his mouth to throw some excuse back to Locke, or Locke explains what is going on with Izzy in the other room, I feel my heart pick up speed. Each word that comes out of their mouths makes my world slowly rock and rumble, knowing that the things Izzy has believed for so long are so far from reality.

It's like when you see a car accident and you just can't look away. Or when you're watching a horror movie that you know will keep you up at night for years to come. You know you shouldn't watch, you know there is something coming, but for the life of you, you can't look away. This is one of those moments for me. I know in my gut that I need to stop listening, but I can't look away. I can't plug my ears as a toddler would, and then drop to the floor, throwing a fit that demands these men to shut the hell up.

So I stand here and take it all in. Then, Axel does the only thing that can break me out of my shocked induced stupor. He mentions the one man that not only ruined Izzy's life, but mine as well. The one man that still has the power to ruin hers, and the one man that I would do anything to see wiped off this planet.

Brandon Hunter, Izzy's ex-husband.

At my gasp, his face turns to me. I flinch again at the hard look that's come over his otherwise handsome features. "Are you fucking okay?" he spits with a tone that lacks all sympathy. I'm the annoying one here? I don't fucking think so!

How in the hell can he turn this around, and make it everyone else's fault? Any sympathy that I've felt for him over the last hour or so vanishes instantly. I feel the adrenaline starting to fire through my veins. He has the misfortune of pissing off the mama bear inside of me. I have years and years of being Izzy's rock and strength on my side to fuel my anger. You do not piss off the one person who would go to battle to make sure that the woman in the other room doesn't turn into that powerless blob again. Especially when, in all reality, all of this is in a way his fault. Even if he doesn't know it, HE is the reason she is so screwed up.

And, just like a man, he can't keep his mouth shut when he pisses off a woman. You would think that he would know better. But his words prove otherwise. "Seriously, do you need something? Water, a chair, a fucking Midol?"

All that adrenaline, fire, and pent up, stone cold fury rushes to the surface, and all I want to do is charge this man. I walk right up to him, step into the middle of the small space between him and Locke, and do my best to meet his angry glare with one of my own. "Listen here you... you big asshole, you will *not* sit here and be a little shit. You have no clue what's going on, but I promise you this, it's bigger than your need to 'chat'. Do you understand *me*?" I jam my finger into his rock hard chest a few times just to make sure my point is clear.

He looks down at my finger, still pressed hard between his pecs, before wrapping his fingers around my wrist and removing it. "No, little girl, I do not fucking understand you, not one little bit. So maybe your ass can clue a bastard in?" Just as quickly, that burst of anger seems to vanish, and he looks like the same confused man that he was earlier when he realized the woman standing before him was his long, lost lover.

"I can't, Axel. This isn't my story to tell." I smile weakly, but drop my lips the second his confusion turns a little darker.

"How do you know my name? I haven't gone by Axel in a long fucking time, Sweetheart, so if anyone knows what's going on, my guess would be you."

"Of course I know what's happening, but like I said, this isn't my story to tell." I point towards the door, the door that is protecting Izzy from having to have this conversation. "It's hers. It always has been. I just never thought I would see the day it would need to be told."

His eyes squint, glaring down at me when I refuse to open up and clue him in,   "All right, fine, don't fucking tell me, but let me ask you this, does her fucking husband know she's out, dressed like that, flirting with anything that speaks to her?"

"You son of a bitch…" I don't even think before my hand flies up and cracks against his cheek. It's hard to tell who is more shocked that I slapped him, and slapped him hard enough to cock his head to the side.

"What the fuck was that for?" he rumbles. Behind me, I can hear one of the three other men in the hall laughing, and heat rushes to my face. As embarrassed as I might be for letting my temper get the best of me, there is no way in hell that I feel bad about giving him that hit.

"Oh shit, shit... I am not sorry for that. Get that straight, right now, but you need to watch your mouth, and what you say about Iz. Until you know what's going on, you have no room to say anything. Not one damn thing." I cross my arms over my chest and hold my ground. If he isn't going to listen to anyone, then I'll take him out by myself if I have to.

He sighs deeply before reaching into his pocket to retrieve his wallet, slipping out a white card, and holding it out to me. "Here, give her this, and have her call me."

"I'll tell her, but I won't make any promises to you. If you understood what you are asking of me, well, you would just understand where I'm coming from."

He starts to respond, but the door next to us opens up, and Greg walks through the door with Izzy curled protectively in his arms. The scene reminds me of so many of her 'breaks' in the past that I sway slightly with the enormity of emotions weighing me down. I want to scream and punch something.

What I really want to do is find Brandon-fucking-Hunter and kill him with my bare hands. How dare he take such a perfectly happy woman and turn her into this hot mess. The truth is, not even I am immune to him. Not after *that* night, not too long after he and Izzy were married when he showed me firsthand what she had been living through, and then some. When the memory filters through my mind, I find myself almost on my ass, but Beck steps over and loops his arm around my shoulders, holding me steady.

"I got you," he mumbles in my ear.

"Thanks," I offer, weakly.

Greg walks out a second later and stands in front of me. I know he's just as worried about her as I am. It's written all over his face. "She finally calmed down about ten minutes ago. Let's get her home, yeah?" He addresses me softly so that he doesn't disturb her.

"Sure, G. Let me go get the bouncer to open the side door. They already have your truck parked back there so we don't have to take her through the front." Seeing her like this, and the worry that Greg has, just confirms my thought that this isn't going to be good at all.

I turn and almost crash into the man standing behind me, catching myself just in time.

"Come on, I'll make sure you don't need any more help." Beck reaches over and laces his fingers through mine. He's offering a whole hell of a lot more with that show of support than what his words suggest.

I try not to like the warm feeling that gives me, but I would be lying if I said I don't enjoy and entertain the thought. But right now, I can't even let myself go there. Izzy needs me and just like all the times before, and any time she will need me in the future, I'll be there. I know, all too well, what it feels like when there isn't anyone there, and I will *never* allow someone I love to feel that kind of pain.

CHAPTER 2
Dee

It's been a week.

One week of hell.

My best friend has completely lost her shit. She doesn't want me to know it, and I'll give her some credit, she does a decent job of hiding it. I can see it in her eyes, and I can hear it through the walls when she cries herself to sleep every night. She's been 'busy' avoiding the huge six-foot-six elephant that dropped into her life all week, and all the while, I've been running damage control with Greg. She won't speak to him. He knows this and won't even fight her on it. We both know that if he tries to make her talk before she's ready, it will only end badly. I know it's hurting Greg, but like I told him last night, we have to let her work this out herself.

Hell, at this point, I'm pretty sure there isn't a good way for this to end. Regardless of how Greg and I feel, we both know that Izzy *has* to talk to him. She has to hash this out so she can heal and move on. Whether it's with Axel, someone else, or alone. One thing's for sure, I'm done letting her hide. It kills me to see her suffering, but if I don't put my foot down, she won't ever wake up.

Last weekend wasn't easy. I sent Beck a text letting him know that we had made it home and things were… challenging. Since I haven't heard anything else from him, I just figure he's one of those guys that just wants a cheap run of things, then things got muddy, and he doesn't want the drama now. I'm okay with that, and honestly, I had a feeling that it would happen. Sure does makes it a lot easier for me that way, anyhow. I don't want or need a man right now, and as promising as he seemed in the pleasure department, I can easily see myself getting deep with him.

Deep is something I will avoid like the plague.

Deep is what brings the pain.

Pain when he cheats. Pain when he leaves. Pain when you realize that, no matter how much you wish things were different, you will never be first in a man's eyes.

Am I jaded? Hell yeah I am. I even annoy myself with this, but I've learned enough from my past, that *if* I ever find a man worth trying a relationship for, the chances of him not breaking my heart are slim.

Until then, I plan on just enjoying the ride. If Beck happens to be one of those rides, then so be it. I just have to remind myself that the price of admission is too high to make it a ride I take often.

"Dee?" I lean back from my desk, rub my eyes, and push the work away. I've been staring holes in it for the last thirty minutes while I sit here and fester on all the shit going on.

"Yeah, Babe?" I call back through the open doorway, hoping that my voice sounds better than I'm feeling right now.

Beck

"I want you to take me shopping tomorrow. The whole nine. You know, all those ridiculous things you keep telling me are wrong with how I dress. Well, now they are yours to do whatever with. No limit." I want to call bullshit so bad. I can tell by the way she sounds that this is another way for her to avoid her life. Okay, my rational mind knows, but she also knows how to play the game. She's using my love for shopping and my hatred of all that crap she wears to get her out of the house and away from what I can only assume is Axel. But, my girl hit the nail right on the head.

Direct slam.

So I give her what she needs. I put the smile on my face, and with some screeching and jumping up and down like a demented kangaroo, I readily agree. After all, I'm still helping her out. Right?

****

The next morning, we don't waste any time getting ready and heading off for the mall. We arrive just as most of the stores are opening. I'll give her credit. She hates being here, but she's acting like this idea of hers is the best one yet. She doesn't even fight me anymore when I pick stuff up and thrust it into her arms. The last store we left, she just handed me her credit card and the clothes she had just tried on, before even leaving the dressing room.

At least she's trying to smile.

We walk out of yet another store, and I look over at her. She's still clearly miserable but trying to hide it. I, on the other hand, couldn't be in a better place. I'm in my element. I could spend hours walking around the mall. It's my vice. Some people have booze, drugs, hell even sex. But me? I have shopping.

When I was younger, and my parents just wanted me out of their hair, they would send me with Nanny Amy and their credit card. I loved Nanny Amy. When we would disappear for hours, just walking around the mall, going in all the toy stores that my mother never let me look at, eating all the junk in the food court, or just being *normal,* I could pretend that someone loved me. I could forget the crap that I had to deal with, and the fake mask that I felt forced to wear.

I could be me. The real Dee. The girl who wanted desperately to just have someone who loved her for her, and didn't hate just looking at herself in the mirror.

When I was out shopping, buying whatever I wanted to fill that void, I could pretend. I could forget. So, I get what Izzy is doing here. She's using me and shopping to forget the giant mess of 'what the fuck' her life has become.

It's nearing lunchtime when she takes a call from Greg. Her tone is light and teasing, and she finally agrees to meet up with him. I know it's not what he wants, but baby steps are better than nothing. She isn't closing him off anymore.

We are on our way to meet up with Greg, and find him waiting outside the newest store that we had just left, when I see him. Beck. Mr. Panty Soaking himself, and just like the night we met, the pull is just as strong as it was. Only this time I don't want to stop it. I want to enjoy him and all the promises I see hiding behind his eyes.

He looks at me as if he only has eyes for me. With a devilish smirk on his face, and his brown eyes smiling, he's saying everything that he can't say out loud with just a look.

This gorgeous man wants me, and for once, I'm going to let my hair down, and just enjoy the waves that life wants me to ride. He's a guy, after all, so he shouldn't have any issues with the whole 'this is just sex' thing. I need him to take my mind off of everything else going on around me.

We leave the mall right after meeting up with the guys. Greg is the type of man that gets hives just from being near shopping, so it doesn't surprise me that he wants to get out of here. We head over to Heavy's, our favorite restaurant, and settle into a long afternoon of eating, drinking, and much needed laughter. The tension between Beck and me is tangible. Half of the conversation just floats around me as I look into his eyes. The flirting, sex talk, and uncontrollable lust are just too much to handle.

When Izzy drops the bomb that she wants to go get a tattoo, I do the only thing I can. I put my friend hat back on and go along for a ride. I can tell that Beck is confused and worried, but he still tags along.

We have only been at the tattoo place for about thirty minutes before she is called back. Beck comes over to my side and wraps his arm around my shoulders, pulling me in close and offering his support. It's obvious that Greg is about to come unglued. I can't stop worrying about Izzy, and the fact that it was a huge mistake to let her come here.

I swiftly stand up and get ready to march back and drag her out of here, but before I can get a step away from the couch, the front door opens, and Axel comes storming through the entrance. One look at his face has me dropping back down next to Beck.

"It's okay. He won't hurt her," he whispers in my ear.

"He already has," I reply cryptically. He looks at me in question, but I just shake my head and watch the shit storm unfold.

After the most intense ten minutes, we all end up on the curb. When Axel all but forces a stoic faced Izzy into his massive truck, I breathe a deep sigh of relief, and one of massive anxiety, all at once.

"Do you want to be alone?" Beck asks when he pulls me into his arms. I stand there for a second, and watch where Axel's taillights just disappeared before shaking my head. "Come on, I've got you now." He presses his lips to my temple, and I shiver. He growls low in his throat before lacing our fingers together and leading me to his truck. I steal a glance back at Greg where he's still standing on the sidewalk. He waves me off before heading to his own vehicle. I should be mad at him for what he pulled tonight, but I know he did what he feels is best for Izzy.

Knowing that there isn't anything I can do for her tonight, and hoping that she opens up to Axel, I get ready for the new turn in my night. The man I haven't been able to get out of my head is taking the lead, and I have every intention of letting him.

And now, here I am, after a night that I still can't really process, in his house, and by the heated look he is throwing at me from across the living room, there is no doubt in my mind that we both want the same thing here.

"Do you think she's okay?" I finally break the silence. The way that Izzy 'left' the group earlier still isn't sitting right with me.

"Sugar, I think we can both agree that enough is enough with those two. Axel isn't the kind of man that will sit by and wait when there's something he can do about it. I think a week is about as much patience as we will ever get out of him." He starts to walk over to me, but I stop him with my hand.

"I don't like the way I left her," I stress, hoping he understands me.

"There really isn't anything you can do about it now. Those two are adults, and they need to figure out their own mess without dragging everyone else into it as buffers. Let me take a guess here. You've been her shield for a while now? You and Greg?" At my nod, he continues. "Right, well, I would say it's time to set her free, and let her stand on her own two feet. You aren't doing her any favors by holding her hand." He's right in my space now, the heat from his chest warming my own.

"I don't know if I can," I whisper as his hands come up and take my face between his warm palms. His thumbs stroke my cheeks softly before he brings my face up to look into his, making sure that I see him and understand what he's trying to tell me.

"Let go, Dee. I saw it the moment I met you. You hide it well, but while you work so hard to protect her, you forget about yourself."

I gasp, and he just offers an understanding smile. It shouldn't shock me since he's right, but this man, who has known me all of a week, can see right through my walls. It's unnerving.

"You don't know me," I throw at him, almost defiantly. I don't want him to get in and worm his way past my walls. This is just supposed to be about letting loose and having something for me.

His eyes go warm for a second. "Not yet, but I will. It was my job, for too many years, to see what others didn't want to be seen, so I'm sorry if I hit it on the head, but don't get pissed because I'm right."

I have no idea what I'm supposed to say to that. He's right. I'm pissed because he figured me out in no time, and the two people that I love more than life itself still think I'm happy-go-lucky Dee. I break eye contact when it becomes more than I can stand. It's like he really does see right inside me. It's almost as if he can reach right in and pull out my secrets.

"Right. Are we going to do this?" Desperate to change the subject and steer him away from seeing too much, I bring my hands up and slip them under his shirt. I shake off the nagging feeling that getting into bed with this man might be more than I can handle. The warmth of his soft skin causes the butterflies to pick up speed, and chills to break out. He is completely scalding and hard all over. Every part of him that I touch makes my body get hotter and hotter. I lick my lips when I think about running my hands down his back, digging in as he pounds into me.

"We were going to do this before you even knew you would be coming home with me, Babe." And before I can blink, his lips are on mine. He is consuming my mind, and completely branding me straight down to my soul.

Shit. I knew he would be more than I could handle, and if I feel this 'owned' after one not so simple kiss, I have no idea what I'll feel like come morning.

When he pulls back from the sweet seduction his lips have been making against my own, the look in his eyes almost makes me lose my footing. His eyes are so dark now that they look like the richest, most expensive chocolate money can buy. Twinkling with lust and alight with desire, they rake over my face, taking in my swollen lips, and my hooded eyes. When he sees the state that he's brought me to, his lips curl in to a heart-stopping smirk.

"You want this, don't you, sweetness? Because I can tell you right now, after just one taste of you, I want you more than my next breath." His deep gritty baritone wraps around me like a blanket. I feel as if he's spun a web of desire that I'm completely stuck and hypnotized in. "Dee, you've got to give me the words. Once I start down this path, there isn't any way I'll be ready to pull the brakes."

I clear my throat, hoping to clear some of the fog from my brain before speaking. "Yeah, Beck I want this, but *this* is just going to be fun. No attachments, no love notes, and no promises." I try to stay strong, keep that mask of indifference firmly in place, but the look he's giving me is my undoing. That sexy smirk, eyes twinkling in mischief, and one brow raised as if even it is mocking me. Whatever. "I mean it. I'm not looking for forever, Beck."

"I didn't ask for forever. You want to live in the moment, and get off while you're at it, I won't judge you. But fair warning, I'll do my best to change your mind." And with a wink, his lips are back on mine. His tongue, warm against my mouth, traces the seam of my mouth. He slowly caresses my lips with lazy licks, bringing his teeth into the seduction, and nipping slightly until I open up and let him in. The second his tongue meets mine, I feel like my whole body has caught fire. Flames lick up my legs, arms, all the way to the top of my head, completely engulfing me in an overwhelming, burning to the core surge of lust.

I don't even realize we are moving until my thighs hit something solid. Beck's big hands reach down, burning my skin as he travels from my hips to the backs of my legs, and with an effortless movement, he has me in the air and my ass on the kitchen table. I break free from his mouth and look around in a daze, wondering how we made it from his living room to the kitchen. Before I can ask the question, his lips latch onto my neck, and with his light bites, swipes of his tongue, and hot breath against my neck, I swear I could come on the spot. Just a small amount of friction is all I need against my core, and I'll be off like a rocket.

"Your taste is intoxicating," he mumbles against my neck, his lips moving from my collarbone on a blazing hot trail towards my cleavage. The only sounds I can hear are his soft grunts when he licks my skin, and my panting. Yes, panting. I'm sure I should be embarrassed that I sound like a bitch in heat, but it's been so long since I enjoyed the pleasure of a man that I don't think there is one single thing that could ruin this moment.

"I want to feel you," I plead, trying to pull his shirt over his shoulders without losing his mouth on my skin. "Please..."

He pushes himself off of my body, and in seconds, his shirt is ripped off and thrown over his shoulder. He reaches forward, and in a swift move that would make a magician proud, takes mine and tosses it away, both shirt and bra flying across the room. I look down at my tits, wondering when in the hell he managed to get my bra off but the second his hard body moves back between my spread legs, and his warm mouth closes around one of my painfully hard nipples, all rational thoughts fly out the window.

The next few minutes are a flurry of limbs, wet mouths, and flying clothes. I vaguely register the sting of his hardwood floor when we roll off the kitchen table and crash to the floor. I hear, almost as if I'm standing in a tunnel, the splinter of wood and a crash in the distance, but with his mouth and tongue dancing against my body, I'm happy to ignore everything but this man.

"Are you ready for me, Dee?"

I look down my body and see him up on his knees, stroking with lazy movements, the largest cock that I have ever had the pleasure of seeing.

"Holy shit," I whisper. I have no doubt in my mind that even when Beck isn't ready for some fun, this man looks just as impressive then as he does now. Rock hard, thick shaft, and mouthwatering, smooth skin makes me lick my lips in anticipation, and just nod my head.

"I'm not sure you are. I can smell how much you want me, and let me tell you, it is taking all my strength to stop from taking you hard and fast. I bet your pussy tastes as sweet as the rest of you. I'm going to get you good and ready for me, and enjoy every damn second of it." He removes his hand and I whimper when he stops touching himself. "Don't worry, you'll have me soon enough."

And then, he bends forward and licks from end to end with one agonizingly slow stroke before closing his mouth around my clit and sucking. Hard. Just like that, I slap my hands against the floor, arch my back, and come. I can feel his growl of approval against my oversensitive skin, which does nothing more than intensify my orgasm when I feel the vibrations.

"More." His demand has me shaking my head and mumbling incoherent words. "Yes, more." He slows down his assault, licking and nibbling, paying attention to every inch of my drenched pussy. Every inch, but the one spot I want his lips back on. He leans up, and I take in his glistening lips and chin. With one brow arched, and his smirk in place, he brings his hands up, and with two long, thick fingers, enters me with one firm push. Curling his fingers slightly, and finding that bundle of nerves guaranteed to drive me over the edge, again he whispers, "More." Then his lips, his full and perfect lips, are right back against my clit. He sucks, licks, bites, and in seconds, he hits my spot again, and I fly. I don't just fly, I freaking soar.

I'm pretty sure I blacked out. Hell, I might've died and gone to Heaven, had tea with Jesus, and then fallen back to earth. He is that good. When I'm finally able to focus, I can feel his lips kissing a path back up my body. When his face is level with mine again, I notice the smirk I've started craving is long gone. He is looking at me as if I'm the last scrap of food left on the planet. He looks at me like he can see right through me, and if I was smart, that look would terrify me.

"Delicious." One word, spoken with so much hunger, he actually makes me believe it. When his lips press against mine and start feasting again, my toes curl, and another whore-like moan slips up my throat.

"Please, Beck, I need you inside of me." I'm not past begging at this point. I would probably sign my soul over to the devil for just a taste of him pounding into my body. "Please, take me."

"My pleasure," he rumbles before reaching between us. I feel the head of his cock rub against my clit, and my eyes roll back. He rubs against me a few more times before I feel the solid length at my entrance, pressing against the resistance my body seems to be giving him.

"Condom..." I squeeze out between gasps of pleasure.

"Already on," he pants. "When you were passed out from pleasure." My eyes fly open at his smug tone. I meet his hypnotizing stare before his lip turns up and he pushes forward. In one swift thrust, he settles himself balls deep. My nails bite into the skin on his sides, my toes curl, and I throw my head back, screaming his name so loudly, I'm sure the windows will explode. His forehead is resting against my shoulder, his warm breath bathing my skin in rapid bursts as he struggles for control.

I squirm, trying to get him to move, and his head pops up. His eyes, so dark and full of promise, narrow slightly. "Do. Not. Move." He pants. I grip him, tightening not only my legs, but also my walls, as they close around his thick cock. He groans and drops his head against my shoulder again. "Please. I want this to last, not be over in two seconds." If there hadn't been so much desperation in that almost begging request, I might have tormented him a little longer.

When he finally starts moving, I have a brief thought that he has ruined me for any other man. Fireworks are going off, my ears are ringing, and my throat is raw from screaming out in the pure, raw pleasure he has me drowning in. Every single nerve ending seems to be firing at once; my skin is slick with sweat and on fire as my orgasm builds strength. All sense of time and reality fly out the window as he takes me hard against the kitchen floor. When my climax hits, I lift my hips off the floor and grab his firm ass tight, grinding my clit against his pelvis, and screaming out his name.

"BECK! Oh God! Beck!"

"More." His voice sounds almost animalistic. His eyes drink me in. They look completely black to the point that you can't tell where his pupils are. All traces of the chocolate color are gone, and in their place is the hunger he feels for me. It completely takes over, and with it, the control he's held in check all night snaps.

We move together as if our bodies have been made just for each other. We switch positions, and when I drop my weight onto his lap, and feel him hit deep inside me, I almost lose it. Our dance for dominance continues when he flips me onto my back again, driving his pelvis in deep. Minutes, hours, days... I'm completely lost as this man takes me. The smell of our arousal is as intoxicating as the man driving himself into my body. There isn't an inch of our bodies that isn't touching.

"Ouch!" When my head hits something solid, he flips us again, and his hands, so large they almost touch, grab my hips, lift me off his lap, and then ram me back down. And just like that, my core clenches tight, and I feel the ribbons of pleasure starting to uncoil. Knowing I'm seconds away from yet another climax, I bring my hands down against his rock hard pecs and look into his eyes. His handsome face is drawn tight, his brows furrowed, his nostrils flaring, and his plump bottom lip between his teeth. I know, without a doubt, that he's just as close, if not closer, than I am to reaching his relief. I can feel it building, our pleasure reaching its peak together.

I've never thought it was possible to lose consciousness, but still be aware of your surroundings. He seems to have gained some third wind, and in a speed I can't quite understand, we are rolling again. Furniture crashing, glass breaking, and through it all, his hips keep a steady rhythm against my body. I bring my hands up and grab ahold of his ass once again, enjoying the feel of his firm muscles flexing under my hands.

His balls slap painfully against my ass, and his grunts pick up speed. In a tangle of limbs, slick skin, and grunts of pleasure, we both come undone. Completely spent and connected, he crashes his big body down against my chest. Neither one of us is ready to break the spell.

I've never felt as vulnerable as I do in this moment. Not even my brief past relationships have ever made me feel like all my walls have crumbled so instantaneously. My mind is telling me to run, and my body is telling me to never let go.

It scares the ever-loving shit out of me.

I know in this moment, trapped between a rock hard body, and an even harder floor, that this man has all the power in the world to completely crush me.

When he seems to come back to earth, he leans up on his elbows, gives me a sweet kiss, and just looks at me.

It feels as if he is looking right into my soul, and seeing everything I have never wanted anyone to see. He sees *me*.

"Come on, let's take this upstairs. I'm nowhere near done with you." He kisses me again, offering a few, small, barely there presses against my lips before pulling out of my body with a groan. He looks around, shakes his head a few times, and softly chuckles under his breath. "Looks like I need to call a housekeeper and a furniture shop. And what is that smell?"

I must look as confused as I feel over that comment, because he throws his head back and laughs. "Look around you. You could level a house with that powerful pussy."

My jaw drops at his crass comment, but when I look around at the destruction of his once perfectly organized kitchen, I can feel my cheeks fire.

"Oh my God! Did we do this?" He pulls me off the floor and before answering, he pulls off the condom. Turning to look where I assume the trash can used to be, he lets out another laugh. I forget, for a second, the mess around us when he bends forward, and picks up the can and small amount of trash that spilled when it toppled over. My palms itch to take his firm globes in my hand and squeeze. He is head-to-toe tan, hard, and full of deliciously bulging muscles.

Shaking my head a few times before he catches me mentally molesting him, I take the room in again. The kitchen table is toppled over with at least one broken leg. Three of his four chairs are broken and in pieces around the table. There are a few pieces of what looks like a broken plate scattered around. Two bar stools are on their side. A house phone ripped out of the wall, mail on the floor, a hole in the wall near the floor, and peanut butter covers most of the floor around us.

What the hell?

"I had a feeling that you would be a wildcat." He laughs softly, taking my hand in his and pulling me towards the stairs. And me? I just follow him, even with my mind still screaming to run, trapped completely under his spell and not ready to find the cure.

CHAPTER 3
Beck

It's been two months since I first took Dee home with me. Two months of the best sex I've ever had in my life. Two months, and I still don't feel like she's opened up once. I can see the war behind her eyes. She wants to want me, to want us, but it's almost as if she's afraid to let go of whatever fear I still see dancing behind her eyes. It's not as strong as it was when I first met her, but it's still there, and I don't know what to do about it.

I've given into her whole 'this will only be sex' bullshit, because honestly, I never thought she would be so bullheaded about it. I think I'm an okay guy. I still call my mom every Sunday to check in, and my little sisters say I would make the best boyfriend. Some crap about how being raised by women means that there is no way I can screw a relationship up.

Never, not once, in my thirty-two years have I craved a woman the way I crave Denise Roberts. She gets under my skin like no other. She walks into the room, and I want to be near her. If one of the guys talks to her, I want to gut them, skin them, and maybe even behead them. She laughs, not one of those fake as hell ones she always gives Izzy and Greg, but the soul expressing belly laugh that she only gives *me* when we are alone. I'm near her, and the only thing I want is to claim her, make her mine, and let everyone around us know.

It's not for lack of trying that I haven't been able to break down her walls. I can see past it all. The happiness that doesn't touch her eyes. Those moments when we're out as a group and she looks like her world has crashed. The times that she sees a happy couple strolling down the street, and immediately, her face is full of deep longing. I just don't understand why. I can tell, deep down, that she wants someone to hold her hand through life, but damn if she'll let anyone do it.

There isn't even any doubt in my mind. She's worth sticking this out for and finding the diamond hidden beneath all the dirt.

Now, here we are after two months of constant companionship, almost nightly sex, and just about everything else a 'couple' does without the label. I've tried. She knows where I stand, but she is firm. She wants all the exclusiveness without the title. To her, there will never be an 'us', and if I'm not happy sharing her bed, then I can take a hike.

It's those moments when I want to wring her fucking neck.

"Still chasing after the uncatchable, huh?" I look away from where Dee is standing with Izzy, her head thrown back in laughter, and her rich brown hair falling in curls down her back. Her jeans tightly hug her ass, begging for my hands, and her tits are about to burst through the thin material of her tee. Jesus, how pathetic am I?

"I'm not chasing."

Maddox raises his brow. Yeah, I'm pretty sure he knows I'm full of shit. Even to my own ears, it sounds like a lie, because chasing is exactly what I'm doing.

"Right. And how's that working out for you?" He takes a pull of his beer, glancing around the room before his dark eyes return to me.

I don't say anything because really, what is there to say? I look around the room, trying to find a distraction. "What do you think about that?" I point my beer towards where Axel is sitting on the couch.

"Don't know. Shit doesn't make sense, though." And with that, he gets up and moves over to the couch, turning his attention back to the game.

At least I'm not the only one in relationship limbo. Fuck, I sound like a damn chick. *Relationship limbo?* My sisters would have a field day with that one. Dee saunters back into the room and drops her fine ass right in my lap. It takes everything in me not to throw her down on the floor and claim what's mine. Rip her clothes off and ram my dick so far into her warm, wet body that she won't be able to walk for weeks. I grunt and try to adjust my erection, only to get a giggle from Dee when she realizes what she's done to me.

"Need some help there, Big Boy?"

Her warm breath against my ear only causes me to get even harder. Painfully hard.

"Don't tease me unless you want an audience when I fuck you." My words come out harsher than I meant, and her eyes widen before filling with the same desire that's coursing through my veins.

"Later, I promise." She leans in and whispers, her lips against mine before laying her head against my shoulder, and turning her attention to the football game.

It's moments like this that remind me why I'm fighting so hard to make this girl mine. She's close; I can see it in her eyes when she looks at me. She looks at me like I'm sure I look at her. As if just being around each other makes the world a little easier. I sigh and pull her tighter against my arms, just enjoying the moment.

I'm not sure how much time has passed when the doorbell chimes. Dee and I have been so wrapped in our bubble with the lust turned up high that we've been pretty much ignoring everyone. Dee goes to get off my lap and answer the door but Izzy waves her off.

The events that follow will forever replay in my mind. Izzy had been gone for a few minutes before all hell breaks loose and complete chaos erupts around us. When we all make it to the porch, and see the state that Izzy is in it is like living a nightmare. Having someone attack her right under our noses doesn't sit well with any of us, but amidst the insanity that follows, I can't do anything but watch as *my* girl slips a little further away. By the time the ambulance arrives she has crawled so far into herself that I doubt I'll ever get her to turn it back around.

I hold her while she tries her hardest to keep it together for Izzy, and it breaks a little piece of me. I would give anything to take this from her, but I know she won't let me.

"It's okay, Dee. We'll leave now and meet them at the hospital. Axel won't let anything happen to her." She doesn't move for the longest time, so I repeat myself. Once my words finally filter through her haze, she jumps.

"I need to be with her, Beck. She needs me." Her eyes are frantic, but her tone is deadly calm. It's almost as if she's trained herself how to act. I narrow my eyes at her, watching her take in everything. Her eyes keep sweeping around the room as if waiting for another threat. What the hell is going on here?

"All right, Wildcat. Let's get the truck, and we can drive them." She doesn't seem to hear me so I try again. "Come on, Dee. Axel has Izzy, see? He told the EMT that he was taking her, so let's go get in the truck, and we can drive them. Okay?" She nods but continues to look around in her manic way. I keep my arm tight around her, and call out to Axel to follow us to the truck, and just like that, Dee seems to relax. Not much, but it's something.

****

We make it to the hospital in record time. Axel still refuses to leave Izzy's side, and Dee is in no shape to take over care, so after telling the staff he's her fiancé they don't give us any issues about him staying with her. Coop and Maddox sit silently in the waiting room while Greg paces in tight rotations around the room. Doesn't take a leap to see how upset he is.

I'm more worried about Dee. She hasn't stopped shaking since we left her house. Her hands are literally vibrating with nervous energy. Her eyes are still crazy, and every few minutes, she lifts her head up from where she's been staring at her lap and takes in every single square inch of the room. She then drops her chin back to her chest and watches her hands fidget once again. She's shutting down, and I have no clue how to stop it from happening.

"Let's go get something to eat, all right?" I speak softly, but she practically jumps out of her seat. Her hands fly up to her mouth, and her eyes do another sweep of the room. "I've got you, Dee. I'm right here. I won't let anything happen to you." She still won't stop her worried gaze around the room. I try to calm her down by whispering reassuring words, but she can't calm herself down. I'm about to open my mouth to try again when Maddox steps in front of where she's sitting. I raise my head and give him a questioning look, waiting to see what he's up to.

"Let's go. Now." Even though I knew he was about to speak, Maddox's biting tone has me instantly on edge. Who the hell does he think he is, talking to *my* woman like that? But to my dismay, Dee stops her crazy eyes and takes his outstretched hand. I sit here in disbelief as a man close enough to be my brother, and the woman I'm close to falling in love with, just walk right out the door.

What the hell just happened here?

$\mathcal{D}ee$

I can't stop the chills. This fear that Brandon's attack on Izzy has brought on. That he was even able to get that close to Izzy. That close to *me*. My whole body feels like a jackhammer, violently shaking. I've never known fear like the kind that Brandon-fucking-Hunter can induce in me. And the worst part, I can't talk about it. Izzy has no clue, and Greg is so worried about Izzy's mental stability that he remains pretty blinded to the rest of the world around him. I'm trapped in my own personal hell with no chance of escaping. It's been so long since I felt this darkness closing in on me that I can't figure out how to push it back.

It's better this way. I remind myself. Izzy has too much going on right now, and even before now, there has never been a good time to tell her what he did to me. I've kept it locked inside, and hidden it behind my mask.

Goddammit. I'm so sick of this. I thought all this Brandon shit was behind us, and then bam, he's right back in our faces like some bad venereal disease. Just when I'm ready to tell Beck that I'm ready to try. For the first time in my life, I'm ready to trust a man, and then like a reminder from hell, stone-cold reality smacks me in the face.

Now, it doesn't matter what I do. I can't separate all the bad runs I've had in the past with men, and most importantly, what Brandon did to me when I was just a fresh-faced, college student trying to make Izzy's life a better place. All the amazing moments that Beck and I have shared over the last few months seem to vanish when the shadows pull me back under water.

Beck might seem perfect. He might act perfect. Hell, he might BE perfect. But that means nothing in the long run. I've never met a man that could have a relationship without it turning sour eventually. I've been a revolving door for assholes my entire life. It isn't a stretch that all of my 'man issues' start and end with my father. Try as I might, I can't shake the feeling that it's just impossible for me to have love.

I'm pretty sure that Beck is the closest thing that I will ever have to happiness, but after today, there is no way in hell that I'm taking that chance. I can't, because deep down I know, *I know*, if I give him a chance, he will steal my heart. I'm just not sure what would happen to me if I let him in, and he ever changes his mind.

So, it's best that whatever this is between us ends now before something bad happens. I take a deep breath, trying to get the images of Izzy, broken and beaten again, out of my mind. I tremble violently when the painful images of her filter through my mind again.

"You going to keep huffin' and puffin' over there like a damn brat?"

My eyes widen and my spine stiffens before I look up and glare at Maddox. How dare he! How freaking dare he!

"You don't know me well enough to judge me, Maddox Locke." I've never been good at throwing sass around. Izzy is better at giving those stank eyes out to get her point across. I can tell that I'm doing a crappy job when the corner of his mouth tips up slightly. "This isn't funny." I pout, crossing my arms over my chest.

"It's pretty damn hilarious."

My jaw drops, and I stop right in my tracks.

"Excuse me?" I don't have to fake the displeasure that laces my words.

"You want me to lay it out for you?" At my nod, he just shakes his head before continuing. "Here's how I see it. Two months, give or take a few hours, you and my boy have been fuck buddies who act more like a couple than some married people do. I've watched you, Dee. I see you pushing back and at the same time, running forward. You're hot and cold, but when you're cold, it's fucking frigid. Last couple of weeks, I've seen that fear leave you. The crazy emotions, ups and downs, all those stupid games you've been playing with him, have stopped. You were finally ready. I won't act like I understand your life, but if you let what happened today ruin what could be something worth trying for, then that's on your shoulders."

"Are you done?" I spit out. Literally, spit the words out at him. I'm sure I look hilarious. I might even be frothing at the mouth at this point.

"Yeah, I'm done. For now." He starts walking again, and after a second of stunned shock, I rush after him.

"You have no right to judge me, Maddox. You have no idea what I'm going through right now." I almost stumble, but he reaches out before I can nosedive to the asphalt.

"Really? Want me to let you in on a little secret? This," he waves his hand around us, "isn't even close to being about you. Your best friend is up there with God knows what wrong, and you're stewing in your own shit. We all have a jacked up past, all of us. You aren't special because you've been fucked over. Do you know how much I would love to have someone solid to share my life with? Both of you girls, running and running. Where exactly will you run when there isn't anywhere left to go?" His chest is heaving, and his black eyes are just taking me in, judging me without knowing what he's judging.

"You don't think I want that? I *crave* that! But I know better than to ever let someone hurt me again! I will never, NEVER, be at the mercy of another man. I'll tell you that much, Maddox! You want to stand there and stare at me with those judgy eyes, that's fine, but you better have all the facts before you condemn me to hell!" His eyes narrow slightly before he gives me a slight nod and starts walking again. "Seriously! Where are you going?"

"Food. You need to eat and calm the hell down. When you're done eating, we'll talk."

Beck

Bullheaded, asshat, infuriating MAN!

We're sitting at a small diner around the corner from the hospital. He's already had a meal that could feed a small army, while I've been picking at everything and anything on my plate. His words from earlier are still slapping me in the face.

Slap.

Slap.

Slap.

What is it with these damn men and their ability to see right the hell through me? He's hit the nail right on the head, and I'm silently freaking the hell out. If he can see past my mask right into my deepest hurts, then I'm sure Beck can, too.

"My father used to slap me around. My mother wasn't as bad, but she was still bad. I've had a few boyfriends. All used me and left when they got what they wanted. Some more bad relationships and friendships with men scattered here and there. My track record with female friends isn't much better. Izzy and Greg are the first real friendships that I've ever had in my life. Ever. I don't trust easily. I don't really even believe that I could love someone. The last time I felt what I thought was true happiness and love is when Izzy met Brandon." I continue to move my food around, trying to find the right words. I'm not even really sure what it is about this man that has me opening up, but now that I've started, I'm not sure I can stop. We've known each other just as long as I've known Beck, but there is something about him that

60

makes me feel like he could take my secrets on and lock them tight.

"Izzy's story isn't pretty, Maddox. It's about as bad as you can imagine, and a little worse than that. When she met Brandon, he was a great guy. Hell, I was actually for the first time in my life, rooting for someone to get their happily ever after. But, just like all the other men that have come into my life, his true colors came out. I can't even remember how long they had been married before it happened. Small things, so insignificant that you only could catch on if you really know the person. I missed the signs. Izzy sure as hell missed the signs." I stop what I'm doing and look him dead in the eyes. I want him to feel what I'm about to tell him. I have a feeling that is the only way I will gain an ally.

"They hadn't been married long, maybe a year or two. I was working late, trying to get some last minute stuff done so I could take the following week off. I'm not even sure what I was doing. Anyway, I was alone in the office when I heard something fall in the backroom. I know what you're thinking. Stupid little female taking off to check on the bump in the night. Oh, how stupid I was. I had just enough time to turn my head before I caught the first slap. He didn't hit to leave marks; he just hit to hurt enough to get his point across. Ten minutes of hell, absolute hell. That was the day that I realized there really weren't any good men left. My best friend's husband beat the shit out of me for ten long minutes. I counted. Do you know how many seconds are in ten minutes? Six hundred. The last thing he said to me before he gave me one more kick in the ribs was to stay away from Izzy, or he would kill her. And you know what? I believed he would do it, so I left my friend alone with that monster."

When I finish, I drop my fork, jumping when it makes a loud clatter against the plate and table before falling onto the floor with a loud bang. I've never told a soul that story. Now that the words actually left my lips, I want to grab them, shove them back in, and pretend that this conversation, as one-sided as it is, never happened. The only sliver of relief I feel right now is that I didn't tell him everything.

"You've had a lot of shit in your life." Well, leave it to Maddox to break it down like that.

"Yeah." I laugh a little at the assessment of my life story.

"You going to continue to let that control your future?"

My head shoots up from where I've been picking apart a napkin, and once again, I find my mouth wide open.

"Uh..."

"You going to let the ghosts of assholes past ruin your chance at something good?" His brow goes up in question and immediately, I think of Beck. His handsome face and those eyes I love so much filter through my mind. The way he looks at me as if I'm the last woman on earth.

With a deep sigh, I nod my head.

"Right. You let them win then. Push away a good man, but when all this shit blows up in your face, I'm going to remind you of this conversation. No man in this world is worth the pain you have on your shoulders. There is also no way I believe that you aren't able to love. Seen you with Izzy, seen you with Greg, and I've seen you with Beck. You're wrong, Dee."

"I have to protect myself, Maddox. I can't... I don't, I don't know how to let go."

He reaches over and grabs my hand. His huge palm covers it whole. He gives me a gentle squeeze, and for the first time since I've known him, I see something close to regret in his eyes. "Just because you let someone in doesn't mean you have to stop protecting yourself. It just means you have someone to share the job with."

We sit there in silence for a little while longer before he pays the bill and then head back over to the hospital. There really isn't much more to say, at least on my end. Right before we hit the entrance to the hospital, Maddox asks me to stop.

"Can already tell you're going to run. Promise me, you need to talk, you'll find me?"

"Yeah, okay, Maddox." My voice is just a whisper, but he hears me. He gives me another one of his nods before closing off his face again.

When we get back inside, everyone is standing around Izzy's bed, waiting for her to wake up. I know she won't be happy, but these people need to know this isn't the first time we've been in this position. So, I open up and spill my best friend's secrets. I watch as the men in the room grow rigid and the mood is waist deep with fury. My eyes move from Axel's wrecked expression to Beck's stoic one. He's just looking at me. His face is expressionless except for his eyes. His eyes are begging me to come to him, to let him be my rock. When I give him a small shake of my head, his lips thin, and he drops his gorgeous eyes to the floor.

Just like that, regardless of my stupid, no strings rule, my heart breaks in two.

And, I have no one to blame but myself.

CHAPTER 4
Beck

Bullshit.

Yeah, that's what my life's been like the last few weeks. Absolute fucking bullshit. Dee's walls are up higher than ever. Last weekend was the real kicker. I showed up at her condo with movies, snacks, and flowers. The fight in her eyes when she opened the door, shocked to find me standing there, was almost painful for me.

The smile on my face when she answered the door died a slow and painful death when she told me she wasn't free. Something about 'Stewart from the office' was on his way over. I checked the time again and frowned when I realized 'Stewart from the office' wasn't coming over to get work done. Not at eight o'clock on a Saturday night.

What could I say? Not a damn thing, because she made it clear she didn't want a relationship, and whatever progress I had made went poof the second Izzy got hurt by her ex-husband. So I smiled, handed her the crap I bought, and left with my pride intact.

Then I sat in my truck like a goddamn stalker and waited. No 'Stewart from the office' ever showed up. The lights went out, and her house went dark and silent.

I'm pissed that she's using excuses to push me away, but I'm even more pissed that she isn't letting me be there when I know she needs me. She's slipping so far away that I'm not sure anyone will be able to catch her this time.

I can tell she's going through some heavy shit. Izzy and Axel have finally worked out their issues. The boys and I have a running bet on how long it's going to take for those two to either get hitched or knocked up. I know she is happy for her friend; she genuinely looks happy when she's around Izzy, so whatever her issues are, they have nothing to do with jealousy.

With their reconciliation, Izzy moved out of the condo she shared with Dee. I could tell Dee's heart was breaking when she helped her best friend pack up her life and move in with Ax. No one else noticed because she kept the smile in place and the laughter flowing. But I knew. I saw it the second I walked in the door and all I could think about was taking her in my arms and easing her hurt. The worst part was the fear in her eyes when everyone went to leave. I could feel the terror rolling off of her, but she just smiled weakly and shut the door.

Looking down at the mess I've made out of the kitchen table I've been busy putting together, I throw the screwdriver against the wall and stand up from the garage floor. Note to self, no home improvement projects when I'm pissed off.

"Goddammit!" With a kick that would make David Beckham proud, the table I've spent the last two weeks making from scratch is nothing but a good, wood burning pile.

"What's that wood done to you?"

My head shoots up, and I watch as Coop walks into the garage and picks up a piece of wood before laughing softly and dropping it back into the ruined remains.

"Didn't work the way I thought it would." Ha. How true is that?

"You talking about the little Tim the Tool Man project or Dee?"

"That transparent, huh?" I huff, and walk over to the fridge I've got set up outside and grab two beers.

"Yeah, Beck. Not sure why you even waste your time when you can have different pussy every night." He lifts up his drink, giving a toast to the fact that he's a complete man-whore.

"Not everyone is content waiting for the next outbreak of crabs."

He laughs awkwardly before adjusting his crotch. Disgusting. If I didn't know how anal he is about getting checked, I might be concerned that he is really worried.

"Funny. You need to wake up out of this funk you've been in. What happened to the guy that couldn't wait to get to a new town and start fresh? Hell, you didn't even really date back in Cali." He shakes his head and laughs. "No pussy is worth this much work."

"Damn, Coop. I didn't know you were such a giant douchebag."

He doesn't even flinch at my sarcastic tone. If anything, his smile gets larger.

"Nope. No way in hell I'm a douche because I don't want my nuts tied down."

"Yeah, you pretty much are. I'm not even sure how you get chicks in the first place, but I promise you this, you're the last person I would take relationship advice from." I start picking up the heap of wood and cleaning up the results of my temper tantrum.

"You're going about it all wrong, Brother. I'm going to give you some free, Coop 'the Cooter King' special advice. You need to make her see what she's missing. Right now, she's playing hard to get. You know... Working the power of the pussy. She thinks she has you wrapped around her little finger. Make her see you aren't her bitch."

"Did you just refer to yourself as the Cooter King? Jesus Christ, what the hell is wrong with you?"

He just shrugs his shoulders. I shake my head and continue cleaning up. As ridiculous as it is to take advice from him, I've got to give him some credit. He makes a little sense.

He finishes his beer before letting himself in my house, calling over his shoulder that he's using my shower AND my shit to get ready to go out tonight.

I keep cleaning up and continue thinking about what he just spewed out. Normally, when Coop starts running his mouth, we all just roll our eyes and ignore him. But, what if he's right? What if Dee *is* just playing hard to get?

My whole body feels the charge of determination. It's game on time. Coop might be full of shit most of the time, but he really has a point. All Dee sees is me, waiting and chasing. She hasn't even seen me look at another woman. Hell, I'm not even interested in another woman.

I can see it in her eyes when we're in the same room. She wants this just as badly as I do.

Well, Denise Roberts… get ready, because I'm coming for you.

****

After Coop finished primping like a damn woman, we headed off to Heavy's to meet up with everyone. I feel like I've been pounding energy drinks all day. The anticipation of making some headway with Dee has my senses going haywire.

My body craves her. And ever since she's cut me off and started avoiding me, I feel like I've been living in hell on earth.

Coop laughs when he sees me check my phone, again, to see if she texted me back yet. Her messages earlier today were more of the same.

Me: Why did you run out of the office before I could see you?

Dee: Needed to take care of some work things.

Me: Really? Using work as an excuse again?

Dee: Yeah, sorry just really busy.

Me: You coming to Heavy's tonight? I get that you're busy but I would like to spend some time together where I'm not chasing you around like some stalker.

Dee: Funny, Beck. I'll be there but not sure if I'll stay long.

Me: Save me a dance?

Dee: We'll see.

Me: We could always go out tomorrow night. Like we used to.

That's all it takes for her to go back to her silence. The second I mention just the two of us doing something, she turns cold. It's been almost a month, and she hasn't made it possible to be alone in the same room with her. It's as if Izzy's attack turned some switch in her brain that has her afraid of her own shadow.

When the light turns green, I throw my phone into the cup holder. Coop is rambling on about this new bartender at Heavy's, something about how he just knows she is the one. Yeah, the same douchebag that was talking about not being tied down earlier is now convinced there is one woman that he would spend some extra time with.

Sure, maybe he would devote an extra day to her.

"You know, you could actually make an effort with one? Test the waters. It isn't a hardship to enjoy the company of the same woman. I don't know, maybe grow a real relationship?" He snorts, rolls his eyes, and then continues on.

"You know, I've tried every trick in the book, and she won't budge. Not an inch. I'm going to enjoy breaking this one."

"How are we friends?" Shaking my head, I laugh when I think just how different Coop and I are. Don't get me wrong. I love the little shit like a brother, but we couldn't be more different.

"Because I'm the king of the fucking world?"

"You're delusional."

I turn the radio on to distract myself and to try to calm the anticipation fueling my nerves. It's time to make my woman understand she wants me.

****

Heavy's is packed when we arrive. When we walk in the door, Izzy waves us over, and we begin picking our way through the crowd. Ever since the girls brought us here the first time, this has become the place of choice when we all want to get together for a little 'family dinner'. Of course, that always turns into pitchers and pitchers of beer, and before we know it, someone is being carried out.

The classic rock is already turned up, and since Coop and I are late to arrive, it looks like the alcohol is already flowing freely.

"We ordered a bunch of wings for you two." Emmy smiles up at me and moves in so I can squeeze past her. Dee has effectively blocked my chance at getting close to her by holing herself between Izzy and Maddox. I try to make eye contact with her, but she's looking everywhere but at me.

"Have you been here long, Em?"

She shakes her head, and the light blush that we all find so adorable covers her face.

"No, not too long." She peeks up again and looks over at Maddox. I laugh softly, which earns me her wide-eyed shock. It's no secret that she has a major crush on our resident Mr. Untouchable. He's either clueless, which I have a feeling isn't the case, not with Maddox, or he just doesn't want to see sweet Emmy change. He's not an easy man to deal with, and even I worry that her little crush could end up going sour. One of these days, she's finally going to come out of her shell though and give that man a run for his money.

"That's good, Sugar."

"Yo! Who's ready to get this party started?" Coop screams when he finally detaches himself from the blonde that grabbed him before he had two feet in the door.

Leave it to Coop to break the ice and have us all eating, drinking, and laughing in no time. I look over at Dee again to see her smiling and joining in, but like always, I see right through her. She's laughing, but not like she used to. She's smiling, but it doesn't come close to making her eyes dance. She's eating, if you call picking up a fry every few minutes and nibbling, eating. How is it that everyone else is blind to the fact that she needs someone to lean on?

I take another long swallow of my beer, wipe my hands against my jeans, and settle in. I'm just biding my time before I take a risk and try to shake some sense into her.

Let's just hope I'm not making a huge mistake here.

Dee

Thirty more minutes, and I'm getting out of here. Normally, I have no issues being around Beck, but after last weekend, seeing the devastation wash over his face when I told him Stewart was coming over, almost had me giving in.

It's been so hard to stay away, to keep my distance, and try to squash this thing between us. I feel like my mind and heart are in a constant battle, each wanting something different. But deep down, I know I'm doing the right thing. There is just too much at stake if we give in and attempt a relationship.

For the last hour, Izzy's been sitting on Axel's lap, and I'm pretty sure if they could, he would be bending her over the table. It feels so good to know she is finally happy, but watching them is almost nauseating.

Beck

I reach out to take another drink when I remember the pitcher went dry a little while ago, sending Coop and Beck to the bar for refills. I lean back in my seat and pick up another French fry that I know I won't eat.

"Want mine?"

I jump when Maddox's question tickles my ear.

"Jesus, Maddox... Scare much?"

His lips tip up slightly, and he shrugs.

"I'm not drinking it, if you want it." He holds out his full glass, and I gladly snatch it from him. The longer I stick around, the more tempting getting fall down drunk seems.

After a long pull, I look around the room again. *Where the hell is he?* Just when I'm about to give up my stupid search for Beck, my eyes hit the bar and the couple I had overlooked the first sweep through the crowd.

Before I can stop them, the words fly out of my mouth. "What the fuck?" Izzy's head snaps up and looks over at me before following my eyes across the room. I know when she sees him because her hand reaches out and grabs my arm. I don't even notice the biting pain of her nails because of the red-hot fury that is pulsing through my body.

How dare he? He acts as if he wants me, but the second things get difficult, he runs. Typical man. And a Heavy's Slut? He had to pick the regular trash that never seems to leave and is always here, always dressed like a prostitute, and never with the same man.

74

"That stupid, little fucker. I hope his dick rots off." There's no way in hell that I can stop the verbal vomit now. I can hear Axel laughing softly, and all it does is fuel the inferno blazing through my body. I want blood, preferably the hoochie grinding her crotch rot all over his leg, but I'll settle for his. I want to hurt something, destroy something; I want him to know this is wrong.

It takes me a few more seconds before I can't stand it any longer, and I shoot out of my chair and stomp across the wooden floor. My heels threaten to snap with the force of my steps. My hands clench at my sides, and my breathing is coming in short bursts. When I get closer, and see how she is shamelessly grinding against his leg, my eyes narrow, and I pick up the speed in my walk.

His hands are holding her loosely by her hips. Those hands I know as well as my own are on her body, against her bare skin where her scrap of a shirt has ridden up during her imitation of a bitch in heat.

In all my life, I have never felt this kind of madness. Not when my father slapped me so hard I couldn't hear for a week, not when I got dumped for the seventh time when a job opened up under my father, and not even when Brandon 'filthy ass' Hunter put his disgusting hands on me.

No, this is a new kind of anger, and deep down, I know the only way to make it feel better is to take out the trash.

When I get close enough to get my hands on this troll, I don't even have to think. I reach out, take the badly dyed, teased to the roof hair, and pull. With a yelp, her mouth loses its suction against Beck's lips, and I rip her body off of his.

"You stupid, little slut. What makes you think you can walk into this fine establishment and start rubbing your disgusting, crusty crotch all over a man you do *not* know? That one, the man whose leg will need a case of bleach now, is not up for your filthy, used, and pathetic shit." Her nails are making purchase against my wrist, trying, without success, to detach my hand from her hair. "And wash your hair, you nasty bitch." I push my arm out, and with every single ounce of anger possessing me, I toss her to the side. I don't even spare her another glance before turning on the man who has me in knots.

"And YOU!" I scream in his face. "You make all these promises. You have me questioning everything I have ever told myself, and second-guessing every single carefully planned path. YOU MAKE ME FEEL, DAMN YOU!" I jam my finger into his rock hard chest, taking another deep breath before continuing. "How could you make me feel, and then just give up?! I knew you would be just like the rest of them."

I finally stop, drop my hand, and work to catch my breath. I feel like I've just run a marathon. I take a few more deep breaths, calming myself down slightly before looking back up at his too handsome face. But when I see his smirk, that infuriatingly hot smirk, I'm knocked slightly off balance. When he lunges forward, I jump back with a shriek. That shriek turns into a grunt when he bends, puts his shoulder to my stomach, and before I know what's happening, throws me over his shoulder.

By the time he puts me in the passenger seat of his truck, buckles my seatbelt, and has the truck speeding down the road, I finally wake the hell up from my shock.

What in the... "You did not just kidnap me?" I yell.

"You're damn right I did, Wildcat. I'm sick of you ignoring me, running, and fucking hiding. Tonight we're talking, and there isn't a damn thing you can do about it." He turns the radio up, and Papa Roach's *Last Resort* blasts through the silence.

Real subtle, Beck.

With no choice but to go along for the ride, I start preparing myself for the showdown that's to come.

CHAPTER 5
Dee

When he pulls his truck into the driveway, I push the door open and stomp up the stone pathway to the brightly lit porch. I watch him as he makes his way to the door, shaking his head with that damn smirk in place, and I want to scream. My anger has hit the point of no return, and all I want to do is smack that look off his face. Then, kiss away the pain. God, I'm so sick with my own constant, mental tug-a-war with this man.

"Is this a game to you, Beck?"

He looks shocked for a second before his eyes turn hard. Turning to unlock the door, he holds it open for me to step through before he follows me in. After dropping his keys on the table he disarms the security system before looking at me. His eyes are still hard, and his body strung tight.

"Which part do you think is a game? You refusing to be more than a bed warmer? Not answering the phone when I call because I'm worried about you? No, wait, I've got it. It must be the time that I told you I wanted more than to be just an itch to scratch and a dick to ride. Please tell me, Dee, because for the life of me, I can't figure out just what game *I* could be playing with *you*!"

Oh. My. God. Never. Not once, in the months that I've known this man has he ever yelled at me. Standing here, right now, looking at his wild eyes and flaring nostrils, I want to slap myself for taking such a strong man and turning him into this. He doesn't deserve this. He deserves a woman that can love him freely. A woman who won't be waiting for the other shoe to drop, and the perfect man to turn into the perfect nightmare.

He deserves the best. And as much as I wish I were that person, I know that it isn't me.

"I don't know what you want me to say here." Even though my words are whispered, by the look on his face, I might as well have just screamed them at him. "I don't think I'm capable of being the person that you want me to be."

"Are you serious? I don't want you to be just anyone, Dee. I'm not sitting here demanding that you be anyone else but YOU." He walks over to where I'm standing, taking each measured step slow and steady. His hands are relaxed at his side, and his body is screaming comfort. "All I want is you." He stresses with his deep velvet voice, caressing my ears and warming my heart. If anyone has the power to make me believe, it's this man right here in front of me.

When his feather-light kisses dance across my face, it's almost my undoing. He takes my head between his large hands and tilts it to give him better access. I look into his pleading eyes, and silently beg him to stop.

"I'm so scared of you, John Beckett."

His eyes widen a fraction before an emotion I've seen a few times takes over his face. He looks at me as if I'm his whole damn world and he isn't afraid to admit it.

"You've got nothing to be scared of with me. Not one damn thing. You've had me in knots for months, Dee. Fighting for you, us, and this relationship might drive me mad at times, but it's a fight I want if it ends with you in my arms." Between his words and the soothing promise, I find myself relenting. Knowing this might blow up in my face, and prove once again that I'm right about men, doesn't even bother me. I crave him just as badly as he craves me.

His lips meet mine, and it's a kiss full of every ounce of love he's been trying to convince me of but I've been too afraid to see. I'm still terrified of the unknown, but when I look into his eyes I know he means what he says. I can feel the emotion pouring over me, drowning me, and I want more than anything to believe him.

"Tell me you're mine. Tell me that you'll stop running and working on those damn walls so hard. Just try. That's all I'm asking, please." He doesn't even give me a chance to answer him. Scooping me into his arms, he carries me up his stairs, down the hallway, and into his bedroom without removing his lips from mine. He places me softly on the mattress, and continues to look at me with his eyes blazing, just taking me in. I go to sit up and remove my clothes, but my movements must have looked like another flight attempt, because he places his hand lightly on my chest lightly, his eyes begging. "Please, Dee. Take a chance on us, and I swear to you, Baby, you won't regret a day of it."

Sighing deeply, I look him in the eyes and hold his stare. Yes, I'm scared out of my mind, but if I leave here tonight and deny him this, I know I'll regret it until the day I die. "I'll try." The smile that takes over his face makes my heart skip a beat. His eyes crinkle at the corners and lose all traces of worry. He looks like a man that has the world. And, in that second, I feel lighter than I have in years. I feel like *I'm* the one who has the world.

"Thank you." Kiss. "Thank you." Kiss. "God, thank you." I laugh when he pulls back from peppering my face with kisses, and I see the smile is still firmly in place. "You won't regret this. I'm going to make you the happiest woman in the damn world, Dee. Just you wait."

We come together roughly. I pull him down on top of me, and his solid weight hits me, causing my breath to leave with a whoosh. God, I've missed this feeling that only he gives me. We're a mess of limbs and flying clothes. The room echoes with our loud kisses, panting, and moaning. Neither one of us wants to miss one second of our newfound connection.

It doesn't take long before we are both finally naked. His heat warms me straight down to my core, and I want to cry when I think about all the time I've stupidly denied this man. "Hurry, please! I need you."

"Shh, soon." His warm breath against my ear causes me to shiver, and when he pulls my lobe into his mouth, biting slightly before lightly licking up the shell of my ear, my toes curl. He laughs when I push my fingers into his hair and roughly pull his head back to my lips.

"I need you now. I need to feel you take me hard." God, I need him. I'm not even ashamed of my begging.

Beck

"I'm not taking you hard, yet. Not this time. This time, I'm going to show you just what it feels like to be loved." His words have my eyes widening, but when his lips trace down my body in a trail of fire and latch onto my clit, I forget every second of fear that had previously washed over me. His talented lips and tongue feast at my center, and I lose myself in the pleasure that overcomes me. It doesn't take long for our normal, out of control lovemaking to take over. No matter what, the carnal passion we always create together blows to maximum proportions. He licks, sucks, and nibbles, causing me to scream a few times when the pleasure almost becomes too intense. No matter how close I get he keeps pulling me back, denying me what my body is craving.

"Beck, please!" I plead when he inserts one long finger inside me, pressing against the one spot guaranteed to have me shooting to the sky.

"Mmmm..." When his deep rumble hits my clit, and the vibrations shoot up my body, curling around me, and setting fire to every single inch, I scream. Scream so loud that my throat burns, my ears ring, and my eyes water. He kisses back up my body and takes my lips roughly, and when I open to accept him, I can taste my desire on his tongue. Never in my life did I think I would enjoy the taste of myself, but on him, I feel like I could lick his whole face and never get enough. His tongue sweeps in, dancing with mine, and after a few minutes of the most soul-consuming kiss, he pulls back. My lips feel as bruised and swollen as his look.

We hold each other's eyes as he slowly trails his hand down my side before taking his hard dick into his hand and slowly pushing into my waiting body. The second he pushes inside me, the rest of the world is forgotten, and we come together like we always do, wild and frenzied. I lose track of how many times we flip back and forth, both of us fighting for the top position of control. When we fall off the bed, he flips so that his body takes the brunt of the pain, and I scream out his name when I land, and his dick hits me deeper than ever before. My eyes roll back in my head, and I ride him like I'm auditioning for the top spot in a rodeo.

I reach out blindly, grab onto his nightstand for leverage, and dig my heels in before lifting almost completely off. He growls, and his fingers dig into my hips, almost to the point of pain. "Dee…"

I wink before roughly dropping back down his length, and we both groan with the pleasure.

He doesn't give me much time to enjoy taking him and being in control. I know he is just humoring me when he lets me have a few minutes of fun. He flips me easily, and I vaguely hear something crash to the floor before he's pounding into me hard and fast, just the way I love it. His strong hands hold my legs by the knee as he comes up on his knees and thrusts into my body powerfully. Each time he bottoms out, I scream his name.

"Beck… Baby, so close!" I close my eyes when the pleasure becomes too much.

"Eyes. I want to see your eyes when you come."

My eyes snap open, and I look up to see his eyes burning with lust. A bead of sweat rolls down the tip of his nose and drops between my breasts, burning my skin as it slowly rolls towards my neck. He takes a few more deep thrusts before he leans back slightly and brings one of his hands between us, pinching my clit in between his fingers, and delivering the most delicious pain.

"Oh, God... Oh, YES!" I try to keep my eyes open to focus on his face, but then the kaleidoscope of bright colors closes in on my vision as the power of the orgasm takes over my body.

"Feels so damn good... so, so good." He pulls out, almost slipping free of my body, before he pushes in quickly. His balls slap against my ass, his hands tighten against me, and he grunts before collapsing against my body.

We lay there for a few minutes before he rolls off of me. I instantly miss the fullness of him inside my body. He helps me off the floor and pulls me close, wrapping his arms around me tightly before kissing me deeply.

"You're a pain in my ass sometimes, but damn, when my wildcat comes out, it's worth every second." I cock my brow at him, not quite understanding at first, and frown slightly when he laughs loudly. "Dee, look around." I pull my eyes from his and look around his room. The sheets are on the floor, the mattress is slightly hanging off his massive bed, nightstand over-turned, and his lamp is in pieces on the floor.

"Oh my God! How do we end up doing this every time?" I bury my head in his chest, enjoying the feel of his laughter rumbling against my face.

****

I should have known better to think that I could be happy. Happiness and love just aren't something that is meant for me. It was stupid of me to think that I could trust that foreign feeling of pure happiness, trust and love I felt that night and the following days when I was wrapped tight in Beck's arms.

All that happiness that I had been feeling died a quick death, when a week later, Izzy's crazy ass ex-husband showed up at my house. Not only did he almost kill Greg, but if Izzy hadn't taken control of the situation, I have no doubt in my mind that she and I wouldn't have made it. The hope, the joy, and the belief that I could do this died that day, and it didn't matter what I told myself, what Beck told me. Nothing was able to shake me from the dark hole my mind seemed to run to.

I was lost. I was afraid. And worst of all, I was alone because I pushed the greatest thing to ever happen to me away when I let my fear take control. The worst part, next to losing Beck, was that I couldn't even pull myself back in. I didn't *want* to pull myself back in. Darkness had become my best friend, and everything bright and happy just seemed to vanish.

Time turned into an endless cycle of gray. I went through the motions, and acted like everything was okay when everyone was around, but the second I was alone, and the webs of my depression weaved their way around me in a cocoon tight enough to suffocate me, the only thing I wanted was for it to all just stop. I wanted the end, and each morning when I woke up and realized I hadn't gotten it, I slipped a little deeper.

And I had no one to blame but myself.

PART TWO
Healing
&
Acceptance

CHAPTER 6
Beck

Almost Two Years Later

"You're turning into the old cat lady on the street." Coop laughs, picking up one of the kittens that appeared on my porch one day a few months ago. "Which one is this? Pussy or Trouble? You know, it's basically the same damn thing. Pussy is trouble, and trouble always comes from pussy." He laughs at his own joke, but I stay silent. I'm always fucking silent these days.

"Yup. You want a beer before we head out?" He just looks at me, so I shrug and head over to the fridge, snagging us both bottles. When I hand him his beer, he's looking at me as if I've grown two heads, not exactly a look I'm used to being on the receiving end of.

"You feeling okay? I know it's been a rough run the last year or so, but drinking before lunch? Not exactly a normal Mr. Perfect move there, Beck." My skin feels like it's too tight as he looks at me with his worried eyes. Jesus, when did I become this guy? Hell, I know exactly when. I just don't know what to do about it.

"I'm fine… just have a lot on my mind right now." He looks at me for a couple more beats before shaking his head and looking out the garage door. I busy myself with cleaning up the tools from my latest woodwork project, cleaning off my worktable, and sweeping up the sawdust. I should've known he wouldn't be able to let this go. I know they all worry about me. I see the way that they watch me, waiting for me to crack, or maybe, waiting for me to explode. At this point, I'm pretty sure both are options.

"How long are you two going to play this game, Beck? You don't think I know how you spend your nights, sitting at home like a fucking old man? You don't date; you work, which I'm sure everyone loves since you do all the hard shit before we ever even crack the file open to start a new case. But you aren't doing yourself any favors. If Dee doesn't want a relationship, or whatever the hell you're fighting this one man war for, I think it's time to move on." He walks over, puts his beer back in the fridge, and takes a deep breath before continuing. The whole time, I'm statue still. "Whatever her issues are… they aren't yours to worry about."

What can I say that won't be betraying her confidence? I wish I could scream the truth in his face, because he doesn't even know half of it. For almost two years I've watched the woman that owns my heart struggle to keep her head above water. Not even her best friend sees the pain she's carrying on her back, because she hides it so well. But not from me. No one else was there to pick up Dee's broken soul and fight to keep her whole after Izzy's ex-husband attacked them. No one else saw how many times her beautiful, dark eyes completely lost their spark. And, while everyone else has moved on after the incident, I was the one by her side for months before she finally pushed me away.

The only thing I've thought of is the deep-seated worry that, one day we would show up at her house, and she would be gone. I do what I can from the sidelines, but even I know that isn't enough. Izzy is too busy with Axel and their son, Nate, to even notice how far Dee is slipping away from us. Greg and his new wife, Melissa, and son, Cohen, are enjoying their new life as a family. Honestly, after everything those two have gone through recently, it isn't a shock to me that he hasn't noticed. Having your son kidnapped can do that to someone.

No, the two people closest to her, who that would be able to see through the veil of bullshit she wears around, are too busy. And the one person who wants more than anything to be there for her, has been locked out. So, yeah I'm just a little screwed up at this point.

"I can't help it, Coop, and I know you don't understand, so spare me the bullshit. I can't just turn this shit off." I finish sweeping the last pile of sawdust, and after dumping it in the bin, I look back over at Coop. "She needs me. I don't know how to explain it, but when I look at her, even when she's smiling and laughing with the girls, all I see is the need."

"Right, well, I won't pretend to understand where you're coming from because I've never felt that, but you have to ask yourself if you're just seeing something you want to be there because you're still fighting for something that used to be. Did you ever think that maybe, she isn't the same chick you first met?"

"No, because if I thought like that, I would be just another person to give up on her. Come on, we're going to be late if we don't stop talking like a couple of damn chicks and get over to Greg's house."

I take a few minutes to change out of my work clothes and throw on some old jeans and a faded black tee before we head over to Greg and Melissa's for Cohen's birthday party. The closer we get, the more nervous energy flows through my system. I feel it every time that I know I'm about to come face to face with Dee.

God, please don't let her have a date.

****

The party is in full chaos mode when we walk in. Coop, being Coop, heads straight for the kids and starts acting out some weird impression of a ninja. Kicking his legs and flapping his arms around, he looks more as if he needs medical attention by the second. Cohen's in the middle of about ten little boys his size, all of them laughing at the weird man in front of them.

It takes Coop about one second too long to notice what he just walked into.

"Coopie!" And in a flash of blond hair, black spandex, and a gold cape, Sway jumps into the fray and hugs Coop tightly. Cohen starts laughing hysterically when Sway starts jumping around, flailing his arms, kicking his legs, and swishing his long, blond ponytail around. Coop, never the one to be out done, joins in, and before long all the kids are acting like cracked out little hyenas.

"Hey, you, glad you could make it." Melissa's voice breaks through the insanity, and she wraps her arms around me, giving me a small hug before pulling back. Greg is right behind her, giving me one of his hard stares, which just makes me pull her in for another hug and kiss her lightly on her cheek. When she is pulled out of my hands and into Greg's arms, we both laugh. Yeah, it's way too easy to pick on him these days. Ever since she found out that she's pregnant with twins, he's become almost unbearable with his possessiveness.

"Calm down, you beast." Melissa laughs, swatting his arms away.

His eyes are still burning at me when he finally speaks. "Don't touch her. You want some cake?" I laugh before following them through the craziness and into the kitchen. The tension that has slowly rolled off my shoulders when we first got here comes flinging back with vengeance. There she is, as beautiful as ever, laughing with Izzy and Emmy.

She's wearing one of my favorite pair of jeans that hug her ass perfectly, and showcase her long, toned legs. Her shirt is one of those blousy things that kind of hang loosely in a sexy way. It's sheer, so I can still see her tight body and full chest incased in a tight, black tank. I almost swallow my tongue when I see her shoes. That woman could have me licking the floor just to have her in those heels, and those heels alone. Red-hot and sky high.

Temptation on legs.

I clear my throat and will my erection down. Last thing I need is to look like some creepy, old man getting hard on at a four-year-old's birthday party. Yeah, that wouldn't go over well at all.

Her eyes snap over to where I'm leaning against the doorjamb that leads into the kitchen. I can tell the exact second that her wall she has up starts securing all their extra locks, and the bulletproof glass starts to rise. You can literally see her protecting herself. And the worst part, the part that guts me right to the fucking heart, is that she is protecting herself from me.

"Izzy, Em, Dee... good to see you." I turn and walk back into the living room. No sense in sticking around where I'm not wanted.

CHAPTER 7
Dee

What a mess. I should know by now that my body will react to being around him, even if I beg it not to. My therapist keeps telling me that it's time to trust. Time to stop letting my fears, and the ghosts of the past stand in the way of my happiness. She says I can't keep condemning everyone around me for the crimes of others. The rational part of me knows that she's right, but then I remember, for the billionth time, what happens when the good guy turns into the devil. It's getting easier, though. I feel stronger, and that in itself, is a huge step for me.

I look around at the happy faces of my friends and feel the usual tug at my heart. The love so clearly painted all over them, is almost too much to take. Hell, even shy, little Emmy seems to be smiling and laughing more.

Everyone is happy.

Everyone is loved.

Everyone is blinded by that perfection.

I smile, donning my 'I'm so happy' look, and excuse myself from the group. I know I saw Maddox walk in a little while ago, and if I plan on getting the information I need from him without others around, I have to do it soon, or it will be hours before I get a chance to corner him alone.

For the last few months, I've been trying to avoid letting one of these overprotective apes in on my issues at the office. The North Carolina branch of my insurance agency has been having issues. Big issues. I only caught wind of it because one of our larger clients called to inform us that they would be moving their account to another agency. One they claimed could give them better rates. Knowing damn well that wasn't true, I started digging and when I found the number of times their account had been overbilled, I was shocked. When I began to understand that the problem was bigger than I had realized, or ever imagined, I knew it was time to call in help.

Enter Maddox. He's been helping me, with the promise that he will keep his mouth shut unless he notices something potentially dangerous. How dangerous could this really be?

The only plus to the giant cluster fuck that my company has turned into is that I don't have time to miss Beck. Well, I don't have time to miss him with the same bone crushing intensity that I have been. Still, it won't ever be easy to be in the same room with him. Not when I can feel the invisible line that seems to connect us pulling tight every time we're around each other.

There have been a handful of times over the last two years when I haven't been able to hold those walls up anymore, and we've come together with the same ferocious lovemaking that we always create. And each morning after, I make sure I'm long gone before he even wakes. Neither one of us mentions those stolen moments, but I know him... I know he wishes that just once, I would be there in the morning. I've made a promise to myself that last time would be it. No more hurting him because I'm too weak to keep my walls up.

"Looking for me?"

I am so lost in my thoughts that I almost run right into Maddox. He doesn't give me a chance to fall because his hands shoot out to steady me until I catch my footing.

"Uh, yeah." I look up into his unreadable eyes. Maddox has always been the master of giving nothing away when you look at him. His face is almost always expressionless, his bottomless eyes hard, and his large frame is never anything but intimidating. To be honest, he would scare the daylights out of me if I ran into him on the streets. Maddox Locke looks like a man that eats babies for breakfast.

"Found me." His gritty, deep voice rumbles his normal 'as few words as possible' way of speaking.

"Yeah, I noticed when your hard ass chest almost knocked me out. Were you just going to let me break my neck?" My patience, for the most part, is in small supply these days, but for some reason, Maddox, and all his asshole tendencies, just works for me. I know that part of it is him knowing something about me that no one else does.

"Probably. Seemed pretty lost in thought there, so I'm not even sure you would've heard me say anything anyway. Noticed you and Beck doing your normal bullshit, too. Which do you want to avoid talking about more?"

"Don't be an asshole, Mad. Did you find anything out from the files I sent you?" I'm pretty sure I sound as desperate as I feel, maybe even borderline manic at this point. I know he told me he wouldn't say anything to the others, but depending on what he's found, that could change everything. And the last person that I need to find out that I'm in trouble is Beck.

"Yeah."

That's it? Are we serious right now?

"Please, don't play games with me. This is serious, Maddox."

"Yeah, I know it is. I know it's serious because I've dug deep enough to know just how dangerous this can be for your pretty little ass if you keep being so obvious with your detective work. Hell, you might as well just show up and tell the whole office what you're looking for." He narrows his eyes and does that stupid manly huff and grunt thing that is supposed to put me in my place. Fat chance of that happening.

"Tell me what you found. Please." I know, before he even opens his mouth, that I'm not going to like what he tells me.

"Adam Harris. Age thirty-six, single, agent in your company for the last eight months?"

"Yes, I know who you're talking about. I hired him myself. He had a good resume, and all of his references checked out. He might not have finished top in his class or anything, but he had enough work history in the insurance field for me to give him a go. Hell, his last employer told me he didn't want to let him go!" Okay, I might be close to losing my calm, because this guy was nowhere near my radar.

"That would be the one. Seems like Mr. Harris has a nasty little habit. The kind of habit that costs a lot to keep up." The confused look on my face must have clued in the fact that I'm not exactly following him, because almost as an afterthought he added, "Drugs, Dee. He's so far in debt with his drug dealer that I'm not really sure how he's still breathing."

"What?" I gasp.

"Dee, I checked his financial history, and best I can tell, he's in the red everywhere. Mortgage is in foreclosure, truck repossessed, and that doesn't even count the negative bank statements, and at least fifty thousand in credit card debt. Looks like from all the company reports you've given me, he's only done this to the one account. It wasn't enough for them to get suspicious, until recently. My guess is that he was getting close to desperation, and that makes people like him sloppy."

I just stare at him in disbelief. I know Adam. Hell, I've gone to dinner with him a few times on my trips back to North Carolina. I've told him about my life here. He can't be doing this to me. "You have to be mistaken. He doesn't look like he would be so... evil." I try to calm my breathing, and when I'm not successful I lean against the hallway wall before sliding down to the floor.

Maddox sighs before he crouches in front of me, takes my face between his hands, and forces me to look up. "Calm your shit, Dee. I told you I would look into it, and I did. Now that we both know what's going on, it's time to let the others in. There is no damn way it's safe enough for you to try and fix this on your own."

Before I can reply, an angry voice cuts through the silence, and I jump so high that my chin knocks into Maddox's nose. I watch in horror as his legs give out, and he falls on his ass. He doesn't even seem worried about the blood pouring from his nose; he's more worried about pulling down the leg of his jeans where it's ridden up mid-calf. His head snaps up when my gasp echoes around us. His expressionless eyes are now full of anger and panic.

"I'll keep your secret for now, Dee, but don't you dare say a word about that to the girls." He jumps up and stalks away, roughly hitting Beck against the shoulder.

I must be in shock because I don't even move. My mind's spinning out of control with all the information Maddox told me, and with what I just saw when he fell. I don't even notice when Beck stomps up into my space. Still staring into the distance, when I feel his hands close around my biceps and lift me to a standing position in front of him. His body is vibrating with anger.

"What the hell was that?"

It takes me a second to put the pieces together, but when I do, my eyes widen. He thinks that me and Maddox... That Maddox and me... Oh, shit.

"It's not what it looks like, Beck," I whisper.

"Right, so you weren't sitting here in a dark hallway, all cozy with one of my closest friends? Huh? I'm not good enough for you, but Maddox is?"

I've never seen Beck this pissed before. I've seen him mad, but never like this.

"He was just helping me out Beck. It's not easy being here, and I was having a bad moment. All he was doing was talking to me, trying to get me to stop being upset, and enjoy the party. Can you please calm down?" It's not exactly the truth, but it's not a lie either.

He takes a second; I can clearly see him calming himself down. One of the things I love about him is his ability to control his emotions. He doesn't hide anything from me. I can see the anger fade, and in its place is confusion, which just as quickly turns to hurt. Hurt because it wasn't him that was able to comfort me. And finally, understanding dawns. He might not like it, actually, I know he doesn't, but he still puts his feelings aside and understands. It wasn't Maddox and me being together in a lustful way. It was about Maddox being there *for* me as a friend. For everything I've put us through, the only thing he cares about is that I'm okay, even if he isn't the one that's making it possible for me to be that way

I don't deserve him. I know that now. But the worst part, in this moment, I know there is no way that this man in front of me could ever be anything other than Mr. Perfect. He could never be what I've been running from. All along, he's been right in front of my face, promising me the world, and I just couldn't see it. That's all it takes for the waterworks to start, and my whole body shakes with silent sobs.

I broke us.

I broke him.

And I just continue to break myself.

CHAPTER 8
Beck

My heart is still rapidly pounding from the sight of Maddox with his hands on Dee. The logical side of me knows that he would never make a move on her, but the jealous and possessive ex-lover only saw her in his arms.

Now, I'm still close to losing my mind, but not because of jealousy. This time, it's because the woman I love is breaking down… again. I can't even remember all the times that I've been in this position with her. Right after Brandon's attack, she spent the better part of eight or so months like this. It might have been more, but she pushed me away and wouldn't let me in for another two months following that.

The only reason that I know how bad it got was because I refused to leave. Before she closed me out completely, I was with her as much as I could be, as much as she would allow. She lived with Izzy and Axel for a while, but she still came over. It still amazes me that not one of these damn people in our lives noticed the pain she was dealing with. She was living under her best friend's own roof, and even she didn't notice. When it got to the point that I was more concerned about her doing something to harm herself, I knew it was time to get her more help than I could provide.

I know she is still seeing Dr. Maxwell. She's slipped up a few times over the years and told me. We've had our handful of reunions, those times when I think I might just be getting my girl back, only to have the hopes die in the morning.

Everyone around us looks at our fucked up relationship and does nothing but judge. They see only the outside, the window dressing. They don't see *this* side of Dee. They don't see her when she hits her lowest points and calls me at two in the morning because she is terrified that someone is in her house. They haven't gotten the call from her telling you that the world would be better without someone so damaged. No, everyone sees perfect Dee, happy Dee, and the Dee that never stops smiling, even when she's dying on the inside.

I've watched this happen to plenty of my brothers when we would come back from a mission gone wrong. I've watched them completely crumble, and I've even watched a few of them lose the fight. It doesn't take a doctor to tell me that she has been, and most likely still is, suffering from post-traumatic stress disorder. I've seen the signs that she's getting stronger over the last few months, but she still isn't the Dee that she was before that asshole violated her safety.

"Shh, I've got you Dee." As I pull her into my arms, I press her head against my chest, and do the only thing I know how to do. Just be there. Regardless of how the people around us think I'm wasting my time, I refuse to believe it. I know the woman hiding under all of this pain. "Calm down. Everything's okay."

I know we can't sit here in the hallway. It's not going to be long before someone comes looking for a bathroom and walks into a very private moment. Without losing my hold on her, I bend and scoop her legs up into my arms. She curls even further into my body and presses her head tight against my neck.

I walk further away from the party noise and enter Greg's office, shut the door, and walk over to the couch. When I sit down, she still doesn't remove her face from my neck. Her arms are clamped tightly around my torso. I know there isn't anything I can say right now to make it better, so I just hold her, offering her the one thing I wish she would take and never let go of. Me.

When the last tremor leaves her body, and the vice-like hold she has on me lets up slightly, I can finally breathe a little easier. I wait a few more minutes until she lifts her head from my neck. She looks around the room before finally making eye contact with me. Her beautiful, brown eyes are bloodshot and swollen with her mascara running down her face. Her cheeks are puffy and splotchy red. She looks terrible, but she's never looked more beautiful to me. She's stripped bare and vulnerable right now. This is Dee, my Dee, and not some fancy farce that she projects to the world around her.

"Are you better now?"

She nods, never looking away.

I press on. "Are you ready to knock some of those walls down?"

She nods again.

I want so badly to ask her if she's ready to be mine again, but I know she isn't ready for that. "Are you done running?"

Her eyes go wide, and I can see the wheels start to turn, trying to find a way out of this question.

"I don't know, Beck. I know that isn't what you want to hear, but I just don't know." Sighing, she drops her eyes to her lap where she rests her hands. I reach out and cover both of her hands with one of mine, stroking her soft skin with my thumb.

"That's okay, Dee. You know I'm here when you're ready. Are you still seeing Dr. Maxwell?" I hold my breath, waiting for her to answer, because if she tells me no, then this breakdown means that she is headed back to that dark place she lived in for a while.

"Yeah, I'm doing a lot better. I still have moments, obviously, but I haven't had one in a few weeks." She sounds so weak. All I want to do is fix this for her, but I know that I won't be doing her any favors, and I know if I rush her healing just to make myself feel better, our relationship won't be built on anything sturdy enough to stand on.

"I believe you. Now, what's been happening that has you getting low again?" I keep my voice at a whisper so she knows I'm not mad, just trying to be here for her.

"It's nothing, just had a moment." She won't look at me, so I know she's full of shit, but I don't press.

"Dee, you know you can talk to me. After everything you and I have been through, you have to know you can trust me with anything."

She hesitates slightly, looking me in the eyes again before she drops her gaze back to our hands. The pain in her eyes is almost too much to take.

"I want to tell you. I do, and I will. I just need to do this on my own. I need to be strong enough alone." For the first time in almost a year, I feel the first spark of hope. She isn't falling again; this is just a speed bump in her healing. I want to jump off the couch and shout. This is the first time she's admitted to me that she wants to let me in.

"All right, Dee. I understand, but you know I'm here. I want to be here, and when you're ready, all you have to do is say the word."

"You really get it, don't you? That I'm trying?"

"Yeah, I really do. I know you're hurting. I've watched you hurt for so long and, Baby, you know I would take that from you in a second. But right now? Right now, I can see the fight coming back, and I couldn't be happier. We've been through so much together, Dee, and right now, I couldn't be more proud of you."

Reaching out, I pull her into my arms and just hold her tight. In my gut, I know that something is going on, but I have to let her do this. I have to let her fight for herself before she'll be ready for someone to fight with her.

CHAPTER 9
Dee

After I calmed down, Beck left the room to grab my purse so I could clean myself up before returning to the party. He walked back in the door with his too handsome for words smirk in place.

It seems like whatever that was that happened between us lightened some of the weight off his back. If I'm honest with myself, I feel lighter too.

Right before he opens the door to leave me alone to get ready, I speak the words I should have told him a year ago. "Thank you for being there, for always being there, and not letting me fall."

His body gets tight, and I see his knuckles turning white from how hard he is gripping the doorknob. His head drops for a second before he turns and stalks over to where I'm standing in the middle of Greg's office. Without giving me a second to guess his intentions, he grabs my head with gentle strength and crushes his lips against mine.

It feels as if every single inch of my body is on fire. He doesn't make a move to deepen the kiss, but it still feels like one of the most intimate kisses we've ever shared. My hands resting against his sides dig in when he brings his body closer until he has me pressed against the wall. He keeps his lips pressed tightly to mine, before lifting off and giving me a few smaller pecks. He pulls his face away, but keeping his hold on me, he smiles; all the love he wants me to believe in shines so bright that I feel physically warmed by it.

"Don't you know by now? You couldn't keep me away if you tried." He winks and presses his lips once more to mine. Then he's out the door, and even though he closes it softly, the click as it shuts echoes throughout the room like a shot. I can still feel his delicious kiss for minutes after he's gone. I stand here in the same spot, with my fingertips pressed to my lips, and for the first time in a while, I smile a true smile of pure happiness.

Maybe things are starting to look up.

****

It takes me a good thirty minutes before I look normal enough to return to the madness erupting inside of the Cage household. The second I round the corner and enter the kitchen, I run right into the birthday boy himself.

"What are you doing in here all alone? Looking to steal some ice cream when your mom isn't looking?" I smile, but like always this kid can see right through me. He crosses his little arms over his chest and tilts his head to the side, studying me with an intensity that makes me nervous.

"Aunt Dee, your face looks funny." Leave it to Cohen; I swear that kid has no filter.

"Thanks, little dude. Your cape looks funny." I stick my tongue out at him, and when his adorable face breaks out into a huge smile, I know he's forgotten all about my 'funny face'.

"My cape is awesome. It gives me magic, and makes everyone love me." He plants his hands on his hips and looks at me as if all this should be common knowledge, which it is, but it's still cute to listen to him explain it. His tiny brows are crunched together, and his lips are pulled into an adorable little pout.

"Uh huh, and I bet that magical cape keeps you out of trouble, too?" Bending down and kneeling in front of him, I look into his brown eyes that are so full of innocence that uncomfortable longing shoots through my heart. "You really are the coolest four-year-old I know."

"I know." He smiles big.

"And how many times since you put it on this morning have you gotten in trouble?" I ask with a smile.

His grin gets even larger, to the point where it looks like the creepy is coming out of him. "Two times!" he screams in my face, holding up his fingers. "Two times, but it was Mommy's fault the first time. Daddy's wiener was out, and I was just trying to keep her from seeing it." He leans into my face, so close that our noses touch. "Girls aren't supposed to see wieners, Aunt Dee. And Daddy's wiener was mad that Mommy saw. It was so mad, it was pointing at her!"

Oh. My. God. How the hell I'm able to keep from busting out a laugh is beyond me. When I look over his head, and see Greg shaking his head with a slight blush on his cheeks. I lose it, laughing so hard that I fall onto my ass. Cohen, completely oblivious to the fact that he just let me know he busted Greg and Melissa, just starts laughing with me. I try to stop, but the laughter just keeps coming. Maybe some of the tension from earlier is still trying to escape, but hell, this kid could make the worst of days better.

"All right, all right... come on, Birthday Hero, you need to go use the bathroom and get back to your party." Before I stand up, I pull him into my arms and give him a big hug. His little arms wrap tight around my neck, and he squeezes me hard. "I love you, Cohen. You're right, that cape sure does work."

"I know!" He gives me a kiss on my cheek before rushing past me and slamming the door to the bathroom.

Well, guess I'll join the party by myself. I stand up and dust off my rear. When I look up, I notice that Beck has joined Greg in the kitchen. He gives me a warm smile, and I can tell just by looking in his eyes that he caught that moment with Cohen and me, too.

"I love hearing that laugh, Dee. It's been too long." And with that, he turns and walks back through the doorway and into the living room.

I must have been standing there for a while, just zoning at the doorway that he walked through, because when Greg clears his throat, I jump slightly.

"Must have been pretty far away just then. You didn't even notice Cohen run flying right past you." He smiles, but it's guarded.

"Yeah, must have."

"Are you doing okay? I know things have been pretty crazy around here lately, but you know you can come to me if you ever want to talk." It's times like this that I just want to scream at him. It's not his fault. He's had a lot going on in his life the last few months, but it still hurts to know that someone so close to me, has been completely blind. I want to scream for all the times I needed him, but he was too worried about Izzy. All the times I needed him, but he was too busy falling in love. I know it's not fair to pass any blame onto him, but for someone who knows me better than most of our other friends, he doesn't know me at all.

"I'm fine. Just going through some stuff, that's all." I plaster on my perfectly practiced, 'I'm on top of the world' smile, and wait to see if he can see past my mask.

God, I'm so sick of this mask.

He looks at me a beat before he shakes his head. "I've been a shit friend lately. I know that, but it's no excuse. You might be able to fool the girls, but I'm on to you, Dee. I wouldn't have even noticed if it hadn't have been for that little breakdown I saw. And before you flip the hell out, no one else saw it. When I saw Beck had you, I cleared the kitchen and kept them out of the back hall. You don't want to tell me what's on your mind? Tough. We're talking, and we're talking soon."

I'm thoroughly shocked when he basically stands there and scolds me like a child. What the hell is going on today? No one, not a single one of these people, has noticed anything at all ever since I first crashed and burned. They didn't notice when I slipped so far past the level of okay. They didn't notice when I thought about taking my own life. And, they didn't even notice when I started trying to drink away the fear.

Not a single one of them, except for Beck.

"Can we please just forget about it for the day? Let's not let my issues be the dark cloud on your son's birthday. Please, Greg."

He gives me a look of sympathy before holding his arms open. I walk into the familiar, comforting arms of one of my best friends, and take the support he's offering.

"And don't you dare mention Cohen's little wiener story," he says against my temple. "You had your laugh, but damn, Dee, that little kid was born with an internal cockblocking sensor. I'm just now living down the last time that Cohen told the group about him seeing Melissa 'hugging Daddy under the covers'."

I start laughing again, and just like that, my mood lifts slightly.

"My lips are sealed, but G, you might want to consider getting a deadbolt or something more secure for your bedroom activities." I laugh even harder when I notice he's really considering my comment. "Come on, you freaking weirdo, let's go have a birthday party."

The rest of the party passes with laughter, presents, and a few tantrums, all of which are from Coop when we tell him that he can't drive Cohen's new, kid sized, four-wheeler. I swear that man is just a child trapped inside a grown man's body. When Sway offers to hug it better, Coop shuts his mouth real quick.

"God, I'm so glad those kids are gone," Melissa says as she drops down onto Greg's lap. "But I'm definitely not ready to clean up this mess." She laughs before laying her head against his shoulder. I watch as Greg subconsciously tightens his hold, never once breaking his conversation with Axel and Maddox, and brings his palm up to rest on her adorable belly.

"That was an unbelievably long day. Even Nate crashed before his lunch, and that boy never misses a meal." Izzy laughs, shaking her head a few times.

I look around the room and take in my 'family', getting lost in my thoughts again. It seems like just yesterday that our Greg, Izzy, and Dee trio turned into this big, loving family. Even at my darkest, I think I knew that these guys wouldn't hurt me. Just the opposite, they would protect the women in their lives to the extreme. I didn't always think that, but they have proven themselves over and over again. It still stings when I think about how well my protective mask hides my pain from every single one of these people I love... well, all but one of them.

That one person who is currently looking at me from across the table without hiding a single one of his emotions. Nope, not John Beckett. He's looking at me like he always does. With love, longing, and complete rapture.

Jesus, between my issues with the company, my screwed up head, and my heart that beats for just one man, I can't even tell which way is up anymore. With a mental note to make an extra appointment with Dr. Maxwell this week, I shake myself from my checkout and focus back on the conversation around me.

"… in concert next month," Emmy says in her soft voice. She's looking right at me, so apparently, I've missed something.

"I'm sorry, what was that?" I ask.

"Dee, get your head out of the clouds." Izzy laughs. Oh, my stupidly wonderful best friend. If she had any clue about how my life has been, she wouldn't make jokes. But, it isn't her fault that she's looking at life through her rose-colored glasses and is completely oblivious that I've needed her more than ever.

"You caught me." I laugh, but even to my own ears, I can hear how fake it sounds. "Who is coming to town? Sorry, Em, all I heard was concert."

"That's okay, Dee. Sam Grow's coming back to town. I think it's the last weekend, next month. They're doing a big charity show. I think it would be neat if we made a girls' night out of it." She smiles and I can't help but return it. Emmy is so easy to love, and even though she's in a situation similar to Beck and me, it never stops her from making the best out of life.

"And I told her how much I love that idea. Ever since Greg used his Rico Suave skills and serenaded me with one of Sam's songs, I've been a huge fan." Melissa smiles at Greg, who is still rubbing her rounded belly.

"That sounds good to me. I think Izzy gave me his CD a few weeks ago, so I'll make sure and listen to it beforehand. It's been a while since we've had a girls' night."

We make plans, with Emmy promising to purchase the tickets tomorrow. After a few more hours, pizza, and more conversation, we all head to our separate homes. When I tuck myself into bed that night, even with all the worry still on my shoulders, I feel lighter than I've felt in a really long time.

CHAPTER 10
Dee

After Cohen's party, things got crazy again at work. Chelcie, my personal assistant, calls and tells me that she needs me to go up to the North Carolina branch. We have another big client that is requesting a meeting, and only wants to speak with me. In my gut, I know what the issue will be, but I still hope I'm wrong.

Not knowing how long I will have to be gone this time, I pack heavy and hit the road before lunch. Thankfully, traffic is light since it's a Sunday afternoon. After checking into the hotel and grabbing dinner, I settle in for the night. Not much different from when I'm at home, just this time, I don't have my stockpile of ice cream.

Having my phone ring in the middle of my Sunday Bravo TV shows is a sure fire way to have my mood go straight to crap. When I see 'Greg Calling', I hope that he'll take a hint when I send the call to voicemail. Not even two seconds later, he's calling again. Sighing deeply, I grudgingly answer. "Hey, G."

"Oh, she speaks. Thanks for sending me to voicemail. Really sweet of you." Sarcasm is dripping from every word.

"Sorry about that. I hit ignore instead of answer. I was just about to call you back." I lie smoothly.

"Ha, try that on someone a little more gullible than I am."

"Anyway, what can I do for you Greg?" I turn off the TV and toss the remote to the side in frustration.

"I told you yesterday that we would talk, and I meant it, Dee. I went by your apartment, but you weren't there. Figured that you were either ignoring me, or you were out, so which is it?"

I could lie to him, but really, there isn't any sense in it. He won't think anything is up just because I'm out of town. "I had to come up to the North Carolina branch. Chelcie called me right when I got home last night and said I was needed up here. So, here I am."

"Chelcie called you... on a Saturday night, to tell you to drive right up? What the hell, Dee? Did you just jump in the car first thing to avoid talking to me, or do you really have a need to be over there?"

I shouldn't get pissed, but the flash of annoyance that washes over me is so overpowering that I can't keep my mouth shut. How dare he act as if I'm doing something wrong here? I've been living my own life without one damn care from them for a while, and now that *he* wants to chat, he's pissed that I'm gone.

"I'm not really sure why you feel like I need to check in with you? I've been doing just fine for a while now. Just in case you missed the memo, I'm a big girl now, Greg. I don't even need my training pants anymore."

"Whoa, snappy much. Someone must be on the rag." He chuckles before sobering. I know he isn't going to just drop it, so I wait, my breath held, for him to ask the questions I don't want to answer. "I'm worried about you, Dee."

"I'm fine," I snap, a little too harshly.

"You're not fine, and I'm insulted that you think I would believe that lie." His voice, which had been friendly and calm, now has a hard tone to it.

"Excuse me, but you've been believing it for two fucking years!" I scream into the phone. It takes me about two seconds to realize my mistake. *Shit!* I slap my hand over my mouth to stop the overflowing verbal vomit before I say anything else.

"What did you just say?" Dammit. Damn. Shit. I know Greg doesn't mean to ignore everyone around him. He has every right to be worried about Izzy and his recovery from his injuries sustained that God-awful day. It isn't fair to hold anything against him, but in my mind, I just can't seem to separate my pain and loneliness.

"It's not important. I'm fine," I stress, praying he'll just leave it alone.

"Goddammit, Dee! I know you aren't fine. I saw you breaking down like your world just crashed in around you yesterday. That isn't how someone that is *just fine* acts. You can't push that shit off on a bad day, your period, or someone stealing your newspaper. There's something going on, and you aren't *just fucking fine!*"

"Okay, Greg, I'm going to say this the nicest way I can. Don't worry about me. You have enough to worry about, and honestly, you know I love you like a brother, but right now, I don't need your protectiveness. Give Cohen a hug and tell Melissa I said hi. I'm going to bed now. I have to be in the office early tomorrow so I can get everything done and get home. Greg, I mean it... Stop. Goodnight, I love you, go hug your wife." I disconnect the call without giving him a second to protest or pull his crap. He'll be pissed, but he'll also get over it. After turning off my phone and pulling the covers up, I settle in for another restless night of sleeplessness.

****

My wake-up call comes at 4:45 A.M., about an hour after I finally manage to stop freaking out about the dark, jumping from every sound that I heard coming in from the window, and my mind finally shut down. I never sleep well when I'm away from my house, so I'm not sure why I thought this time would be any different.

Groggy, annoyed, and a whole lot pissed off isn't a good way to start the day, especially knowing that I'm about to have another pile of shit land in my lap when I get into the office.

My office back in Georgia is decent in size. I have three other agents and a few other staff members. It's not the largest, but it works for us. Back home, I've just moved into the same strip of businesses where Corps Security is located. When the building came up, I jumped on it. It isn't that I need a new office, but my old one was out of an old house that had been remodeled into an office. The downside, it was in the middle of nowhere, and I had become scared to even be there by myself. So, I

Beck

didn't waste time signing the paperwork for the new space.

Here, my office is slightly larger. I've got six agents, plus they each have their own assistants. I had the building built from the ground up, and when it was finally finished and open for business, the sense of pride had been overwhelming. I've always been so proud of this office and the staff, and how we've managed to thrive when other small businesses have crashed.

This is my baby.

And every day that a new fire starts within the office, I want nothing more than to give this 'baby' up for adoption. The thrill is gone, and more importantly, I don't feel even an ounce of pride when I walk in the doors.

Being that I'm about two hours early, and the staff shouldn't even be in until eight, shocked would be an understatement when I pull up and see some lights on. I have been so lost in thought that, when I drive up, I don't even check the front lot before I pull my car behind the building. I guess this would explain the ridiculous power bills; idiots keep the lights on all night! Since I'm the only one that ever parks back here, it doesn't even cross my mind to wait until normal hours to go in.

My phone chimes a few times before I make it to the back door, and with a huff, I dig it out of my back pocket and start checking my alerts and emails. Unlocking the door quickly, I walk into the back break room, kitchen area, with my phone still in front of my face. Bad habit of mine, having the phone be a constant

120

attachment to my body, but when you're running two companies in two different states, you need to be available at all times.

I brush off the tingling feeling that makes my skin crawl. Being this early, I'm not surprised that I'm having another one of my ridiculous fears creep up on me. I make another mental note to talk to the doctor about that. I'm too damn old to be afraid of every bump in the night.

Speaking of, I clear the alert reminding me of my appointment with Dr. Maxwell, and switch over to my emails again and surf through the crap while I wait for the coffee to brew. My mind is struck stupid when I see a message from my mother, asking me to schedule in a call at my earliest convenience. Ha, I don't think so. Deleting the rest of the junk, I pull up my text screen to send Chelcie a message to let her know that I've made it in and will see her when she arrives.

I shove my phone back in my pocket and reach for a mug. Right when my hand closes around my favorite University of Georgia mug, it hits me why I had such a sense of unease when I walked through the back door.

The alarm.

It wasn't armed, and from what I can tell, the door sensors didn't even chime.

Suddenly, that nagging sense of dread doesn't seem so ridiculous. I set the mug down quietly, and with a deep breath, turn to face the door leading into the open reception area. My head does a nice imitation of a bobble head as I look between the door to the offices, and the one that leads outside. Fight or flight.

God! I'm so sick of being afraid of everything! I feel like this is a defining moment. Run again, or stand up and fight for my life.

I should know better. Doesn't every horror movie have that scene that has you screaming at the stupid bimbo who runs straight into the dangerous killer? Yeah, I should know better, but unfortunately, my mind has decided it's had enough of the two-year freak fest, had enough of being a scared little pussy.

Ever since yesterday and my 'moment' with Beck in Greg's office, I've felt different. Not different enough that I can pinpoint the change, but I don't feel so... damaged. I almost feel a little like the old Dee. I want that Dee back, and I'm ready to fight to get there. That's the only reason I can think of that would make me take the steps needed to bring me to the solid wood door leading into the offices. When my hand touches the cold knob, I jump slightly, but pull my strength, and try to muster up some of that courage I thought was long gone.

You can do this, Dee. Just open the door and when you see the office is empty have a good laugh. Nothing to it.

Turning the knob, I silently push the door until there's just enough space for me to see into the brightly lit room. I gasp when the first thing I see is a tall figure dressed in black with a mask over his face, standing right in front of the open doorway. I scream loud enough that my own ears ring and try to pull the door shut. The beefy hand that reaches out and stops the door from closing scares me enough that I lose my footing and fall to my ass.

Panting in fear, I quickly back up, knocking my head against the table in the middle of the room. I keep crawling as fast as I can backwards until my spine hits the wall with a thump. All the while, the tall figure keeps slowly stalking towards me, like a predator would his prey.

"Where is it, bitch?" The voice isn't one I've heard before, but then again, the blood rushing in my ears is enough to make the most familiar voice unrecognizable.

"I don't know what you're looking for! P-p-please, don't hurt me… If you want to take my purse, you can have it; there's money in there. Cards too. Please, oh God, please!" Tears are streaming down my face and my body is shaking so violently that my teeth feel as if they're rattling in my head. This is it. My miserable life is going to be over before I ever get a chance to tell the people in my life how much I love them.

"I don't want your fucking wallet, you stupid cunt! Whatever you have in that goddamn wallet isn't enough to cover what that idiot owes. Where the fuck is he!" He bends down and roughly pulls me up by the roots of my hair. I yelp, but scramble from the floor to try to minimize the damage. My body is screaming for me to shut it down, to just let him end it. Anything would be easier than living with the emptiness my life has become. But just as quickly as the thought enters my mind, I remember I want to fight. I'm better than what I've let my life become, and I damn sure don't want to go out like this.

"I d-don't know," I whimper. "Please, I don't know!" Apparently that's not what this stranger wants to hear because he rears back and punches me with what feels like all his strength right in my eye. My head snaps to the side, and the pain that radiates from his punch is almost enough to make me pass out. I can already tell that my eye will be useless, and my other one is watering so badly that I can't make anything out but a slightly fuzzy black dot in an otherwise white room.

"That will be the least of your fucking worries if you don't tell me where he's fucking hiding! That idiot owes a lot of money, and if he isn't around to pay up, then it looks like it's going to fall on you. " He gets right in my face, and with my good eye, I can tell his eyes are ice cold blue. They would almost be attractive if it wasn't for the flame of pure evil dancing behind them. "Where. Is. That. Motherfucker!"

"I'm telling the truth. I don't know! I don't come into this office often! I don't know who you're looking for!" Something I've said must have registered as truth because he pulls back slightly before looking me from head to toe. Shockingly, he starts to laugh, a laugh full of demonic tones. I can literally feel the color drain out of my face when his eyes meet mine again.

"Well, well, well... If it isn't Denise Roberts, one and only owner of Roberts Insurance. You aren't supposed to be here and it's just like a stupid, fucking cunt to come nosing her fat ass where it doesn't belong." What the hell?

Before I can open my mouth to ask him... well, I don't know what I would ask him, but before I even have the chance, his hand comes out and clamps tight around my neck. My airway closes as he lifts me off the floor with his hand. I reach up and grab his wrist, clawing and fighting for the air he is stealing from me. "You, little Denise Roberts, are a problem, and I don't like problems. One of your employees has something of mine, and I want it. You see, my problem now is that he's decided to vanish on me, and I don't like it when I'm owed money, and I've got to play hide and fucking seek to find it. When he stopped answering my calls, I figured the greasy little shit was having a come to Jesus with his conscience. I can't have that now. You will either find that bastard, or all of the money. And I mean all of it."

I try to answer him, but I can feel my mind start to panic. My lungs burn, and my hands are desperately struggling against him, but are quickly losing strength. I try to communicate with my eyes that I understand him, but he just keeps tightening his hold, squeezing me so forcefully that I feel like my throat is about to snap in two. My arms and legs start to flap around helplessly, as I attempt to gain just a breath of air.

After another few seconds closer to eternity, he lets go, and I drop roughly to the floor. As I gag and gasp to breathe, tears stream down my face, and my throat burns like I've swallowed a ball of fire.

He gives my fallen body a swift kick right in the ribs, which snap with a sickening crack. "I wouldn't think about crossing me. I know all about you. I mean every single thing about you. I know all about your little friends, too, and I'm not even slightly worried about those dumbasses. I've got to hand it to you; I never thought you would show up before I had a chance to cover my tracks."

When he goes to grab me again I pull my body in tight and scream. Big mistake on my part, because all it does is piss him off more.

"Shut the fuck up, bitch!" Unfortunately for me, I don't have the strength to block the blow that hits me right in the temple, and instantly, everything around me fades into darkness. I try to fight it, but when my vision starts going, I know that I'm at his mercy. I just hope that he gets bored with me and stops. I'm not ready to die. I have things I want to do. People I need to set things right with. And a man that I know would be devastated if this was my end.

My last thought before everything goes blank is how badly I want to live, and if I make it through this, I'll do everything in my power to learn how to let love in.

CHAPTER 11
Dee

When I start to feel the tugs of awareness, the first thing I notice is a shrill sound. The annoying beeping that won't shut the hell up. I try to move my arms to find the offending noise, but they don't move. When I attempt to open my eyes, nothing happens. I go through the checklist, trying to make something, *anything,* respond to my mental command. Nothing. I lay there trying to come up with a reason why I can't feel anything, can't move anything, and can't see anything. Nothing.

I can hear the beeping start to pick up as my mind continues to panic. With every rapid burst, my mind and body start to freak out even more. I want to scream, but nothing happens. Right when I think my panic might be too much for me to control, I feel something cold hit my arms, and in seconds my heart calms, and my mind goes blissfully blank.

The blackness returns, and I fly off to dream again. This time, Beck's here, smirking with his beautiful full lips and his brown eyes darkened with desire. My smile comes easy when I realize he's here. He's always here when I need him. I don't waste a second before I rush into his arms and soak in his strength.

My last thought before I let my dream carry me away is that I'm so happy that his arms are holding me tight again. I've denied us this for so long, and even though he understands why, he still doesn't deserve it. When his lips touch mine, I want to cry out against the unfairness, but the blackness clouds my vision again, and I fly away.

****

That damn beep is back.

What the hell is that noise?

After attempting and failing to move my body, I take a deep breath and try to figure out what's going on and why I'm unable to move. I can hear a voice somewhere in the room, so I direct all my attention on that and try my hardest to pick up on something that might be useful.

With every fiber of my being, I strain and concentrate, but only manage to pick up a word here and there. "… asleep still… days… haven't caught… should call her family… optimistic… should come." I try to focus some more, but it's taken so much of my energy just to understand those twelve stupid words. I want to weep when the fear seeps into my bones. I have no clue what's happening, or where I am. The last thing I remember is going into the office and getting that stupid email from my mother.

I try to keep my mind alert long enough to figure out what the hell is going on, but after only a few moments, I'm flying away again towards the darkness.

****

God! Every single part of my body hurts. My head is pounding like I've just come off a weeklong bender, my throat and lungs burn with every breath I take, my arms and legs feel as if I've just worked out at that torturous spin class Izzy likes to drag me to, and oddly enough, even my hair hurts.

What the hell?

After accessing my body, and realizing that yes, every inch does in fact hurt, I fixate on the sounds around me. I can hear voices again, but this time I know who they are. Or at least I think I do. I definitely recognize Maddox's low growl. It takes me a second to place Coop's voice, though. He doesn't sound like his normal playful self. Chelcie's voice is the next one I catch, talking in a rushed low tone; I think she sounds scared, but I can't understand her words clearly enough to be certain.

Just when I think that I know all the players in the room, one more voice speaks up, and my heart stops in my chest for a minute before it picks up speed. I don't even need to have my eyes open to know he's sitting right next to me. Now that I'm becoming more aware of my surroundings, I can *feel* him. Not just the warmth on my arm and hand, but I can feel his energy in the room. The ever-present love and strength is pouring all over me like a warm blanket. But I also feel his darkness, that vibe of menacing violence that is just itching to come out. He's pissed and trying to contain it.

I try to remember what happened that could cause this type of reaction from him, but my mind keeps coming up with a big fat nothing. It's there, the answers that I need, but they are just out of reach.

"She'll wake up when she's ready, so I'd appreciate it if you would stop talking about her like we need to start planning her goddamn funeral." Beck's snarl shocks me for a second until his words penetrate my brain. Why would they think I'm dying?

I want to cry out and scream that I'm awake, I'm here, and everything is going be okay, but when I open my mouth, nothing comes out but a strangled choke. I feel the vibe in the room change instantly when they realize I'm waking up. The waves of sadness, anger, and confusion dissipate, and a burst of joy and relief zaps through my body.

"Shh, it's okay, Baby. Let me call the nurse and have her come check you out. I don't know if I can give you any water, so let me go get her."

I grab his hand with what little strength I have when he goes to move away from me. Tightening my weak fingers around his hand, I desperately hope he understands that I don't want him to leave my side. My eyes refuse to budge, so I slowly turn my head to where I think he is. Opening my mouth, I try to tell him not to leave me, but that sickening noise comes out again.

"Dee, please don't try and talk. I'm not leaving, I'm right here. Coop, go get the nurse." I feel him move closer from where he must have been standing, his free hand brushing against my hairline. "I'm not leaving," he vows.

The energy around me goes still, and he continues to murmur in my ear. I can't tell what he's saying because he's speaking too low, but it's still comforting. His soothing tones calm my out of control heart in seconds.

"Well, I see sleeping beauty decided to wake for her prince, after all. My name is Destiny; we've been waiting for you. I'm going to move your bed up slightly so that I can move the straw into your mouth. Okay, Honey?"

When the nurse's soft voice starts explaining to me why I hurt, I start to panic again. What the hell happened to me?

"All right, Honey, open up and let's see if we can get you talking. Your throat's going to hurt, but let's see what we can do. That's it, small and slow sips."

When I get enough to make my throat feel less like I've decided to eat sandpaper and closer to a dull throb, I unlatch my lips from the straw.

"That's good, that's good. Can you tell me your name, Honey?"

"D-de-nise." My voice causes me to jump slightly. A low moan of pain escapes, and I try to calm my breathing when the pain gets a little too intense.

"I'll get you something for that pain in just a second, okay? You're doing great." I hear as she moves around the room, and then places a cuff on my arm.

When it finishes its tight squeeze, she reads my blood pressure out loud.

I try for a few seconds to calm myself down by taking shallow breaths. My right eye finally cracks open, and I take in the room around me. My nurse, a beautiful woman with skin as dark as night and hair back in a tight bun, is still moving around the edge of the bed. I can see Maddox, Coop, and Chelcie in the corner by the window. Maddox has both of his thick arms crossed tightly over his large chest. His face is hard, but I can tell by the slight tick in his jaw that he isn't holding his emotions in as well as he would like. No, he's pissed. To my shock, Coop has Chelcie wrapped tightly in his arms, slightly rubbing her back.

When my eye finally hits the worried, dark gaze of the man sitting by my bed, I want to cry. His eyes are red, and I can tell he's either been without sleep, or he's been crying, and I desperately hope he just hasn't slept. His brows are drawn in tight, his lips are pressed into a line, and his thick brown hair is mussed and standing in a million directions. Even looking as terrible as he does right now, he still is the most beautiful man I've ever seen.

"Everything looks great, Honey. I'm going to get you some more medication for your pain. It's going to make you sleepy, so let me get the doctor to explain what's going on before you turn into Sleeping Beauty again."

My eyes never leave Beck's face.

"That's right. This prince of yours hasn't left your side once, so I imagine I wouldn't want to stop looking at him either." She lets out a soft giggle before I hear her slip from the room.

I try to offer him a small reassuring smile, but it must fall flat because his eyes look even more pained. He leans in and kisses my forehead softly right before I hear footsteps next to my bed again. I turn my head from Beck's worried face and focus on the new arrival. She's wearing a white coat, so I'm only assuming this is my doctor. She puts me instantly at ease with her calm smile, but it's her eyes that make me feel like I'm in good hands. She has the kindest eyes.

"Hello there. I'm Dr. Knott. I understand you just woke up?"

"About thirty minutes ago, ma'am." Beck speaks, and I'm thankful that I don't have to try out my voice again.

"Good, good. I understand there was an incident at your office, and I know that the police have been waiting for you to wake to speak to you, but I think I can hold them off for a few days. You need your rest. We're going to keep you on the pain meds for at least another day or so, and let your body get a little better before we take the good stuff from you." She smiles again and pats the arm opposite of the one that Beck is rubbing softly. "You have a few bruised ribs, but luckily nothing broken there. Your eye, the left one, is going to look and feel a lot worse than it is, but in a few days, the swelling should go down enough for you to be able to open it. We do want to make sure that you aren't having issues with your vision, so we will need to check it. There are a few other bruises and bumps, but right now, we're keeping an eye on your head to make sure the swelling stays down. You're a lucky girl; by the looks of it, it could have been a lot worse."

She continues to explain various things about healing and home care, but I'm too busy taking in everything she just told me. Beck asks a few questions, but I don't hear them. I just lay there in shock. She asks me a few more things that I weakly answer before she leaves the room with the promise of sending Destiny back in with my pain medication. The second the door closes, it's as if the floodgates slam open, and all the memories, leading up to now, come rushing back. The office, no alarm, light on, the man... oh God, the man!

"Shh, Dee... Look at me. It's okay. I've got you." I turn and focus on him, trying to calm the rapid breathing that has my ribs screaming.

"Did you find him?"

He shakes his head, and when I hear a snarl from the side of the room, my eye shifts to Maddox, who looks as if he's about to snap in half. Beck yells at him to either calm down or leave the room before making me look at him again. "It's okay; I need you to believe me, Dee. We're working on it, okay?" I see his eyes pleading with me... begging me not to close him out.

I take a few shallow breaths and focus on his eyes. "Okay. I trust you, Beck."

His shoulders sag with my whispered words, and his eyes drop for a second before he looks back at me. I gasp when I see the moisture forming in his eyes.

"Thank you, God, thank you..." He leans up, kisses me lightly before sitting back down, and starts to rub my arm again. I can tell from the way his lips are pressed tight, and the slight flare of his nostrils, that he's trying to compose himself.

Destiny comes back in the room, and she gives me the pain meds, and checks the machines one more time before leaving. I try to stay awake, afraid that if I fall asleep, I might not wake up again. Clearly understanding me better than I understand myself, Beck recognizes my reluctance to close my one good eye. He brings his face back to my ear and starts to whisper softly, again.

Between his deep voice speaking softly against my neck, and the strength I pull from just his touch, my eye starts to close, and my heart starts to calm. The last thing to filter through my mind as I listen to his voice is how lucky I am that he's even here. It doesn't even matter that I can't even understand the words, he's here. For everything that I've put him through, my depression and PTSD, and my stupid mind letting the past rule my present, he still hasn't given up. If this isn't proof of just how far he really will go to fight for me, then I don't know what is.

I let his love wrap around me, and drift off to a dreamless sleep with the knowledge that when I wake up he's still going to be here, and it's up to me to fix this now.

Beck

CHAPTER 12
Beck

When the doctor finally told me she would be released, I want to actually hug the lady. For the last week, I've sat by her side, hoping and praying that I would finally get to take her home.

First, they wanted to keep her because of the swelling to her brain from repeated blows. God, just hearing them say that over and over had my body ready for a fight. When her head wasn't the main worry, it seemed that her kidneys were. And finally, a few days ago, she stopped pissing blood. We would've been out of here before now, but they wanted to monitor her kidneys to make sure there wasn't anything else going on.

I think we were all ready to get her out of this room and back to Georgia. Dee was starting to get frustrated with the constant poking by the staff and lack of good food. All I could do was smile, because even though she was here, she was fighting mad. The important part was that she's here at all.

Being this far from home wasn't ideal either. Having to keep everyone back there up to date with her progress had become more annoying than anything else. Somewhere around day seven, I finally passed the phone to Maddox around day seven and told him to keep them fucking happy. To be honest, I didn't really give a shit about keeping anyone up to date.

I only have eyes for Dee, and all my focus is on keeping her comfortable and making sure that she feels

Beck

safe. I look over at her sleeping face and I physically hurt when I see how swollen it still is.

When she finally opened her left eye two nights ago, just a crack, she announced that she could see. We all released the collective breath that we had been holding since the doctor had warned us there was a chance her vision could have been impaired from the injury.

Her eye really was the least severe of her wounds. There wasn't much of her body that wasn't covered in nasty black and purple bruises, right down to a few of her fingers.

I lean back in the chair that I've pulled up next to her bed, and let my mind think about the call that we got Monday morning that all but stopped my heart.

When Maddox came bursting through my office door with enough force to literally rip it off the hinges, I knew something was wrong. All it took was one word— Dee— and I was out of my chair and following him out the door. Coop had already brought the truck around, and we hit the road from there.

He filled me in during the drive. Her assistant called his phone in a panic. She had come to work to find the whole office trashed. She would have missed Dee, but in her panic, she tripped over some overturned boxes. When she fell, she had a direct line of sight into the break room. By the time she had gotten to Dee's side and called 911, she said she could barely find her pulse. That was the last update we got. I spent the rest of the car ride thinking that when I finally made it to her, she would already be gone. The unknown was bad enough, but when I couldn't stop thinking about what I would do if she were taken from me, the crushing agony was almost too much to bear.

Now, here we are almost two weeks after her attack, and still no answers. Those first five days when she wouldn't wake up were the worst. There was enough time for Maddox to fill us in on what he had been investigating for her. I was livid at first, but then I tried to put myself in her shoes, and slightly understood why she would go to Maddox. When she finally woke up enough to tell us what happened during the attack it still felt like we were playing with a deck that was missing half the cards. She didn't know who the man was, and even if she knew how to find the employee he wanted, she didn't even know how to get in contact with him.

The police came and got her statements, documented her injuries, and left with the promise that they would be investigating things. There wasn't anything left behind to give us a single clue as to who did this.

The last call Maddox had with Greg, he filled him in on everything we knew. Our best hope was finding this Adam character, and hopefully, he would shed some light on this mess. I didn't ask Maddox how that call went, and wasn't sure I wanted to know. I logically knew that Greg couldn't help when he didn't know what was happening, but the other part of me, the one that wanted someone to blame, couldn't stop the what ifs from hitting me hard. Knowing that he was probably just as upset as the rest of us was the only thing that kept me from lashing out.

"Beck, you really need to head back to the hotel for a few hours and get some sleep. You aren't doing her any favors by running yourself into the ground." Coop smiles sadly. "I'll stay with her, but please, Man… you look like shit."

"I'll walk out that door the second she's ready to go with me. Not a second before, so shut the fuck up about it."

He opens his mouth to argue some more, but snaps it shut tightly when he sees how pissed I'm getting. He's lost his damn mind if he thinks I'm leaving her again.

"Leave him alone." Maddox hasn't said much since we've been here, but when he spits those words out, Coop wisely shakes his head a few times before walking out the door. Maddox is silent for a beat longer then laughs with no humor. "That douchebag. I got back to the hotel last night and walked in on him banging Dee's assistant. Shouldn't be shocked, but fuck, you would think he knows when he should keep that shit locked up." He shakes his head a few times, clearly still not believing just how bad Coop has gotten when it comes to sleeping around.

Well, to be honest, I didn't even see that one coming. Chelcie is always a real quiet girl, but I know she loves Dee, so this whole situation is really messing her up. I should have been paying more attention to Coop's level of comforting.

"Did he say anything about it?" I ask, not taking my eyes off Dee.

"Yeah, some bullshit about helping her to remember she's still alive. Said she kept freaking out, and he didn't know what else to do. What a dumbass."

"That's... well, I'm not really shocked. It is Coop." What can I say, we all know he's an asshole when it comes to chicks, but I really hoped he could keep it in his pants until we got back home. Chelcie doesn't deserve the hit it and quit it approach that he takes, regardless of why she slept with him.

"Talked to Axel this morning. He's having one hell of a time keeping Izzy in Georgia." His condescending tone has my head snapping in his direction.

"And you sound so pissed about that because?" I don't think anyone else has noticed how far apart she and Dee have become recently, but if anyone has noticed, it would be him. I swear this man sees everything.

"Right, don't play me for a fool. I've seen Dee since that motherfucker got ahold of her and Izzy. I've seen her struggling, and you picking her back up. I saw her breaking in two, and it wasn't anyone but you gluing those pieces back together. Not once did her best friends even see one damn thing. Not Izzy, not Greg, not one of them. So yeah, I'm a little pissed about it." His eyes stay on her battered face for a few more beats before meeting mine. "Everyone else kept giving you two shit, thinking you were playing some stupid fucking game, but if they would've opened their eyes for one second longer, they would've seen her hiding in plain sight with you fighting all her demons for her."

I don't keep eye contact with him. Hearing Dee's and my private struggle broken down into a few sentences brings it all home.

Two long fucking years.

Two long years of me worrying that she might never come back from the place inside herself when she had become lost.

And now, right when I felt like she's finally healing this happens, and I honestly don't what kind of lasting effect this is going to have on her. I can only hope that she's become strong enough to realize that she has all the power in the world to become whole again and a man who's willing to fight tooth and nail to help get her there.

"How long have you known?"

I feel Dee's hand tighten on mine, silently letting me know that she's listening, too.

"Since you carried her out of Heavy's."

My eyes shoot to Dee's face. Even with her eyes still closed as if she's sleeping peacefully, a lone tear sneaks out and slides down her face, telling me that she knows just how much Maddox has seen.

"You never said anything, not once. I don't understand why you would be pissed if you watched it right along with them." I keep my tone light, but inside, knowing that I am apparently as transparent to Maddox as it gets, and he still kept his mouth shut is a little hard to stomach.

"Wasn't my place. And before you get pissed, I didn't just sit back and ignore it. I watched, and if I thought for one second that you didn't have it handled, I would've stepped in. Not going to lie. There was a time, when you both were attempting to make each other jealous, or pissed enough to stop trying, that I almost said something. Wouldn't have done me a bit of good, though. She doesn't need me sticking my nose where it doesn't belong. It's always been you. Not everyone would have the patience to stick around when that end result is a big unknown."

Dee's hand clenches in mine so tightly that it's starting to hurt, even though her face still remains relaxed. I don't even know where to begin to respond to all that. I can't be pissed, because he's right. I had it under control, but it would've been nice to know I wasn't fighting alone.

"Patience wasn't even a factor. When you love someone, you fight. You fight for them, and you fight with them. She needed me to fight for her then, and I'll continue to do that until she can fight for herself again." I feel him come up behind me and clasp my shoulder in his strong grip, offering me his strength.

"That right there is why I didn't need to say anything." He walks to the other side of the bed, dips his head down to her ear, and talks low enough that I can't hear him. Her eyes snap open, and she looks right at me. Maddox leans up, kisses her on the forehead, and walks out the door.

"What did he just say?" I whisper, not breaking eye contact.

"He… he said it's time for me and you to start fighting the same war and not different battles."

I nod my head. He's right. It's always been Dee fighting me, fighting herself, and running from her fears. And I've been fighting the world for her while she does it.

It's time. Time for her to let me in and let me help her heal.

Easier said than done with Dee, but when I look into her eyes, it isn't the same force field barrier that she normally has in place that I see. No, I see right into her soul, and the love she keeps carefully hidden, for once, isn't masked. That right there is all the hope I need.

CHAPTER 13
Dee

"If you don't stop treating me like a damn child, I'm going to lose it. I mean it, Beck. I want to go home. I want to sleep in my own bed." He laughs, actually laughs in my face before turning back to the stove and flipping the pancake he's working on.

Oh, the infuriating man. And damn him for making pancakes worthy of me kissing his feet.

It's been two weeks. Two damn weeks since I've been released from the hospital, and he hasn't left my side once. He's becoming Betty freaking Crocker and Suzie Homemaker all rolled into one, too good looking for his own good man. He cooks my meals, does my laundry, and I bet if I asked, he'd wipe my ass for me.

Don't get me wrong. I'm thankful for the assistance, but I haven't left the house once since we've been back. The first week, I don't think I could've left if I'd wanted to. My ribs screamed in pain whenever I moved, and my face would've given small children nightmares. I still look like I fought a semi and lost, but at least the bruises aren't as ugly and vibrant as before, and the swelling has gone down enough that I look somewhat normal.

Now, I just want out. I want to go to my own house, sleep in my own bed, and put some space between us. Oh, who am I kidding? The main reason I want out is because he's making me feel things that scare the shit out of me… making me believe that whatever I've been avoiding this whole time is possible.

He's making me *want* everything he's laying down at my feet. He's making me *crave* everything that I've been running from.

And he's got me so turned on that all he would need to do is say 'come', and I'm pretty sure my body would detonate like a perfectly crafted bomb.

Yeah, I have to get out of here.

He sets the spatula down on the counter and turns to look me in the eyes. "We've been over this before. It's not safe for you to go home until we can finish the investigation, find out who attacked you, and get to the bottom of all this crap you've been dealing with, in secret I might add, at work. So, no… you aren't going anywhere because right here with me is the safest place for you to be." He gives me his trademark smirk and turns back to his flipping.

"I'll be fine! My apartment is secure. I won't even leave. I can work from home just as well as I've been working from your house."

"No."

"No? That's it?" I'm fuming. I know I'm acting like a brat, but I'm terrified. Those walls, that mask, all the protective measures that I've perfected over the years disappeared that last day in the hospital. I can't get his words out of my head.

"Yeah, Dee, that's pretty much it. I know what you're trying to do. You're running, or I should say, you're trying to run. Well, guess what, Babe? You aren't going anywhere. I finally, fucking finally, got back in, and I'll be damned if I let you push me away again." He dishes out the pancakes and brings the plate over to me, turning back to grab some orange juice from the fridge and the syrup from the counter before joining me at the table. I stare at him with my jaw hanging open as he starts shoveling food in his mouth.

"I'm not running," I whisper.

He puts his fork down, wipes his mouth, and looks at me. His eyes are soft and caring. "You're right. You aren't running. You're trying to build that fortress back up around you. You're trying to *hide*. I've watched you since we've been back. The old Dee, the one that's been hiding behind fake smiles and laughter, that's what I expected to deal with when we got home. I was so worried about you after Brandon's attack. There were times when I really thought you would be dead when I came to check on you." He pauses and looks away for a second. With every word he speaks, my heart starts to pound harder in my chest. "You've come so far, Baby, and you've gone through hell. But the difference is now you aren't hiding anymore. MY wildcat is back, and I'll be goddamned if I let her go again."

He gives me a guarded smile, picks up his fork, and starts eating again, as if he hasn't just dropped this… this emotional bomb in my lap. I don't even know what to say. He's right, and dammit, I don't even think I want him to let me go anymore.

"I'm so confused," I confess.

"I know. That's why we will figure this out *together*. I'm right here. All you have to do is reach out and take my hand. One step at a time."

Looking into his eyes, I can see the honesty there, but I can also see the desperation. I've done this to him, to us, and a lesser man would've given up a long time ago.

"I don't deserve you, Beck." I don't, I know this. I've been a bitch; I've pushed and pushed, closing him out. I can see it now, and my heart breaks for all the time he's wasted on me. "Why didn't you just give up? I'm so messed up, Beck... so messed up. I can't even remember half the times you came running when I called because the desire to let the fear get the best of me was too strong. But you did, every single time. Even when I tried bringing other men around to make you mad enough to leave for good, you wouldn't budge. How can you stand by my side, even from a distance, for so damn long, and not hate me? Hell, I hate me." I take a deep breath, and wipe away a few tears before looking up and meeting his gaze. When I see the emotion and adoration in his eyes, I let out a small gasp.

He pushes his chair back and stands, walking the short distance to my chair. I don't look up, but keep my eyes still trained to the spot he just vacated.

"Dee, stand up."

I don't move.

"Dee..."

I can't move, I just let it all hang out and I'm not sure if I'm ready to hear what he's about to say.

"Denise." His tone is harder this time; clearly, he's losing his patience.

I sigh, push my chair back, stand, and turn slowly to look at his chest.

"Eyes up here, Dee." His tone is still hard, but I can hear it, the emotion giving his voice a slight wobble.

When I meet his eyes they are shining brightly, and his lips are curved into a small smile. My breath catches in my throat. He's looking at me like Axel looks at Izzy and Greg looks at Melissa.

He's looking at me as if I'm the only woman on earth.

"I stand by your side because this is where I'm meant to be. I stand by your side because you didn't have the strength to hold yourself up. That's what you do for the person you love. Right after the attack, we were so fresh, but I knew that our relationship was worth fighting for. For months, you would have nightmares, and every time you would wake up, it was *my* name you were screaming to help you. You aren't messed up, Baby. You lived through something terrible, and you needed time to process that. Your mind needed time to heal. I'm not going to lie and tell you I wasn't hurt when you pushed me away. I had just spent eight months at your side trying to be who you needed, but I understand that you had to find your own way." He frames my face in his warm hands, his thumbs brushing the tears that are falling from my eyes in rapid succession.

"Every single time we would get back together, I thought for sure you were back, you would be ready for us. And I won't lie. When I would wake up in the morning expecting to find you naked in my bed, only to meet cold sheets? That hurt. Then I would see you a few days later, and that pain would still be there like a neon sign in your eyes. That pain is gone now. Not even one trace of it is left. Even after all the stuff that went down in your office, it's gone now. You need a little more time to figure it out for yourself? That's fine, but you're going to be doing it, with me, right here." He bends down and presses the softest of kisses against my lips before pulling back and smiling. "Understand now?" I nod. "Good, now let's eat."

I sit lamely and eat my breakfast, because after all that, I'm positive I wouldn't be able to form a word anyway, much less argue with him. Every single thing he just said is true. I don't remember a lot of the early months after Brandon's attack, but I do remember needing him like a life raft. And after all the running, the therapy, the fear, I can also feel that the webs I've been trapped in have cleared. It's almost as if this recent attack has proven to me that I am strong enough to fight for my own happiness. Most importantly, I feel like it's possible now.

****

After breakfast, I clean up our mess and continue to try processing what the hell just happened. Ever since his grand speech, my mind is spinning, and my heart is beating like a marching band has invaded my chest.

Can I forget everything I've ever thought? Is it possible that, maybe, I've just had the worst luck possible when it comes to men, and that he really is this perfect? Even the reasons I've used to push him away in my mind don't hold true anymore. There's no way that he could ever be like Brandon, that bastard. There is no way that he would ever treat me like my father treated my mother and me. All he's ever shown me is love.

I put the last dish in the dishwasher and finish wiping down the counter. The only things I can do now is wait and see if I can convince my head that my heart has been right all along, and then take the leap. The only problem is, I'm just not sure if I can turn off the part of me that keeps thinking he's better off without me and my many suitcases of emotional baggage.

I spend the rest of the day in my head. I know he's giving me time to think and take in everything he said, because he hasn't come out of his office since this morning. One thing I know for sure, if I'm going to do this, I need to let go of my past. That means that I need to finally have that conversation with my parents that I've been avoiding since I graduated high school. And I also need to have the one conversation with Izzy that I know might be the hardest one I need to face.

In order to give Beck all of me, I need to let go of the pain two men in my past have caused me. My father and Brandon.

With a new resolve and the clarity to make it happen, I call Izzy and make plans to meet tomorrow for lunch, and then I call my mother, only to leave a message with her staff requesting an appointment. She must have another new housekeeper because when I said my name she didn't even know who I was. For the first time that I can remember, it doesn't even hurt that my own parents have wiped my existence from their house.

I feel lighter than I have in years, and it feels liberating. When I look in the mirror and see my eyes shining with life, I feel hopeful that I might be able to face the past and win this time. Knowing that I have a one-man army standing at my back has me convinced that I can finally see the light at the end of the tunnel I've been trapped in.

Later that night, when Beck finally comes out of the office for dinner, he takes one look at me, and I know he sees the change, because after he looks down at the floor for a few seconds, he looks back into my eyes with the biggest smile plastered on his face.

"Well… all right," he says, giving me a hug just shy of painful.

Yeah, I can do this. For this man who has been fighting for us alone, I'm finally ready to start fighting with him.

CHAPTER 14
Beck

"I didn't expect to see you actually come into work. I was half tempted to just send these bastards to your house for the meeting today." Axel's laughing voice carries all the way down the hall when I walk into the office the next day.

I knew when I came in today that I would have to deal with comments like this; hell, I've been gone for almost a month, so they've been a long time in coming.

"Very funny. I'm here now, so let's get started."

"Where's Maddox?" Coop asks, coming into the conference room with a box full of donuts. I reach out to take one, but before I grab it he slaps me on the hand like an unruly child. "Mine," he growls.

"You're so fucked up." I laugh. I turn back to the group when they all start laughing. Everyone's here except Maddox, and I can tell by the look Axel's giving me that he didn't know about this. Dammit. "Uh, Maddox isn't coming because he's with Dee."

"Jesus Christ, are you serious? I get it, you wanting to make sure she's safe. I really do. I can understand you being worried about her, but this is getting ridiculous. You're gone for weeks, and hey, I can't get pissed because you're keeping your cases current and shit gets done, but now you have Maddox babysitting her so you can pop in and say fuck you very much?" When

Axel finishes, it takes all my strength to remain in my seat.

Why I thought these assholes would understand, when they haven't seen shit going on right under their own noses for years is beyond me. Hell, they just see Dee being in the wrong place at the wrong time. They don't know shit, and it is making me see red.

"You know what? I'm going to let that shit slide because you don't know the whole story, but if you ever question my actions when it comes to Dee, I won't hold back when I beat your fucking ass." I look around and meet all three sets of eyes looking at me in shock. Hell, Coop still has a donut hanging out of his mouth, just looking at me like I've lost my damn mind. "Okay, I'm sorry, but just don't go there." I finally say after I calm myself down slightly.

"Yeah, I'm sensing that might be a sore subject." Greg laughs, trying to lighten the mood.

"You think? This douchelord just had a PMS fit, and all you're saying is it might be a sore subject. Ha! That's some funny shit." Coop finishes stuffing his food in his mouth and ignores the rest of us.

"Want to tell me why Maddox is with Dee instead of sitting in on this meeting? The meeting that was supposed to be a brief on all this shit we've been investigating for Dee?" Axel's tone is less angry now and more confused.

I should just lay it all out but what goes on between Dee and myself isn't their business. Not that stuff, not until she wants it known.

"He's with Dee because you called me and said I needed to get my ass over here. You asked, and I'm here. Maddox is there because she trusts him, and right now, that's all I need to ease my mind when I can't be there. You've got Izzy, he's got Melissa and Cohen, and this idiot has his insatiable dick to worry about. Are you telling me that one of you would've been there to make sure she's safe?" I continue my sweep of the room. Axel's earlier anger seems to be coming back, and Greg's carefree attitude is gone. Yeah, might as well just keep pissing them off this morning. I look at Coop to see him searching under the table and not even paying attention.

Unwrapping my fingers from their white-knuckle grip on the chair arm gives me a few seconds to figure out just how I want this to play out. I can continue to let them think I've been following Dee around like a lost puppy, or I can give them enough to have them off my back without betraying her trust in me.

"Ha, found you, motherfucker!" My head snaps over to Coop who climbs back up from the floor, blowing on the donut he must have dropped. He finally notices how thick with tension the room has become, because he looks at all of us with one brow cocked for a few seconds before he shrugs his shoulders and stuffs his mouth with half of his rescued snack.

"That's disgusting, Coop," Axel grumbles from across the table.

"Whatever," he mumbles around a mouthful. "What the hell has all you fuckers getting all twitchy? Greg looks like he just shit his pants." He laughs but continues eating without care. Pretty typical Coop, he hates getting into our shit, always has. He's always preferred to be the lover of the group. It's just turned into a different kind of loving as of late.

"Do you maybe want to explain to me why I feel like I just got in trouble with daddy?" Axel asks sarcastically.

"Not really." I cross my arms over my chest and pray that I have the strength to stay in my seat if they continue with this conversation.

"Fuck that! Maybe let's go with why you would think I wouldn't be worried about Dee when I've been around a lot longer than you have. You're acting like you have some claim to her, and we all know she moved on from whatever fun y'all had early on."

Just like that, I jump up from my seat and slam my palms down on the table with a loud pop. Axel looks on as if he is bored with the conversation. I don't have to look at Coop to see that he's stopped eating and has finally given us his attention.

But, Greg? This motherfucker has the balls to actually look smug. He stands up, and with the table between us, moves in so he's right in my face before he continues running his mouth. "What? Hit a little too close to home there, Beck? Maybe it's time to just stop trying to get her to notice you. Stop feeding into her games. I held my tongue when you told me not to drive up when she was in the hospital, but I'm getting sick and fucking tired of watching you two play your little, high school bullshit."

I don't even give him a second to take a breath after he delivers that pile of shit. I reach back and clock him right in the jaw with enough power to have him on his ass. I palm the table again and swing my legs over, landing right next to his fallen form.

"What the fuck!" Axel stands and moves to pull me away from Greg, but stops in his tracks when I look up and meet his eyes.

"Don't you even think about touching me right now. You might have me in size but right now, I've got anger on my side, and I'll level you on the goddamn ground if you take one more step."

I turn back to where Greg is leaning against the conference room wall, wiping the blood from his lip. I can see the anger in his eyes, but he looks more confused as to why I just laid him out. We've fought before, all of us have, but never have I laid my hands on one of my brothers in anger.

Leaning in close enough that he knows I'm serious, I keep my voice low and level. "Do not sit here and pretend to even have a clue what's been going on between Dee and me. I'm going to say this once, and only once, because it still makes me so fucking mad to even think about it." I take a deep breath, not once breaking eye contact with Greg. I want him to understand why I'm livid.

"Months, Greg, hell, close to a year and a half, that woman has needed you, and you couldn't even fucking see it. You have no idea what the hell she's been going through, and I'll tell you right now, if you want to know that's up to you, but you won't hear it from me. What I will clue you the fuck in on is that these *games* you think I've been feeding into? These games kept the woman I love alive. They helped her heal, and more importantly, these *games* you think I'm playing give me more claim on her than you ever had. Do not ever question my relationship with Dee when you have no clue what the hell you're talking about."

He keeps staring at me, his jaw hard, and his eyes spitting fire. Right when I think he's decided to pout in the corner instead of responding, he opens his mouth. "You're really going to stand there and act like you haven't been so pussy whipped for two stupid fucking years? Hell, you have it so bad you can't even see it."

"Don't keep running your mouth because you're pissed I laid your ass out."

He climbs to his feet and moves forward so that we're toe-to-toe. I keep flexing my fist, trying to purge the violence from my body.

"Not running my mouth, Beck. Can't handle a little truth? We've all seen her running around, dating, laughing, and having fun. You can't sit here and act like she's been living two lives! I would have noticed if she needed me."

My jaw drops after that load of shit, and then I laugh. I laugh so hard that I have to step away from him and hold my sides.

It takes me a few minutes because the anger is still very much present. Holding my hand up to tell him to wait, gives me a few seconds to compose myself. I just stand here hunched over, trying to get my breathing under control. Now that the hilarity of just how blind he is to someone he claims to know and love like a sister has passed, and I sober quickly.

"You know, I don't know who I feel more sorry for right now. Dee for hiding behind all that false happiness because she didn't think you could be bothered to be there, or you! You're the one who claims to love her like family, but you're so fucking stupid that you couldn't see it." I throw my hands up and walk away from him before I knock his ass back on the ground. "I can even overlook the time that you met Melissa, and the shit storm that followed. You had your own heavy issues, and believe me, Brother, I get they were as heavy as it gets, but before that, there was almost a year that you couldn't see shit. Hell, maybe you did and just didn't care, because hey, she was still smiling, right?" I throw his words back at him and turn to Axel. He's just standing there, but now, he's looking at me with all the questions I knew he would have if I opened this can of worms.

"Fuck you, Beck. What gives you the right to sit here and act like you're better than any one of us?" Greg growls at me, but makes the mistake of grabbing my shoulder to get my attention back on him.

I turn quicker than he expected and grab him by the front of his tee, pushing him back into the wall hard enough that I swear I hear the wall crack. "I gained that right the first time I had to stop her from swallowing a bottle of pills." I shove off, pissed at myself for giving into him when he clearly wanted to bait me. "I've got a lot of anger built up about this Greg, and it really would be wise if you shut the fuck up. Now." I pace the length of the room, my hands on my hips, and my breathing still coming rapidly.

"I think it's time you cleared the air, Brother," Coop says from the table. I look over and meet his eyes; he gives me a small nod, and the tension in my shoulders drops.

"Fuck!" I kick over one of the chairs before turning back and walking over to my seat. Greg, still clearly pissed, rights his chair, and sits. Axel keeps his gaze on me for a few seconds before taking his seat next to Greg. I laugh at the irony of those two on one side and me, alone, on the other. Coop clears his throat from his seat at the head of the table, and I take that as my signal to talk.

"This isn't my place to tell you, and I feel like I'm betraying Dee by even opening my mouth." The fight, all that anger, leaves in seconds, and I just feel... alone.

"It sure would make it a lot easier if we understood what the fuck that shit was all about," Axel says in frustration.

"I don't like my loyalties being questioned, Beck. And I damn sure don't like being punched in the face. Melissa's going to kick your ass, pregnant or not."

"Honestly, you deserved that and more, Greg. I've kept my mouth shut out of respect for Dee, but mainly because I had it covered. I was there when she needed me, and I will continue to be there for her." I turn my attention to Axel, taking a deep breath before addressing him. "First, I mean no disrespect, Ax, for what I'm about to say, so understand that and keep your temper in check." He gives me a tight nod. Looking back over at Greg I continue. "Right before that shit went down in Izzy and Dee's old townhouse, Dee and I started dating. It was new, so new that we didn't even get to announce shit to anyone before that all went down. Then with Greg in the hospital, almost dying and shit, there wasn't a good time. Izzy needed Axel, and Greg was healing. So, Dee was alone."

"What the hell do you mean she was alone? She lived in my damn house! Izzy was there. I was there. She wasn't alone!" Axel's growl pretty much confirms what I thought. Of course, he's defensive.

"I told you I didn't mean any disrespect, Axel, and I mean it. But, even though she was right under your nose, you were so busy with Izzy that you didn't see a thing. Think back, and I mean, really think. How many times would she sit in that little corner in your office that you gave her to work? How many nights would you catch her roaming around downstairs? Really think about what you couldn't see, because your whole focus was Izzy. I'm not even faulting you there because Izzy needed you, but Dee needed someone, too." I look down and gather my thoughts. I hate thinking back to those months. "She would call me every night, and I listened to her cry herself to sleep. Every single noise in your house terrified her. Then, I finally talked her into getting the apartment in Maddox's complex, thinking she would be better off. I spent another few months never leaving her side." I have to stop and clear the lump in my throat. Jesus, this is harder than I thought it would be.

"The first time she almost took her own life, she called me first. It gave me enough time to get there, and it took me almost a week to calm her down enough to get help. She only tried once after that, but she had me there. That happened a month before she pushed me away. She started seeing a therapist, and I kept a close eye on her. It's taken almost a year for me to see the signs of life coming back into her. She hid it, but if you all would've taken a good look at her, you would've seen just how broken she was." I look up to meet their eyes.

Coop has a look of understanding on his face that makes me think he wasn't as clueless as I thought he had been. Axel's face is clear of emotion, but I can see the shock in his eyes. When I finally meet Greg's eyes, the raw pain that is washed over his features shocks me.

"I had no idea." His voice even sounds flat.

"Yeah, I know." I offer him a small smile but no understanding. These people should've seen it, and knowing they've thought she was playing games just breaks my heart for her. "Those games you think she was playing, the guys she was dating, all of it. That was her way of acting like she's fine so you all wouldn't ask questions. She didn't want you to know, and I still don't even know why she was so determined that you all stay clueless."

"What can we do?" Axel's holding it in tight, but he looks like he's about to start breaking things soon. He doesn't like his family hurting, and he's got to know that when Izzy finds this out, it's going to be hard for her to know she's been just as blind as the rest of them.

"You three don't do shit. She trusts Maddox. I know she's already talked to him about some of this, but I don't know how much she's told him. Plus, with him knowing everything that's been going on, it all makes it easier for her to talk to him. She's meeting with Izzy for lunch today, so Axel, I wouldn't be surprised if you're needed not long after. Right now, Dee is mine, and I'll keep doing what I've been doing. We figure out who this motherfucker is, and he's mine to deal with. Then we move on like the family we are."

They nod their heads in understanding, but Greg pushes back from the table. He pulls the door open, walks out, and slams it behind him.

"Give him a second to get a handle on this. You can't expect him to just brush off the fact that he's basically ignored Dee when she needed him." Axel's right. At this point, it's a tossup for who's going to handle this better, Greg or Izzy.

It takes almost thirty minutes before Greg comes back in. He walks up to where I'm standing by the window and pulls me into a hug. I slap him on the back a few times and let him have this. As frustrated as I am with him, I know how seriously he takes his relationship with the females in his life. I knew it wouldn't be easy for him to know that someone needed him, and he didn't see it.

"Don't beat yourself up, Greg. She's on the other side of it now. Even after that shit at the office, she's got this strength about her that makes me know she's going to be okay."

He pulls back and looks at me with pain clear in his eyes. "Thank you for being there for her when I couldn't see it."

I nod my head and we return to the table. I know this isn't over. Dee's going to have to finish this and forgive him before they can move on. And judging by the look on his face, he knows this too.

We spend the rest of the morning going over what we know about her attack. Which basically, is pretty much nothing. Adam Harris hasn't been back to work since the Friday before the attack. Everything is still in his apartment, except it's been trashed as though he had to leave in a hurry. His family doesn't have one clue as to where he could be. Dee's attacker had parked far enough from her office that his vehicle didn't get caught on any of the security footage, and he never took his mask off when in range of the cameras.

We have nothing. And all I take away from this meeting is the feeling deep in my gut that this is going to get worse before it gets better.

CHAPTER 15
Dee

I'm more nervous for my lunch date with Izzy than I thought I would be. I know this isn't going to be a fun catch up and gossip date. She's going to be devastated when I tell her everything I've hidden from her.

Beck left this morning worried for me because he knew what would happen today. But he also left knowing that I needed to do this alone, and he never once questioned me.

I can only hope that when he gets home, and I tell him what I have to tell Izzy, that he's still willing to stand by my side.

It's time for me to free myself of all this pain.

****

I've just stepped out of the shower when I hear a knock on the door. I think about locking myself in the bathroom and hiding, but after a few seconds of calming my breathing, I'm able to fight the panic.

Dressing quickly in the sweats and tee that Beck had left on the floor this morning, I set off for the door with only a slight tremble in my limbs. As silently as I can I creep up to the door and look through the peephole. When I see Maddox glaring at the solid wood, I smile slightly, take a deep breath to calm my nerves, and open the door.

"Hey Mad." I smile and stand back for him to enter.

"Hey." He looks me over, his lips twitching just barely, before heading off in the direction of the kitchen.

"I'm going to get ready, okay?" I call after his retreating form.

"Yup."

I shake my head and lock the door before heading back upstairs.

It takes me longer than normal to get ready. What does one wear to lunch, knowing that you're about to rip your best friend's heart to pieces? I settle for a pair of skinny jeans, a teal blouse, and my favorite teal four-inch heels. Light makeup and a few motivational pep talks later, I'm ready to take on the day.

"Izzy's on her way." I tell Maddox when I enter the kitchen. He's standing next to the stove, eating some of the bacon left from breakfast. "Do you want a plate? Maybe let me make you something fresh?"

"I know and no."

"Uh, okay? You know you don't have to be here, right? I'll be okay by myself." I smile, letting him know that I really will be okay, but he doesn't move.

He just looks at me with those scary eyes, finishes the last two pieces, and washes his hands. "You might think you're okay to be alone, but I'm still going to be here. You and Izzy do your thing, and if you need me when you're done until Beck gets home, then I'll be here. If not, then I'll still be here." And with that, he turns and makes his way through the house. I hear him settling in the living room, the TV click on, and the low sounds of some sports crap fill the air.

Well... okay then.

I set about cleaning the kitchen, trying to keep my mind clear. Izzy comes bouncing in about an hour later with a wiggling Nate on her hip, and what looks like her whole house in the bag around her shoulder.

"Hey, you!" She drops the bag and sets Nate on his feet before coming over to give me a hug. "I missed you! Beck seems to only want to keep you all to himself."

I try to smile but the butterflies in my gut are going crazy. She notices and gives me a weak smile. I look away from her when I hear Nate's little feet take off and the sounds of his squealing.

Oh, wow.

"Oh, wow." She echoes my thoughts. We both stand here, staring at Maddox who has Nate up in the air, and he has the biggest smile I've ever seen on his face. His whole demeanor changes right before us. The hard, unapproachable look that he normally wears is gone, and replaced with a man seriously too good looking for his own good.

"I can see why Emmy is so hung up on him," she whispers in my direction.

"You aren't lying."

We both laugh and Maddox jerks his head in our direction. The carefree smile that was on his face only seconds before is now long gone. He almost looks mad that he ever let it appear in the first place.

"I'll take Nate while you two do your chick stuff." He takes off with a giggling Nate in his arms. I hear a door click in the distance, and know he must have gone down into the basement where Beck keeps all his workout equipment.

"So, I'm guessing that we aren't actually eating, huh?" She lets a nervous laugh bubble out, but stops when I look at her and shake my head. "I didn't think so. I just knew somehow that you didn't want to catch up."

"Come on, it's a pretty day, so why don't we go sit out in the sunroom?"

She grabs a water bottle out of the diaper bag and follows after me.

"Just spit it out, Dee. It's killing me. All night, I was worried about what you wanted to talk about. I could tell by the tone in your voice that something's going on, but I can't figure out for the life of me what it could be." Her green eyes look so dark when she's worried. She's biting on her lip and fidgeting with her hands.

I start at the beginning and tell her about my parents, the boys I used to date, and how all those relationships ended. I tell her about how I didn't have any real friends until the day I met her. She takes it all in, nodding her head a few times here and there to let me know she's listening. I can tell she's getting upset when I mention how bad things had been growing up with my parents, but she kept silent.

Then I tell her everything I've only spoken about to Dr. Maxwell and Maddox about. I finally reveal the secrets about her ex-husband that I have held in for so long. She only lets out a few shocked gasps, her hand shooting out to hold mine when I relate how he broke into my office and beat me.

"I should have done more to get you out, Izzy. I was just so scared of what he would do. I could see it in his eyes. I don't know how I knew, but I just did. I sat by and let him hurt you, Izzy." When I meet her troubled gaze and see the tears in her eyes, it breaks my heart, and the tears that I have been holding back start falling freely.

"You've been beating yourself up this whole time, haven't you?" I nod my head, but before I can open my mouth, she interrupts. "Brandon was a sick man, Dee. You have no idea how much it hurts to know he got his filthy hands on you, but nothing that happened during my marriage is your fault." She's trying to keep her emotions in check, but the tremble in her voice gives her away.

I pause for a second to get ready to finish my story, and gaze out on the beautifully landscaped backyard. I must have been silent for a while, because her whispered question makes me jump.

"What aren't you telling me, Dee? I know you. There's more isn't there?" Her voice is begging me to prove her wrong.

"Yeah, there's more." I take another breath and look back over to see her face awash with pain. "When he finally got done using his fist he told me that if I tried to contact you in any way, that he would kill you," I whisper on a sob. Her tears are coming quickly, and I know I have to get the rest out before she starts to cry in earnest. "And then... then he took the only thing left to take from me."

She starts shaking her head begging me to shut up.

"I'm sorry, so sorry I wasn't there when you needed me, but he said he would kill you! I tried to keep my eyes on you, but I was so terrified that if I even tried to warn you, he would take you from me completely."

Her body is heaving with her sobs, and it's hard to tell who is crying louder at this point. She grabs me and pulls me into a tight, painful hug. We sit there, rocking together for a while, before she pulls back.

"He raped you, didn't he?" she asks a few minutes later, her voice calm despite the fact that her hands are shaking violently.

"Yeah, he did."

If she hadn't have jumped slightly, I wouldn't have thought that she heard me since I'd spoken so lightly.

"I'm trying to process this. I really am... I can't even wrap my head around all of this, Dee! Why didn't you tell me years ago? Even after he was gone? Did you think I would blame you? God, never! I'm upset because you had to go through that alone." She wipes her eyes with her shirt and tries to calm herself down. "You're like my sister, Dee. Why couldn't you tell me?"

"Because I didn't know how. It seems so simple now, looking back, but then, all I saw was another man turned monster. It wasn't even about the rape, Izzy. That was terrible, but I survived it. I was worried about you and what would happen if I didn't find a way to save you."

She grabs my hand and holds it tightly. "You did save me. That night that I called you, you saved my life that day and every day after. I wish you had told me about this years ago, but thank you for telling me now. For trusting me with this."

We sit here both with our own pain, for a few minutes when I feel her hand constrict against mine. "You aren't done, are you? If you were done, you wouldn't look like that." Her eyes are wide and panicked with the unknown fear of what else I have to tell her.

"I'm not done."

"Jesus, Dee." She shakes her head in disbelief. "Tell me, please." Her pleading voice gives me the last push I need.

I tell her about the pain I suffered after Brandon's final attack. How his attack clicked some switch inside of me. How it made me feel like I was drowning in the nightmare that he created. How I had no hope in my escape. I tell her all about my fight with depression, and concerning what the doctor has diagnosed as PTSD brought on by the attack. For a second, I think I need to stop, or fib a little and downplay how bad I got mentally, but I know that I need to get this all out in order to move on. She's crying, sobbing, and gasping for air by the time I finish.

"My God, Dee!" She grabs me and pulls me in tight again, crying into the crook of my neck. "I'm so, so sorry. I've been so wrapped up with Axel, Nate, and life that I've been a terrible friend."

"No, Iz. You haven't been a terrible friend. You've just had other priorities, and I never blamed you, not once. Please, don't think that. I didn't tell you this to make you upset. I told you this because, without letting it out, I will never be able to move on. I want to move on. I'm ready to fight for my happiness now, and I couldn't do that with this between us, even if you didn't know it was there." I'm so proud of myself for getting that out without a single tear. I hate seeing Izzy upset, but knowing that I'm strong enough to get through that, and to let her know how hard the last few years have been, gives me a feeling of peace that I didn't have before. I'm one step closer to being healed, and it makes me feel like a whole new person.

"I don't know how you can ever forgive me for not seeing how much pain you were in," she whispers, staring off into the yard.

"Izzy, that's easy. There isn't anything to forgive. I love you."

She gives me a smile, wipes her eyes again with her shirt, and reaches out to hug me again.

"Please, tell me there isn't anything else?"

"There isn't. I know it's not easy to hear, but thank you for listening. You have no idea how scared I've been to tell you all of that."

She leans up and gives me a weak smile. "Don't keep things from me again. I understand where your head was in keeping that to yourself, but don't do that again. You're one of the most important people in my life, Dee, and I don't ever want you to think there's something you can't tell me."

"I know that now. It's taken me a lot of really expensive doctor appointments to really understand that, though. I'm done hiding and keeping parts of myself from those that love me."

We sit here silently for a while, just offering each other the strength that we need. I know she's hurting, and there really isn't anything I can do about it. She's my best friend, my sister, and one of the most important people in my life. But this is something she has to take and process on her own, with the help of the husband that loves her, to get past it.

It's a shock, and I know she's going to be upset about this, understandably so, but I also know that our friendship is that much stronger, because there isn't a single thing standing between us now.

She gets up to leave about an hour later and when I watch her drive off, I do it with the clarity that everything is going to be just fine.

CHAPTER 16
Dee

"Dee? Are you up there?" I smile and drop down further in the tub, enjoying the soothing effects the warm water is having on me. "Dee!" I can hear him panicking slightly when I don't answer right away.

"I'm in the bathroom," I yell through the crack in the doorway. I could let him wonder where I am, but I know he's worried. It wasn't easy to get him to leave this morning to begin with, so it would be cruel to make him search longer than he has.

He comes bursting through the door and skids to a stop when he sees me sitting in the bath, bubbles surrounding me. I give him a wide smile, and enjoy the fact that his body visibly shutters.

"Jesus Christ…" he mumbles under his breath.

"You found me." I laugh when his eyes shoot up from where they've been staring at my chest. I make sure that I'm still covered under the bubbles before looking back at his face.

He clears his throat a few times and adjusts himself. I laugh when I see how much just being in this room is affecting him.

"Are you okay, Beck?" I ask, pushing myself up in the tub. He looks like he might pass out as my naked breasts clear the bubbles. My nipples harden instantly when I see the look of pure lust that comes over him.

"Dee, if you don't want to start anything, then please cover yourself up." His voice is just shy of begging.

My body heats up when I see the outline of his erection against his jeans. My mouth waters and I have to press my thighs together to keep from touching myself.

"Don't look at me like that," he pleads.

"Like what?" I question in mock ignorance.

"You're looking at me like you haven't eaten in years, and I just brought you a steak dinner." He sounds strained, almost to the point of pain.

I smile at him and give him one more, slow caress with my eyes. "Will you please hand me a towel?"

He presses his palm against his crotch and groans when he turns to grab the towel I've left on the sink. He stands there with his hand clenched tightly against it and his head bowed. The water is almost completely gone by the time he turns back around with his eyes pinched shut.

"You have no idea what I would do to be able to carry you off to the bed and show you for hours how much I've dreamed of this moment. It's been six long months since I've been inside that tight body, and when I have you again, and believe me, Baby, I will have you again, it's going to be forever this time." He opens his eyes, and the fire I see blazing deep within takes my breath away.

Mutely, I nod my head and accept the bath sheet he's holding out. He leans in and plants a swift kiss against my lips before walking towards the open door.

When I notice the slightly awkward way he's walking, a nervous giggle bubbles out. I slap my hand over my mouth to try to stop myself, but he turns and narrows his eyes at me.

"This isn't funny, Dee. I'm so hard right now that I wouldn't be surprised if my balls are turning blue."

"I'm sorry, really!" I hold my hands up in surrender, but notice my mistake about two seconds too late. The towel falls from my body and pools around my feet, leaving me standing before him completely naked. He growls low in his throat, the sound so powerful that my pussy throbs. Jesus, that's hot.

With more willpower than I thought possible, he turns stiffly and walks the rest of the way out the door, closing it softly behind him. I spend the next thirty minutes trying to calm my own hormones down, but quickly realize there isn't much that can soothe the inferno raging inside me. I want him with an all-consuming thirst.

****

After our bathroom incident, we walk on eggshells around each other. Both of us dance around, knowing that behind each stolen glance and heated glare, we both want nothing more than to collide together in what promises to be the wildest of reunions.

When he looks at me, again, like he's just finished fucking me against the countertop that I'm fixing dinner on, I slam my knife down. The sexual heat between us has the room thick with tension. It almost feels like a fog of desire is cloaking every inch of space around us.

"I think I might need to skip dinner."

He puts the plates down and walks over from where he was setting the table. I don't move. I continue to hold the marble countertop as if my life depends on it, afraid that if I remove my hands, even for a second, that I might shred the clothes straight from his body.

I don't feel him at first, but I know he's standing directly behind me. I can feel him, and his body heat warming my back. I fight the urge to turn and throw myself at him. When his hand moves my hair off my shoulder, and his lips press lightly against my exposed neck, my body trembles violently.

"I want you so bad, Beck." The desperation in my voice causes my cheeks to heat, and I drop my head, annoyed with my body for its shamelessness.

"And I want you right back just as much, so don't think this isn't hard on me, too. I'm not going anywhere, Dee. You might think you're ready, and I have no doubt that your body is, but I want it all. Mind, body, soul, and heart. I promise you that when we finally get there, it's going to be worth the wait. When you open yourself up to me completely... Baby, you won't even believe how good it's going to be." He nibbles softly across my neck before backing away and picking up the plates he'd abandoned. It takes me longer to calm the heat in my body.

I understand where he's coming from, but it's harder to explain to my overactive hormones that we need to put the brakes on it. The last time I had him inside of me was another moment of weakness, and even though it was mind-blowing, as always, it still left me unsatisfied because I ran off in the middle of the night. Six months is a long time to crave someone else. I pause in my tracks when the very vivid images of him with someone else come floating through my mind. I don't know why it never occurred to me that he could have been with anyone else, but now that the thought has popped in my head, there is no erasing it. My stomach cramps with the idea of him and some faceless woman.

"Beck?" He turns with a frown marring his handsome face, cocking his brow in question. I gulp, trying to calm my emotions. "I have no right to ask this, I know I don't, but… has there been someone… um, anyone else?" I whisper the question, but I know he hears me because his face goes soft.

His lips curl into a small smile and his eyes darken. "Are you jealous?"

I glare at him when his teasing tone hits me.

"Don't poke fun at me, Beck. I know that I have no right to even be bothered by the thought, much less question you on it. I pushed you away and I get it, I do. But… I just want to know. I need to know."

He doesn't walk over to me, and I appreciate that he's giving me some space here. My mind is a jumbled mess of questions. On one hand, I know without a doubt that this is where I'm meant to be. I don't fear that he will change anymore, but I'm still afraid of the unknown. I know now that this is normal with any relationship, but it's still there. Knowing that I've pushed this man away for so long, regardless of what I've had going on in my head, is what kills me. I wouldn't even fault him if there had been someone else.

"Look at me, Dee, and I mean really look at me." He gives me a second, and I just look into his eyes, waiting for his next words. "The day your drunk ass went on and on about how chocolate is better than sex, you had me hooked. It was never a question of whether or not you were it for me. I knew. You might have pushed me away physically, but I didn't really go anywhere, and if you think about it long enough, you know I didn't leave you. Even if we hadn't had the handful of nights together during all this time apart, there was no way I would have even been able to get it up for another woman. Not when my heart has always been yours. So no, Dee, there hasn't been anyone else, and there won't be anyone else. This is the longest we've ever gone without falling into each other, and I can wait as long as it takes for your head to catch up with your heart." He smiles and it isn't a smile of sadness. It's one of acceptance. And right then and there, I know without a doubt that I don't deserve this man, but I'll fight like hell to be worthy of the love he's offering.

"For what it's worth, it's only been you for me, too." I echo his words back at him. His smile gets even bigger before he finishes setting the table.

A comfortable silence fills the air, and after sitting down and starting our meal, he clears his throat. I look up, expecting the question I've known was coming, but not sure I'm ready to answer. "How did it go with Izzy today?" He finishes cutting a piece of his chicken, but pauses with it halfway to his mouth when he sees the nervousness take over my face. Telling Izzy what Brandon had done to me had been a painful conversation, but it will pale in comparison to how gutting it will be to tell Beck.

I think I've always known that he would be the hardest one for me to tell. I have had a very real fear that he would look at me differently if he knew everything that had played a part in keeping me from him. Like he would think I'm damaged goods, tainted, unworthy. Things would have been a lot easier if I hadn't been afraid to tell him. I took a while, but now I can tell that he would have helped me get over it back then and still would've loved me.

"It wasn't easy." He nods his head and waits for me to continue. "I think that was one of the hardest conversations I will ever have in my life."

"How did she take it?"

"Better than I thought she would. She'll be okay because it's Izzy."

He smiles, returning to his meal for a few bites. We both know how strong Izzy is now, and since she has Axel standing by her side, I know she'll be able to move past this and not have it affect us.

In a way, having the strength to tell Izzy is what gives me the strength to have this conversation with Beck.

"I would like to tell you what we talked about, if that's okay." I rush the last part out so that I don't wuss out before I finish.

He stops what he's doing, sets his fork down, and gives me his full attention. "I'm done eating if you want to talk now." His eagerness helps give me the final push to talk. He's been waiting for this moment since I closed myself off and pushed him away. Patiently waiting for me to open up.

"Why don't we get everything cleaned up, and then go sit somewhere and have a drink. I think you're going to need it." I stand up and do my best to ignore the worried look across his face.

I smile when I walk into the kitchen with our dishes, because I know, with not one single shadow of doubt, that I'm ready to have this conversation. Not only that, but I finally can see with crystal clear clarity that, once I get this out, there won't be anything left standing in our way.

CHAPTER 17
Dee

I finished up cleaning up our dinner mess and walked out into the living room where Beck's on the phone with his sister, Julie. The phone rang right when we finished up dinner, and even though he's anxious to get our conversation rolling, he answered with a smile.

I round the couch and hand him a beer before settling in next to him. He pulls me close with the hand that isn't holding the phone, and smiles.

"Yeah, Jules, I know. I promise that I'll be home to visit soon. Yeah. No, I haven't forgotten how to work a phone. Yeah, she's great." He stops talking and looks into my eyes, giving me a light squeeze so I know she's asking about me.

I've talked to Julie, his youngest sister, a few times over the phone, and once when she came to visit. She's such a sweetheart and we connected instantly. His other sister, Peyton, I haven't met in person, but each time I've spoken to her on the phone, I can tell that she's just like Julie. Both of them share the same huge heart and compassionate soul that Beck has.

"I think mom said she would be driving down to visit sometime next month. You know how she is; she wants to wait until you and Pey can come down with her." He laughs at whatever Julie says in return.

I settle into his chest and enjoy the feeling of his voice vibrating against my body. This feels so right, sharing this moment, even though it's just a small one with him. Doing things that normal couples take for granted feels like a huge accomplishment for me. When he hangs up the phone and turns to me, catching my smile, he offers one just as big back to me.

"What's that smile for?"

"I'm just enjoying the moment." My smile fades when I realize that it's time to have this talk with him. "How's Julie?" I ask, trying to buy some time to settle the butterflies in my stomach.

He gives a snort, shaking his head a few times. Obviously, he knows me well enough to know my stalling tactics. "Do you really want to know or would you rather I sit here and let you calm down a little while before we talk?" He isn't mad, just being honest.

"You really do know me, don't you?" I laugh softly. "I really do want to know how she is, but I do also need a second to collect my thoughts."

"I understand that. We've got all night. Jules is good. She's complaining about some class she's taking. Keeps going on and on about how she shouldn't have waited until she was twenty-eight to go back and get her degree. She'll figure it out though. She says mom wants to come down, especially when she found out you had been hurt. Don't worry, I bought us some time." His smile gets big when he talks about his family. He's so lucky to have come from such a loving family. Even without having a father around, there was never a lack of love in his life.

"I would love to see them again." I don't think I realized how true that statement was until just now. Even though I've only met Julie in person, I have talked to the other ladies in his life a few times when he was teaching his mother how to FaceTime.

"I would love that, too." I lean back into him, and we both sit here for a few minutes in a comfortable silence. He takes a few deep pulls on his beer, and I spend the time figuring out how to start this chat.

"I'm really not sure that there is a real easy way to start with this one. I suppose it would be really easy to take the cheap way out and just give you my journals that Dr. Maxwell made me keep." A nervous giggle bubbles up before I can squash it. "Okay. Let's just start with my father."

He sits there and gives me the silence I need, his thumb slowly rubbing against my bare shoulder.

"The first time my father ever hit me, I was five and had forgotten to make my bed. That was also the first time of many that he told me that he wished I had never been born. It wasn't easy living with my parents. My mother was just as nasty as he was, except her words were her weapon of choice. I learned real early in life that I would be better off keeping my head down and making sure I did everything they wanted." I steal a glance at him and can tell he's pissed, but holding it in so I can finish.

"I won't lie and pretend that there was much good about my childhood. I had one nanny that gave me as much love as she could, but when she was caught sneaking Barbies in for me to play with, my parents fired her. I'll skip all the sordid details, but whatever you're imagining is probably spot on."

His hand flexes slightly on my shoulder, but when I look over, he nods tensely for me to continue.

"I know that my father is the seed that started my fear of men and growing relationships. There wasn't a single relationship that I had that wasn't a way for someone to get closer to my father and family money. That helped that belief that men do nothing but change after they get what they want. Dr. Maxwell says that since I hadn't had any positive male relationships until my twenties and my friendship with Greg, that it makes sense that I have some asinine belief that all men will change." I shift my body so I can look into his eyes. I need to see him and make sure he understands this next part. "Please know that I see this now. I really do. I know that I was projecting my fears onto you, but they were so deeply integrated that I don't think I would have been able to just shut them off, and you have no idea how sorry I am for that."

He smiles sadly and takes my hands in his. "I know that, Baby. I never doubted that you were fighting something beyond your control."

"God, I don't deserve your understanding."

"Hey, stop that. Don't doubt your self-worth, not with me." His tone leaves no room for argument and I nod my head.

"I'm learning that. Sometimes I feel like I'm completely lost because I have no idea what I'm doing here, but I can tell you aren't like them. It's just taken me a while. I shouldn't have ever lumped you in with them."

"Dee, we can only ever go off what we know, and you hadn't ever seen anything that would make you believe that I wasn't like those assholes."

I sit there for a few more beats, gathering my strength for the next part. "Did I ever tell you that I was the one that introduced Brandon and Izzy?"

His eyes widen before he shakes his head.

"Yeah, that was me. I set up my best friend with the man who almost took her from me. I always wondered what would have happened if I hadn't ever set them up. Until recently, it was nothing but guilt that would eat at me, but Izzy helped me realize that it wasn't anything I could have known. I understand that now, but it isn't any easier."

"I really thought that he was one of the good guys." I laugh weakly. "What a fool I was."

He takes my hands again and waits for me to continue. "It took about a year into their marriage for me to realize how wrong I had been. She started pulling away and I saw less and less of her. I didn't give up though; I kept calling and trying to come around. I think it had been a good week of my constant calls before it happened. I know I was being a pain in the ass, but I just wanted to talk to Izzy."

I don't realize I have zoned out until his hand squeezes mine almost painfully. I look up from where I've been staring at our hands. I have to close my eyes when I see the pain in his eyes. He knows this is about to get really ugly.

"It's okay, Dee. I'm listening."

"Are you sure you want to know the rest?"

He nods sharply and I sigh.

"I didn't realize until recently, with Dr. Maxwell's help, why I had such a hard time after all that stuff with Brandon went down. I knew I was pushing you away out of fear, but I couldn't even understand it myself. You have to understand that I've never known a positive relationship with a man, so when you started getting close, I freaked out. You are so perfect on the outside that it terrified me beyond imagination that you could change just as easily as all the others." I stop when he grunts, but he motions for me to keep going. "Right. So with that, you might understand a little better why his attack was the trigger for me. About two years into their marriage, he cornered me. I'll spare you the gory details, but how I looked a few weeks ago? That's close to how he left me, only he took it a lot further."

He shoots off the couch, knocking his beer to the floor. I keep my eyes trained to the foaming liquid pouring out of the overturned bottle. I knew he would look at me differently, but it's still painful to be right. Why would he want someone so fucked up?

"He put his hands on you? Son of a bitch! If he wasn't already dead, I would fucking kill him. Gut that sorry bastard." He paces in front of the couch, growling each word out with disgust. "Fuck!" He keeps his pacing up for a few minutes before he stops in his tracks and looks over at me. Shaking his head, a look of stark terror comes over his features. I watch in slow motion as he figures it out before I can tell him. Somehow, he just knows, and when I watch all that anger turn into a pain so great that he drops to his knees in front of me, my world ends. "No, no, no…"

I can't move from my spot on the couch. My chest is heaving with the force of my emotions. My tears burn as they fall down my face and land in my lap. I can't even move to wipe my eyes. He quickly moves over to where I'm sitting, his head hits my lap, and his arms wrap around my waist. When his shoulders start to shake with the emotions warring through him, my tears come quicker, and a loud sob breaks free from my throat.

That sob seems to break him from his silent misery because his he pulls his head up, unwraps his arms, and pulls me down into his lap. His strong arms wrap around me again, and he pushes his face into my shoulder. I cling to him, soaking up his heat, trying to warm my body and chase away the pain.

He doesn't break his hold on me when he pulls us back up to the couch, still making sure that I'm in his lap and safe in his arms.

"I'm sorry." I offer weakly.

He looks shocked, but desperation bleeds off his face. "What? My God, Dee, what do you have to be sorry for?"

I shrug my shoulders and just shake my head.

"You've thought this was your fault this whole time? Oh, Baby." He pulls me back to his chest and rocks us slightly. "What that bastard did to you isn't your fault, Dee. Never your fault. He was a sick, disturbed man. It kills me to think about you going through that, and going through it alone. I wish you could have opened up and told me that before, but I understand why you didn't. That's why you kept running?"

"Yeah. I don't think I can ever prove to you how sorry I am for everything that I've put us through. I just saw you and all your perfection, and it reminded me of how *he* was when I had first introduced him to Izzy. I think I always knew deep down that you would never turn on me, but that fear was so ingrained, that no matter what I did, I couldn't separate you two. And then when all of that stuff happened, it was like a light switch went off. I knew he was gone, but my mind couldn't turn the fear off. He was everywhere I looked, and every time I looked in the mirror, I could see what he did to me. I punished you because of what he did, and I did it over and over." I pause to wipe my eyes and blow my nose. He keeps silent and lets me finish.

"It's taken me all this time to push back those feelings, to clear all of the dark webs of my depression. I can't thank you enough for forcing me to start seeing someone, because without that I don't think I ever would have healed. For a while, it was a lot of trial and error, trying to figure out what worked best with my trauma. Dr. Maxwell tells me that there will still be setbacks. Some people don't ever really beat PTSD, but they do learn how to live with it, and that's what I've been doing. Living with it. I can't sit here and tell you that I'll ever be completely carefree and healed, but these last few weeks with you by my side have given me all the hope I've ever needed that I will get past this."

When he still doesn't speak, but just keeps holding me tightly and staring off into the distance, I start to worry that he hasn't heard me. So I say the only thing I can think of to make him understand where I am now. How I'm finally ready for him and all the love he's ever been offering.

"Your love saved me," I whisper.

CHAPTER 18
Beck

Your love saved me.

Her words keep echoing around me, coiling around the pain that has filled my heart since she started talking.

Your love saved me.

I can feel her body shaking, and I tighten my hold so she knows that I'm still here, but I can't speak past the lump that's taken up residence in my throat. I always knew that she had a rough history, but never in my wildest imagination could I have pictured all of this pain she's gone through.

It makes so much sense now. All the times she pushed me away with fear in her eyes. Every single time she would look at one of the guys and have this odd look about her as if she was waiting for one of them to go all Hulk or something.

There is so much swirling around inside of me. I want to kill that motherfucker all over again. I want to go find her father and teach him to pick on someone his own size. I want to lock her away in this house and never let anyone get close enough to so much as give her a paper cut.

Your love saved me.

All I've wanted since the day I felt her slipping away is to prove to her how much I love her and for her to know that I'm here for her. It kills me to know how greatly she's suffered, but with that comes the clarity that she's *finally*, fucking *finally*, on the same page with me.

I squeeze her tighter into my body when I feel her sobbing get harder. It finally hits me that I haven't said a word since she finished talking. I have to work at swallowing my own sorrow. I wipe the tears from my face and clear my throat a few times until I feel confident that I can talk without breaking down.

"Baby, look at me. Please, look at me."

She shakes her head and burrows deeper into my body.

"Come on, where's my wildcat?" I soften my voice, rub her back, and kiss her over and over. I'm begging silently for her to just look at me, to see the all the understanding and love that she needs from me right now. So she will see that I'm here and will never leave. "Dee, I'm begging you, please, look at me. See me. Let my love in. Please, Baby."

She has her mouth pressed into my shoulder, so when she speaks, I can't understand her. She is still crying, but at least her body has stopped heaving violently. "Say it again. I can't understand you."

She lifts her head and her tear filled puffy, red eyes just stare at me. I smile at her, letting her know that it's all going to be fine, and she lets out a shaky breath. She closes her eyes for a few seconds, but when she opens them, and I can see, not only the old Dee that I've missed with extreme longing, shining back at me, but I can also see all of that love that she's been running from. It's staring brightly back at me, and even with her swollen eyes and splotchy face, I've never seen her look more beautiful.

"Oh, Baby. I love you so much."

Her breath hitches again at my words. It doesn't take long before she opens her mouth, and when she finally utters the words that I've been dreaming of for so long, the sense of peace that hits me is nothing short of a miracle.

"I love you, too, John Beckett. I love you with all of my scarred heart." She smiles weakly and I return it with a smile so big that my jaw hurts.

"You're finally mine?" I ask, my smile never leaving my face.

"No…" She pauses and my heart stops. "You're finally mine." All of the earlier pain and sadness drains from her face, and she looks at me with her smile huge, her bloodshot eyes full of love and trust. She looks at me as if she's a brand new woman, and I give a second of thanks that I'm lucky enough to have this woman in my life.

"Whatever works but we're finally us." I cup her cheek and guide my lips to hers. She tastes like her tears mixed with hope. She tastes like heaven.

"I. Love. You." I punctuate each word with a kiss before I take her lips in a slow lazy kiss.

Her hands are running all over my chest, pulling at my shirt. When her cold hands get my shirt up and she presses against my abs, I shake with the chill that rushes through my body. She giggles and it's like music to my ears. I break away from her mouth to pull my shirt off and then hers. She unhooks her bra and drops it to the floor. I take a second to look over every inch of her exposed skin, drinking in her tan perfection. Her nipples pebble under the attention of my eyes, and I reach up and cup each of her heavy breasts, rubbing my thumb over each nipple before pinching them lightly. Her head rolls back on her shoulders and she moans low in her throat.

I shift her so that she straddles me on the couch and take her ass in my hands before pulling her against my erection. She frames my face before taking my lips and kissing me deeply. Her tongue comes out and tangles with mine while she starts grinding against my lap.

I pull my mouth away and lean my forehead against hers. Both of us are panting deeply. When she shifts slightly and her warm core rubs against my painful erection, I growl. "Dee, it'll be over before I even have a chance to get out of my pants if you move again. Give me a second, and then I'm taking you up to our bed and showing you every single ounce of love I have in my body for you."

It takes me a lot longer than a second to calm my body enough that I don't fear coming in my pants if she so much as breathes. When I can finally feel some blood coming back to my head, I push my hands under her ass and stand. She instinctively wraps her legs tightly around my waist and drops her head to my neck. She starts kissing, licking, and sucking lightly against my neck and all the progress I've just made in controlling my throbbing erection just goes flying out the window.

"Dee..." I warn when she starts sucking on my earlobe. She laughs and her warm breath dances across my wet ear. I have to stop in the middle of the staircase because the urge to come in my pants is almost too much. My dick has craved this woman for months, and she is finally mine. There's no way in hell I'm going to go off unless her wet pussy is wrapped tight around me.

She finally takes pity on me, and I'm able to start climbing the stairs again. When I hit the hallway, it looks a mile long and not the short distance I know it to be. I tighten my fingers against her ass and start walking. Every time my balls rub against the fabric of my jeans, I groan. When we finally cross the threshold into the bedroom, I let out the breath I have been holding.

Finally.

It's finally time to make this woman mine.

I bring my hands from her ass and run my fingertips slowly over her body up towards her chest. When I hit her hips, her legs tighten around my waist so that she keeps her hold on me. The feel of her warm skin against my palms has me closing my eyes and dropping my head back on my shoulders. She takes the opportunity to run kisses and wet swipes of her tongue against my exposed neck. She nibbles on my throat before dipping and kissing a path to one of my nipples. When her teeth bite down almost painfully, I tighten my hold on her waist.

Walking stiffly over to the edge of the bed, I lower her until her ass meets the mattress. I step back when she places her palms behind her and leans back. Her tits are thrusting in the air, just begging for my mouth. I lick my lips before moving my eyes up her body and meeting her gaze. Her eyes are on fire, cheeks flushed, and all signs of her earlier sadness have completely disappeared. I give her a tip of my lips before dropping to my knees, wrapping my arms around her legs, and pulling her until her ass is hanging off the bed. When she falls back on the mattress, she lets out a yelp that quickly turns into a moan as I nuzzle my nose against her stomach and start kissing along the waistband of her jeans.

"You're killing me." She moans, running her hands up her stomach. I have to stop what I'm doing when she takes her hands on a trail up her body and squeezes her tits before rolling each nipple slowly. Her face is showing me just how much she's enjoying this.

"Shit." I have to pull one of my hands from her legs to shove it down my pants and wrap my fist around my dick. I press as hard as I dare so that I can stop myself from coming. Just watching her pleasure herself is almost too much to take. "Dee, please, stop."

She shakes her head back and forth, lost in her own world. "Dee," I snap. Her eyes shoot open and her hands stop caressing and pinching. "Please, let me. You keep that up and I won't be able to hold back."

"I don't want you to hold back. It's been too long." God, I love her voice when she's this close to coming. It gets deeper, huskier. Fuck.

I don't even try to take my time I lean forward and pull her pants off with one jerk, tossing them over my shoulder. Her underwear just pisses me off because it's in the way of the one place my body is craving. Taking hold of one delicate side and tugging has them ripping right off her. I thrust my hand back under her ass, lift her hips off the mattress, and drop my mouth right to her soaked folds.

"Drenched, Baby... so damn wet. Whose pussy is this?" I latch onto her clit and suck hard, waiting for her to answer me.

"Yours! It's yours! Oh, God!" Her small hand pushes through my hair and holds my head still while she brings her hips up and shamelessly rubs against my tongue. I hum when the sweet flavor of her desire hits my taste buds in a rush as she comes all over my tongue.

I lick her slowly, lapping up every single drop of her addictive taste before pulling my head from her hand and trailing kisses up her thigh. Seeing her back in this bed, completely naked and in the afterglow of one hell of a climax, has my dick getting even harder than I ever thought possible. My balls are already drawn tight against my body, just ready to explode at any second.

I take a step back, never letting my eyes leave her body. She doesn't even move. Both legs still hang off the side of the bed, her head tips to the side, and her brown hair spills out around her. My jeans are the first to go. I unsnap and slowly pull the zipper down, holding my dick back with my other hand so it doesn't go off on a mission of its own to find that delicious pussy.

When I'm finally naked, I continue to stand there, slowly drawing my fist up and down my swollen shaft in lazy movements. She finally opens her eyes to see me standing between her spread legs, and lets out a whimper that goes straight to my dick, which throbs painfully in my fist.

Words aren't needed, not with us, and definitely not now. Her walls are down... No, they aren't down; they're completely decimated. There isn't a single speck of the pain that's been in her eyes for the past two years. No, my girl has her love shining brightly, and her heart beating in sync with my own.

Leaning down, I take her lips in a deep, slow, bruising kiss. Our tongues mate together in a slow dance, and when I press my hips to hers, and my dick is nestled between her swollen lips, I moan in her mouth. She breaks her lips away and starts sliding against my dick, letting her wetness coat me in seconds. Her fingers dig into the muscles of my back, almost to the point of pain each time I hit her clit. It doesn't take long before fire starts slowly burning its path down my spine, and the first threads of my orgasm start to race through my body. I have to pull my hips from her wet heat, earning me another bite of her nails when she tries to keep me close.

Without losing my connection to her mouth, I bring my hands up to her hips and lift her up, scooting her back so I can crawl up behind her. Staying on my knees, I shift her body so she's resting on her shoulders with her hips in the air, right where I need them to be to lean up and enter her. Her hands come back up to her tits and start rolling her nipples again. I lean forward, letting go of one hip long enough to line myself up, and then push forward slowly. We both groan when we come together completely. My balls rest against her ass and her walls hug my dick with a vice like strangle. Goddamn, it feels like home.

I take a few slow thrusts before the pleasure becomes too much. I hook her legs with my arms, spreading her wide so I can watch her pussy take my dick. Watch, as she becomes mine.

"Look. At. Us." Each word has my hips pounding in until I can feel her lips against my pelvis. I roll my hips and tighten my hold on her legs before sliding out almost completely. I wait for her to look at me before I slam home.

"YES! Oh fuuuuu, YES!" Her hands slip from her tits and she grabs the bed sheets in her fist, holding on to anything that can anchor her to the world, because if her orgasm is anywhere near as strong as mine is promising to be, she's going to need that hold.

I drop her legs and lean forward to press my chest against hers, planting myself deeper inside her walls. My left hand braces the brunt of my weight from her body, while my right hand starts the slow journey from her hip to her neck. I thrust my hand into her thick hair and tilt her head so I can crush my lips to hers. The way her body feels while I'm buried deep is intoxicating. She wraps her legs around me, and I start thrusting in and out. It's painfully slow, but I don't want this to end. I can feel our bodies becoming one. Her heart is beating rapidly against my chest and mine answers every beat.

I pull back and look into her eyes, resting my forehead against hers. I watch my body rocking against hers. She brings her hands up and frames my face, bringing my eyes back up.

I know she's close, because she's panting and moaning each time I thrust home. She leans up, kisses me softly, and then whispers against my lips. "It feels so... so different, Baby." She moans when I stop thrusting and roll my hips again, hitting that spot inside her that has a surge of wetness coating my dick.

"Yeah, that right there is what it feels like to finally be mine." And with that, I pull back and give her body what it's silently begging for.

Not long after she screams my name and clamps down on my dick, the thirst that's been burning its delicious pain in my balls rushes out as I empty myself inside her body, giving her everything that I have in me.

"DEE..." I groan her name and dig my fingers in the soft skin of her hips, thrust a few more times before pushing in one last time, and roll so her body is laid out over my own. Each of us is breathing rapidly, and her tight walls still grip my dick, begging me not to leave.

"I love you so damn much," she whispers in my ear.

"I love you, too. Always have and always will." I can feel her smile against my cheek, and with our arms wrapped tightly around each other and our bodies connected, we both close our eyes, and for the first time in a long time, I sleep with complete peace.

PART THREE
Believing
&
Letting Go

CHAPTER 19
Dee

Peace.

That's what this kind of love feels like. My mind and heart are working together in complete harmony, and I no longer wake up wishing that I could just disappear. I wake up, and the first thing I do is smile because I have been blessed.

I still have some bad days. Times when I freak out because of some stupid reason, but Beck is always there to remind me that there isn't a thing in the world he won't do to keep me safe and happy.

It's been one week since we had our talk, and since then, we have spent almost every second together locked away in his house so that the world can't touch us. He called Axel sometime the morning after we let go of everything that was standing between us. I don't think he's happy about it, but he still told Beck to take some time off.

Beck left for the office about an hour earlier, and today would mark the first day that we would be apart since he went in for his meeting last week. I brushed him off when he asked me if I needed Maddox to come wait with me.

Truth is, I'm still nervous to be alone, but I know I've got to learn to stand on my own two feet without Beck to keep me up. I have to take the steps to rid myself of this fear.

The main reason I don't want anyone here is because today, I'm calling my parents. Today, I'm finally going to let them know how much they have completely ruined the first twenty plus years of my life. Today, I will put my parents, and every single fucked up issue they have given me, to rest and forever forget that they ever existed.

After eating something light for breakfast, I settle on the back deck with the phone and a cup of whiskey flavored coffee. Yeah, I need all the courage I can get.

I stare at the phone in my hand before I can make my fingers dial the ten numbers to connect me to my parents. When I press the last number and place the phone to my ear, I take a deep breath for strength and get ready.

"Roberts' residence, this is Collette speaking."

"Collette, this is Denise Roberts. May I please speak with Annabeth?" I feel the instant need to wash out my mouth when I say my mother's name. It takes everything inside me to speak normally and keep the snark out of my tone. I really just want to ask Collette if I may speak with the raging bitch of the house.

"One moment, please, Ms. Denise. Let me see if the lady of the house is available for callers."

She has got to be joking. *The lady of the house?* What a fucking joke.

By the time I'm finally taken off hold and my mother's annoyed voice comes over the line, I am about to hang up and just say the hell with it.

"What is it, Denise? I'm in the middle of my bi-weekly massage, so can we make this quick?" I pull back the phone and drop my jaw when her words penetrate. Did I really expect anything different? No. I want to laugh when I realize how unnecessary this call is.

"Well, *Mother,* I'm so sorry that I interrupted your fucking massage."

Her gasp comes out, and I can picture her pressing her hand to her chest in shock over her daughter's 'disgusting mouth'. "You will watch your mouth when you're speaking to me."

"It's a little too late for mothering, Annabeth, don't you think?" She starts to speak but I cut her off quickly before I lose my lead on this conversation. "Here's the thing, you old fucking hag. You might be my mother by birth, but that's only because I didn't get to pick the idiots that decided to have sex once, and nine months later, their accident was born. No, I didn't get to pick then, but I do now. I've wanted to say this to you for years, but until recently, I didn't have what I needed to make this call."

"You are a filthy, disgusting, piece of shit, and I would have been better off thrown into the system than being raised by you and Davison. I hate you. I've hated you for the last thirty-one years of my life, and for once, the thought of telling you that doesn't send me into a panic. I want you to let Davison know that this will be the last time you ever speak to me. From this day forward, you are dead to me. Do you understand that, Annabeth? Your *daughter* is dead."

I take a deep breath and squeeze my eyes shut. My legs are bouncing in place, and I know I'm seconds away from throwing up.

"Well, I think an email would have sufficed here. Goodbye, Denise." The click of her hanging up the phone causes me to jump. I can't seem to remove the phone from my ear. The shock that she didn't even react, not once, when I finally let her know what I think about her, is overwhelming.

I should be sad. Maybe shed a tear or freak out a little, but there is nothing. Nothing, but the heavy weight of the pain that they've caused me over the years, as it vanishes from inside of me.

I grab my coffee off the railing and take a long swallow, enjoying the burn of the whiskey mixed with it. When I pull the mug away from my mouth and feel my lips curve into a smile, I know that everything is finally okay. My life is finally perfect, and there isn't anything that can take this feeling from me.

****

By the time I pull myself off the couch on the back porch, it's nearing lunchtime. Beck's already called twice to check on me, and the last time he called I told him he better not call me again. I love him for wanting to make sure that I'm okay, but we both need to start getting back to normal. Our normal. Together.

Beck

After a quick lunch, I sit down to start answering emails. I've enjoyed my break from work, my forced break, but now it's time to get back on the wagon, so to speak. The first order of business is to start cleaning shop with the North Carolina branch. I spoke with Chelcie the other day about selling the business and having her move down here to help me run things. I'm ready to stop making work my number one priority, and focus on living my life.

Ring.

"Hey, Chelc, I was just thinking about you." When I hear her soft sob, the smile on my face vanishes. "Chelcie? What's wrong?"

"Oh God, Dee. I thought it was over, you know? Things have been so quiet around here, but you… you got a letter today." She sounds terrified, and all it does is fuel the dread slowly closing in on me.

"Chelcie, what did it say?" I'm pretty proud of myself for sounding a lot calmer than I feel. I take a few deep gulps to calm myself and wait for her to speak.

"There are pictures, Dee. They have pictures of you, and they have pictures of me."

My heart is beating out of control. Oh my God.

"Was there anything else?" Tears are streaming down my face, and my hands are shaking so badly that I have no idea how I'm able to hold onto the phone.

"There's a message," she whispers back.

"And?"

"It said... God, it said that if you don't deliver Adam or two hundred thousand dollars by the end of the month, they're going to clear the debt owed in other ways. Dee! What the hell does that mean?!" By the time she finishes, she is sobbing.

I give myself a few minutes to freak out before trying to come up with a fix.

"Chelcie, listen to me. I want you to get your things and go straight home. Lock the door and do not answer for anyone. Pack as much as you can and get down here. I need to call Beck and let him know what's going on, but I want you here where I know you will be safe."

She's silent for so long that I have to pull my phone away to make sure she didn't disconnect.

"Chelc, do you understand?"

"Yeah, Dee. I'll be there by tomorrow. Promise me you're safe?"

"Don't worry about me. Worry about you. Get down here, Chelcie. Everything's going to be okay. Make sure you bring everything they mailed you and try not to touch it, okay?"

"I'll be there."

I quickly hang up the phone and immediately call Beck. After I fill him in, he tells me to check every door and stay away from the windows. I know he's worried, but he's trying to hide it so it doesn't freak me out.

"I'm okay, Beck. I'm really okay. Just get home okay?" I don't think I realized until that moment that I'm not as scared as I would have been months ago. I'm worried, but mainly for Chelcie. I know that Beck won't let anything happen to me, and until she gets down here, I don't think I'll be able to stop the feeling that I have no way of controlling what happens here.

I check all the doors and make sure the alarm is active before making my way back upstairs. The only place that I know I'll feel one hundred percent safe is in Beck's bed, where I can pull the covers around me and let his scent surround me.

CHAPTER 20
Beck

The second that I hang up with Dee, I gather the rest of the guys in the office so I can fill them in on what's going on.

"She doesn't know if there's more. The letter didn't come here, which makes me think that he wants her to believe he knows more than he does. There's a reason he sent it to Chelcie at the office and not here."

Axel looks around for a second, thinking about all the facts that we have. Which is basically is a whole lot of nothing. "I don't like this. How is it possible for this Adam shit to hide for this long?"

"We need the letter. Maybe we can pull something off of it. It's a long shot, but right now, it's all we have." Coop sits down and for once doesn't end a sentence with some smart-ass remark.

We're all worried. This guy has us all by the balls, and it's not sitting well with any of us.

"You need to get home to Dee. Let us worry about the shit we can do here." Maddox pushes off the wall after giving me my marching orders and slams the newly replaced door against the wall in his haste to leave the room.

Greg leans forward from the seat in front of my desk, resting his elbows on his knees. "He's right. We'll handle shit here, and if anything new comes up, we'll call.

Just go make sure she's okay. If you decide to come in tomorrow, then she comes with you."

"You didn't really think I was going to stay here today? Fuck you very much, Greg. All I had planned was filling you assholes in before I went home to my woman." I start packing up my laptop and anything else I think I'll need should I decide to start working out of my house until this shit is over. There's only ten more days in the month, so regardless of what we figure out, there's only a short amount of time before the deadline we're working against runs out.

Greg goes to open his mouth, but I stop him as I round the desk to leave. "Don't, okay? I get where you're coming from and that's fine, but don't mistake my making sure you all knew what is going on as me not putting her first. Everything I do is to make sure that her happiness and wellbeing come before anything else."

"Got it."

I leave him still sitting in front of my desk and head out to the truck. I offer Sway a quick wave as I walk down the golden glitter filled sidewalk and pass by the salon. He smiles and waves in his usual flamboyant way, and as per normal with him, there is no way you can't smile back. One thing with Sway, when things are starting to press in around you and your mood is as close to shit as it can get, Sway always makes the world a little bit brighter.

I throw my bags in the passenger seat and peel out of the lot, heading home to Dee as quickly as I can.

****

Dee throws the garage door open the second my truck shuts off. When I see her standing in the doorway with a small smile on her face, I let out the breath that I have been holding the whole drive home. I knew from her phone call that she is holding it together better than I would have imagined, but I've worried that with the time it took me to get home, she might have started to freak out. Seeing her now, and seeing that she really is fine, helps me untangle a little of the knot that's settled in my gut.

"Hey, you," she whispers when I walk up the two steps leading into the house. She brings her arms up, and wraps them around my neck, hugging me tightly.

"Hey you, back. Are you okay?"

She pulls back and nods. "I'm fine, just worried about Chelcie but I'm okay."

"She's a smart girl. What time did she say she'd get here?" When she lets go of my neck and takes my bag from me, my body instantly misses the contact. I follow her through the mudroom and into the kitchen. She sets the bag down and grabs me a beer from the fridge. As I sit down at the table, I reach over and pull her into my lap. I don't want her more than a foot away from me right now, not until I can calm myself down a little more.

"She's going to leave soon. I talked to her about fifteen minutes ago and she had just finished loading her car. It's going to take her anywhere from six to eight hours to get here, so I would guess sometime in the middle of the night. She's got directions to the house. She knows to call at any time, and we'll be waiting for her."

"How is she holding together?" I'm a little worried about her making that drive by herself, but I know she's much safer here than she'll be up there where no one can protect her.

"I think she's okay. I mean, as okay as she can be when a death threat basically just landed in her lap. What are we going to do, Beck? Unless we find Adam and have him shed a little light on this, I don't see what else can be done."

I study her for a second while I take another pull from the beer. She really does seem completely fine. Maybe a little rattled, but that's to be expected. There isn't any darkness in her eyes that makes me think she could be having a setback. Nope, my wildcat is front and center, ready to fight for it.

"Let's try and focus on the positive here, okay? You're safe, Chelcie is safe, and there is no way in hell some sick fuck is getting close to either of you. When Chelcie gets here, we can take a look at things and see just what he sent to her. For now, let me enjoy your sweet ass in my lap."

She smacks my arm playfully and smiles.

"Pig." She laughs and I savor every second of it.

****

"Beck. Beck, wake up."

When Dee's soft breath and low whispers wake me up from one of the hottest dreams ever, I immediately reach over and pull her closer. Her naked body rubbing against mine further ignites the desire burning inside of me.

"Beck! We can't start anything right now."

Her laugh shoots straight through me, and my already painfully hard dick throbs. Her small hands pressing against my chest make my skin burn. She doesn't protest much when I start kissing down her neck.

"God, you taste good." I continue to kiss along her collarbone, ignoring her protest. The only thing I can think of is pushing inside of her welcoming body. My dick is begging for the release that only her body can provide. "So damn good," I murmur against her breast before pulling one erect nipple in my mouth, twirling my tongue around the tip, and sucking gently.

"Beck, please... I won't be able to stop you soon, and Chelcie just called. Damn, that feels so good." She stops talking and pushes her hand into my hair, holding me to her breast.

Right when I'm about to push deep between her legs, her words finally make sense. I drop my forehead to her chest and try to hold myself back.

"How long?" God, it hurts to stop. I'm close to begging her to just touch me. All it's going to take is a few strokes of her soft hand for me to explode, but I want to be with her... in her.

"What?" Her eyes are clouded with desire, and I know that if either one of us is going to be strong enough to stop before we get any further, then it's going to have to be me.

"How long until Chelcie is here? Please tell me she isn't about to knock on the damn door." I can't even lift my head off her chest. Her pussy is hugging my dick, and as much as I would love to pull back and press into her, I know if Chelcie is close, this is the last thing I need to be doing.

"Relax, Honey. She's a good thirty minutes out." Before I can even move, she wraps her hand around me, lifts her hips so that I'll move off her, and the second she has enough space between our bodies, lines me up. In a move that would make a porn star proud, she pushes off with her feet and buries my cock deep. She doesn't even give me a chance to move at first. She just continues to work her body against mine.

"If you want to do all the work, all you have to do is say something. I can see my wildcat itching to come out and play."

She doesn't speak, just keeps pushing herself off the mattress. Her walls constrict and hug my dick tight when I speak.

"You like working my dick, Dee? You like the way it feels when you take what you need?" She moans and I can feel her growing even wetter. I let the strength in my arms and thighs slacken and press her deep into the bed. "I asked you a question. Do you like working my dick?"

When she realizes that I won't let her move, she finally looks up at me. Her eyes are so thick with ecstasy that the normal light brown color looks almost black. She blinks a few times before a wicked smile forms across her beautiful flushed face. She runs her hands up my chest and wraps them around my neck before pulling me in close until we're nose to nose. "I like it almost as much as when you throw my legs over your shoulders and pound my body so hard I'm sure I could feel you in my throat."

Jesus. Christ. My woman knows just what to say to get what she wants and right now, I can tell that she is begging me to take her hard.

"Is that what you want? You want me to take these long legs and wrap them around my neck like a goddamn bow? Be sure, Wildcat, because right now, I need you like you wouldn't believe." I lean back, holding onto her slim hips so that we don't lose our connection, and take a second to enjoy the view. She's already palming her tits, caressing and pinching her puckered nipples. Her body is raised slightly from my hold on her hips. She is completely at my mercy right now, and when I thrust forward shallowly, I know she is only seconds away from begging for it. Her legs wrap around me and her heels try to dig into my ass to push me further.

"Answer me." I give her another shallow thrust, and when her walls clamp down and a surge of wetness coats my dick, I almost forget everything except taking what we both want. "Now."

Her eyes snap open at my hard command and burn into me. "YES! Fucking take me, Beck. Take me hard."

She doesn't even get the whole sentence out before I throw her long legs over my shoulders, rise up on my knees, and pull her body off the mattress with my hands on her hips. Her arms fall from her tits and help support her body. I've taken her in this position before, with all of her weight bracing on her upper back and shoulders, but never as hard as I'm planning. "You good?" I ground out, flexing my fingers against the soft skin at her hips.

"If you don't move soon, I'm going to hurt you." She pants and squeezes her legs around my head. "Pleas—"

With one swift and powerful thrust, I finally let myself take her. My balls slap against her ass with each slam home, and it doesn't take long before her screams are echoing through my room. She looks so damn beautiful, legs around my neck, perfect tan body flushed with desire from welcoming each rough pump of my hips, and her eyes showering me with every single ounce of love I've ever craved from her.

Complete one hundred percent acceptance of everything I've ever dreamed of giving her.

Stopping briefly, I set her body back down on the mattress, lower her legs from my neck, and slowly glide in and out of her wet heat. Her eyes flash when she realizes I've changed course, but when I press my thumb against her swollen clit, her eyes roll back in her head. I bring our hips together tightly and continue to strum my thumb against her. Right when I feel her about to fall over the crest, I pull back. Her eyes burn with frustration and I laugh. "Does my wildcat want to play?" God, I hope so, because the way her body feels when I'm balls deep inside her wet heat is almost too good.

"Stop playing games and fuck me!"

I shouldn't have laughed, because the second I smile and bark out a laugh, she takes advantage. Her legs push in and her hands shove against my chest. Somehow, I manage to grab her hips and keep us connected as we roll. Her hands shoot out to gain purchase. One hand wraps around the headboard, and the other flies out, crashing against the nightstand. She doesn't even pause when the sounds of glass breaking and wood smashing against the floor mixes with our moans.

She rides me hard and fast. Her strong legs push and she grinds down against my ridged dick. I help lift her up when I can tell she's close, digging my feet into the bed to match each movement with a thrust of my hips.

"You feel so good, so good... love how you love me." I groan when her words wrap around me, and squeeze her hips tight. "I'm close, Baby." And just like that, she drops down, throws her head back, and screams my name. I have just a few seconds to enjoy the view before I flip our bodies once again, and take what my body is craving. There is nothing better than feeling her come against my dick, her wetness so slick that even my balls are coated, and with each thrust, her body holds me so tight that I feel like it's begging me never to leave. Yeah, when my woman is coming hard against my dick, there isn't anything better.

"Oh my, God, Beck! I'm going to come again! Harder, please, Baby, harder!" Her legs wrap around my hips and her fingers dig into my back. The bite of pain from her nails breaking the skin is all the fuel I need. Fire dances down my spine and wraps around my balls. I take one more thrust into her body before I empty every last drop of myself into her.

I don't know how long we stay like that, with my body blanketing hers, and my dick making slow, lazy glides into her drenched pussy. When I fall from her body, the moans that leave both of us are borderline desperate. Leaning up, I look down at her. Her hair is in messy waves around her head, her eyes are closed, and her face is flushed. The only clue I have that she's even awake is the small smile playing against her swollen lips.

I press my lips against her and smile back at her when her eyes open. "I think we should think about leaving this bed before I can't stop myself from taking you again."

She smiles and nods.

"Come on. If we hurry, we can wash off before Chelcie gets here. Probably wouldn't be a good idea to answer the door with you running down my leg." She laughs as she climbs from the bed and starts walking towards the bathroom. When she notices I'm not behind her, she stops and turns to look where I'm still sprawled out on the bed. My once slack dick is rock hard and ready for more. Fuck me, but just the thought of my come inside her, running down her leg makes every possessive part of me roar to life.

Pushing off the bed, I stalk towards her. She looks confused for a second until I grab her body and walk towards the bathroom. Her legs wrap around my hips out of instinct. "Chelcie's going to have to get over it. Just the thought of your body with my come all over you is the hottest fucking thing you could have just said. Fuck, Dee. You make me want to come all over your body so everyone knows you're mine."

"That sounds kind of messy, Honey." She laughs, pulling back to see how serious I am, which causes her laughter to die on her lips. "You can't be serious?"

Not even bothering to answer, I busy myself with turning on the water and walking into the shower, rotating so that the water hits my back until it can warm.

"Oh, Dee, now that you're mine, there isn't much of anything I wouldn't do to make sure the world knows that you are taken."

She doesn't protest much when I push her against the shower and take her body again. Her bright eyes and naughty smile are all the confirmation I need that she understands what I'm saying.

CHAPTER 21
Dee

Lucky for us, when Chelcie said she would be here in thirty minutes, she had really taken an hour. She finally pulled down Beck's driveway and parked behind the garage just as I was walking downstairs to wait for her. My hair was still dripping wet, but at least I didn't smell like sex anymore.

A small smile forms when I think about how energetic Beck had gotten. I love when he takes me hard, but tonight, he took me hard *and* rough, and there wasn't a second of it that I didn't love.

"You look happy, Dee." Chelcie comments from where she's sitting at the kitchen table, pulling me from my daydream.

Beck had gone to pull her car into the garage, taken her luggage up to the guest room, and looked over the letter she had received. I think he really just knew that he needed to make himself scarce while Chelcie came down from her panic. The second she pulled into the driveway, she slammed the car in park and rushed into my arms. She hadn't even shut the car off before she came running.

She just stopped crying about five minutes ago. She hasn't moved from the seat that she dropped into and I can tell that, even though she's stopped crying, she hasn't been able to stop shaking.

"I am, Chelc. I really am." I smile weakly and walk over the mugs of coffee I've just brewed. "Here, I have a feeling we won't be going to sleep anytime soon. Do you want to talk about it?" I grab her cold hand and offer her the only thing I can, my strength. I know without a doubt that if I didn't have Beck by my side during all this, I would be feeling the same way as Chelcie. Alone, afraid, and hopeless. This isn't the first time that I've realized how far I've come in my own healing, but right here, in this moment, I realize that I finally, finally have all the power in my own happiness. I no longer fear the love Beck has to offer, but I also don't have the weight of every single ghost from my past choking me anymore.

I'm mentally free from all the pain I've been carrying around. Now, all I have to do is get past this mess and enjoy the life I've been running from for too long.

It's time to take the love and strength being offered, and fight with every single breath in my body to make sure I win.

Chelcie's deep sigh pulls me from my mental 'ah-ha' moment. I hate knowing she's worried, but I know how strong she is, and if anyone has the power to get past this with no scars, it's my girl.

"I'm here, Chelcie. I've had a little bit longer to come to terms with the fact that Adam has turned my life into this mess, but please, tell me you know that the guys won't let anything happen to us."

She nods but doesn't speak. My heart breaks a little when I see a single tear fall from her eyes. She just looks at me, her dark brown eyes pleading with me to take everything away and make it all better.

"I don't even know how to express how I feel right now, Dee. I feel like just yesterday you were in the hospital, and I was terrified that you weren't going to wake up. Knowing that sicko is still out there, watching both of us now, is so scary."

"I know. I'm not going to lie. When I think about someone out there watching my every move, I feel the same way. We're going to get past this, and then we can look back and laugh." I smile, but I can tell by the look on her face that she knows I'm just trying to make light of the situation.

There isn't anything good about this mess. We have no idea where Adam is, and even if we did, I don't know how I feel about turning someone over to a psycho, regardless of what he's done to get me into this position to begin with. There is no way I can come up with all that money, and even if I could, I wouldn't give it to him. My only hope is that the guys get lucky and find some hidden clue as to who he is... or we find Adam and get our answers there.

"What if they don't find him? What are we supposed to do, spend the rest of our lives in hiding? This guy beat you, Dee! He beat you so badly you almost didn't wake up! This isn't just some small time asshole. This is huge!" She's starting to get hysterical, and I have no clue how to answer her. I just nod my head and hold her hand tighter.

Beck comes into the room a few minutes later and stands at the doorway. His face looks hard, and I can tell from the way he's holding himself that he isn't happy. My gut clenches in fear, but I quickly bat it down. I need to hold it together and prove to myself that I can handle this, but also be the rock that Chelcie needs.

"Coop and Maddox are coming over in a few hours. It's late, and there isn't much we can do at three in the morning, so dump the coffee, and let's get some sleep." He walks over to Chelcie and crouches down next to her seat. He waits for her to look at him before placing his hand on her shoulder, offering her the strength she needs. "No one is going to hurt you, Chelc. You and Dee are safe here, and I'm not leaving you two until we figure this out, okay?"

She nods, gulps a few times to try to calm down but loses the fight. I watch with my heart heavy as her body falls forward and she sobs into her hands.

Beck stands before pulling her up from her seat and wrapping his arms around her. He looks over at me, and I give him a small nod so that he knows I'm okay. He looks more worried about the fact that he's holding another woman in front of me. I give him a smile and reach out to squeeze his arm so he knows that I'm not upset with him. Chelcie needs him and I know how comforting those strong arms are. He continues to hold her while she sobs into his chest, rubs her back, and reassures her that everything is going to be okay. Not once does he take his eyes off of me.

If I weren't already head over heels in love with this man, this moment would have had me sold.

Watching him hold one of my closest friends as she falls apart doesn't register anything other than the knowledge that he really would do anything to make sure that I, and all those that I love, are protected and happy.

I love you. I mouth.

I love you. He returns.

I stand from my seat and dump out our full mugs of coffee. Walking over to where they stand, I wrap my arms around her back, and kiss her cheek before heading out of the room.

The sounds of someone moving up the stairs come about ten minutes after I've left the kitchen. It doesn't take long for the door to open and my heart to swell when I see Beck outlined against the hallway light. He walks into the darkened bedroom, stripping his clothes as he stalks towards the bed. I roll onto my side and wait for it… that moment when he slides into bed and reaches over, pulling me deep into his arms and surrounding me in his protection.

"Are you okay?" he whispers against my ear.

"I will be." I reply honestly. Because, I will be. We will get past this, and nothing is going to stand in my way now. "I will be." I repeat.

He doesn't answer, but then again he doesn't need to. He just pulls me tighter, pressing his chest to my back, his chin to my neck, and his arms tight around my body. It doesn't take long before his steady breathing is matching my own.

CHAPTER 22
Dee

"Rise and shine, you horny little humpers!"

I jump when Coop's voice booms through Beck's bedroom. I frantically pull the sheets over my naked body, but given the look on Coop's face, it's too late and he's already seen my boobs.

"Nice tits, Dee."

Yup, he definitely didn't miss them.

"You motherfucker, stop looking at her like that." Unconcerned with his nudity, Beck jumps out of the bed and rushes toward him. All my embarrassment disappears when I watch his firm 'good enough to eat' ass as he runs out after Coop. It sounds like a herd of elephants running through the house as Beck chases him.

"Dude, if your dick touches me, I'm going to puke!" Coop yells, his voice carrying through the house. He sounds so freaked out that I can't even hold back the laughter anymore.

I start snickering so hard that I lose my hold on the sheet. Not even concerned about my state of undress, I climb out of bed to get dressed, wiping the tears that my laughter has brought from my face.

With my naked back to the door, I bend over to pick up the shirt that Beck discarded last night, but when a masculine cough hits my ears, I jump and stand. *Holy shit.* I know it's not Coop because I can hear his gagging and Beck's yelling from further away in the house. *Shit!*

"Please tell me that you're gentleman enough to have your back to me?" My voice wobbles and my face flames.

"Wouldn't exactly be able to enjoy the view if I did. Nice ass, Dee." Maddox laughter echoes through the room before I hear the door shut and his heavy booted feet walking away from the door.

I rush to throw some clothes on. I'm so embarrassed that my face feels like it might burst into flames. Thank God Beck was busy with Coop because I'm pretty sure his head would explode if he knew that both of his friends have seen me naked.

Beck comes storming back in the bedroom with his hands covering his dick. I want to laugh, but when I see his face, I know that wouldn't be the best move. He takes one look at me, standing at the sink brushing my hair, before stalking towards me. His hands drop and I watch in fascination as he grows harder with each step. I lick my lips and he growls. My eyes meet his in question, and I'm met with pure, raw heat.

He walks right up to me and without a word, strips the clothes from my body, lifts me up so my ass rest against the vanity, and rams into me. His movements are frantic and his pace rushed. He licks and bites along my neck and his fingers dig into my hips as he pounds into me. It doesn't take long for us both to tip over the edge. His lips slam down against mine, eating my screams while I swallow his grunts.

He releases my lips, and with his dick still deep inside me, locks eyes with mine. "Do *not* shower. I want to know that I'm still inside you when you walk down those stairs and sit down at the table. When those assholes are sitting in the same room with you after just seeing what is *mine,* I want to know that I'm still all over this sweet pussy."

Well. Ohhhkay, then. I nod, and when he pulls from my body, we both get dressed in silence before walking downstairs hand in hand.

****

Chelcie looks different this morning. I can still see the lingering fear in her eyes, but now, she also looks... nervous? We've been sitting around the table for about thirty minutes, just making small talk while we eat some breakfast that the boys brought over. The whole time, Chelcie keep looking over at Coop before quickly shifting her eyes away. She hasn't even eaten much, just keeps pushing it around her plate and worrying her lips.

What in the hell?

I know they hooked up while I was in the hospital last month, but Chelcie has told me that it was just one time, and she knows better than to get tangled up with Coop and his playboy ways. I know there aren't any feelings for him on her end, and knowing Coop as well as I do, I know there aren't any on his end, either. He's completely oblivious to the awkwardness. Just stuffs his face with more and more food.

Beck squeezes my leg, and I look over at him. He tips his head towards Chelcie and just shakes his head once. I know he would tell me if he knew anything, so I nod and continue to eat.

We finish up breakfast and I busy myself with cleaning up the mess. I'll do anything to buy me some time before we sit down and talk about everything swirling around us.

"You need some help, Dee?" Maddox asks.

I blush remembering him catching my ass in the air earlier.

"Nope, I got it all under control." I'm loading the last dish into the dishwasher. I can hear Beck and Coop talking at the table and glance over to see Chelcie still sitting there silently.

"Don't worry. Just because I got an eye full this morning doesn't mean I'm going to carry you off and enjoy the view up close and personal."

My shocked gaze snaps to his, and when I see his dark eyes dancing with humor, I want to kick his ass.

"Not funny, Asshole!" I smack him with the dishtowel before walking back over to the table and sitting down.

"What was that all about?" Beck asks, looking at Maddox with a glare.

"Nothing, just Mad being a douche."

His eyes narrow as he looks over at Maddox, who just holds his hands up in surrender.

"All right, so... can we get this over with?" I break the silence, praying that Beck will drop it. Maddox might be the most closed off man I've ever met, but I know he didn't mean anything by his comments. He has apparently grown a sense of humor overnight, and even though it's at my expense, it's nice to see him not so closed off.

"Stop thinking about her ass." Beck growls, taking my hopes that we can just forget about this away in a flash.

"Seriously, just forget it!" I snap.

Beck breaks his heated staring contest with Maddox to look over at me.

"He saw you naked, Dee! You want me to just forget about it?" His tone is low and lethal. I know he's seconds away from going all alpha-man crazy.

"Oh, really... you know, I'm aware that he saw me naked, but it was also an accident. When you were running through the house with your dick flopping all over the place for everyone to see, you didn't see me going all crazy. Oh no, I was laughing, because, hello! It's funny!"

His nostrils flare and his eyes are still narrowed, but he doesn't say anything.

AH! I swear that these overgrown apes are going to be the death of me.

"Stop your shit, John Beckett. So what? Coop got a quick look at my girls and Maddox saw my naked ass. THEY aren't the ones that get the benefits of *possessing* this body. It's all yours! I didn't flip out when everyone in this house saw you, and I would appreciate it if you could tone that testosterone down a little. So, would you please stop?"

"Those two bastards didn't enjoy looking at my junk, but I know they enjoyed the hell out of yours!"

For the love of God! It takes me a second to tone down my frustration, and if I'm honest with myself, it's hot as hell to watch him get all jealous and possessive.

"Are you forgetting about the very feminine set of eyes that got to take in all that is little Beck?"

Coop chokes on his drink when I finish talking. Maddox booms out a laugh that shocks me enough to look his way. If I weren't so frustrated with Beck right now, I might drool over how handsome he looks. How has no one noticed, besides Em, just how good-looking he is? Even Chelcie seems to be zoned in on all that is Maddox Locke smiling and laughing.

"Dee!" His growl has me snapping my eyes back to his.

"What?"

"Eyes. On. Me."

"Oh, you infuriating man!" I stand up, shift until I'm in his lap, and press my mouth to his ear. "Your tits, your ass. No one else's but yours. Yours to touch, lick, and kiss. No. One. Else. Do I need to keep listing all the parts of me that belong to you? Because, Baby, we don't have enough time for me to list every single part of my body." When I finish whispering in his ear, I pull back and look into his eyes. I want him to see how serious I am and how ridiculous his caveman act is.

His eyes are burning with emotion. I can see how hard he's working to control this jealous urge of his. The lust and desire that lights his eyes doesn't shock me, but when I see his face go all soft and my words penetrate his thick head, I know he gets it.

He understands. He out of everyone knows how big it is for me to admit that I belong to anyone, but more importantly, he gets that right here in the midst of his stupid jealousy, that I am completely his.

Mind, body, and soul.

He closes his eyes and pulls me deeper into his arms. Chills rake through my body when he presses his lips against my temple and leaves them there. Just breathes me in and takes the moment he needs.

"Well, as entertaining as it is to watch Beck go nuts, why don't we focus on the shit that needs focusing?"

I glare at Coop, pissed that he interrupted Beck's and my moment. It pisses me off that all this shit with Adam and the asshole sending the letter has come at the worst possible time.

"What have you found out?" Beck asks, never lessening up his hold on my body. His voice vibrates through my back, causing me to shiver.

"Not much from that letter. I'm going to drop it off with a buddy of mine at the police station and get them to run it for prints. No postmark, which we expected, so either he had someone drop it off at the office, or he paid someone to do it for him. Either way, we most likely aren't going to get shit off that letter. Pictures are all local. Most of the ones of Chelcie are her coming and going from Roberts Insurance. Nothing that leads me to believe he knows much about her personal life, which was also to be expected. Chelcie just happens to be his way of shaking Dee up because he knows about their friendship." Maddox pauses for a second, and I take the moment to glance at Chelcie. She doesn't look as scared as she was last night, but she still looks worried.

"I did get lucky on Adam Harris. Seems that he isn't as stealthy as this other douchebag. Picked up a trace on his cell phone. Local tower, so for some reason he seems to be in the Atlanta area. I'm still working on the rest, but he isn't using any bank or credit cards, mainly because he doesn't have any money in those accounts. There are a few shithole motels around where his phone was traced, but no luck finding him. For now, he's our number one concern."

When Maddox finishes talking, I let out the breath I didn't realize I had been holding. They have nothing. Well, nothing reassuring.

"So, you're telling me that this Adam guy is local and very well could reach out and fucking touch me?" I whisper. I notice Chelcie shudder out of the corner of my eye and regret the way I worded that.

"No one is going to get their hands on either one of you." The venom behind Coop's promise shocks me. I don't think I've ever seen him act like that before. He normally hides behind his 'don't give a fuck' immaturity, but this right here is a side to him I've never seen. "I mean it. We won't let anything happen to you two." He looks away and we're all silent for a minute, letting Maddox's news sink in.

When Coop's cell rings a few minutes later, I jump in Beck's lap, causing him to grunt when I land awkwardly. "Thanks for that, Babe." He groans, adjusting me better in his lap.

"Oh, I'll kiss it and make it better later."

Coop checks his caller ID, and a big shit-eating grin takes over his face. In hurried movements, he accepts the call, stands, and places the phone to his ear. "Ash! God, is it good to hear your voice."

What? Who the hell is Ash? I look at Chelcie when I hear her gasp, and like a damn light bulb going on, it all makes sense. Damn, I knew I should have said something to her about getting mixed up with him. Regardless if it was once or a few times, she obviously is upset knowing he's talking to another chick.

"Leave it alone, Dee. We need to focus on other things right now, and whatever is going on between those two is none of your business."

I nod my head at Beck's whispered words and sit back to wait for Coop to return to the conversation.

No one says anything while we wait. I can't hear what Coop is saying, but by the tone of his voice, he's happy to hear from the chick who's on the line. He comes back into the room about ten minutes later with a big, stupid grin on his face.

"What?" he asks when it's obvious that the mood in the room has shifted.

"Nothing. Let's talk about plan of action." Beck is quick to change the subject, and I notice Chelcie visibly relax.

"Right now, we keep doing this. The girls stay here and so do you. Axel knows what's going on, and we all agree that their best protection is either here or at the office. When you need to leave, Coop or I will come stick around. I know you have a few security installs coming up this week. If you would have taught us how to install those bastards, then we could have taken those, but it's those high end, fancy motherfuckers. My guess is this unsub will make himself known when the ten days are closer to an end. Until then, we wait and try to find Adam."

"What the hell is an unsub?" I ask the room when Maddox stops talking.

Coop stops looking around the kitchen before giving me his attention. "Unknown subject, Babe. You have any Cheetos here?"

"Jesus, Coop! Could you at least pretend to pay attention?" Beck barks, causing me to jump.

I can tell Beck is frustrated, knowing there isn't anything we can do at the moment.

"Got it," I say meekly. "So we sit and wait."

This doesn't do anything to help reassure me. Regardless of how safe I feel with Beck, and his ability to protect Chelcie and me, not having answers is downright terrifying.

"Don't worry. We're going to catch this jackass no matter what." Beck's words don't help.

'No matter what' is the part that causes me the most concern. The thought of the happiness we've just now gotten back vanishing to some unknown threat, and not knowing how to prevent it causes my heart to hurt.

"Stop, Dee. Just trust me to do whatever it takes to keep you and Chelcie safe."

I nod my head at Beck's words and try to keep my breathing even, but inside, my gut is telling me that there is no way possible for this to end well.

CHAPTER 23
Beck

"How are you taking all of this?" I ask Dee later that night while we lay in bed.

She lifts her head off my chest and rests her chin against her hand. She just looks at me for a few beats, not giving anything away, before she says anything.

"I'm scared. I know you don't want to hear that, but no matter how safe I feel in your arms, I can't help it. There is someone out there that wants to hurt me, wants to hurt Chelcie, and who knows who else. Beck, he could be anyone off the street. What if it's someone I pass every day and I have no clue?"

"I get it, I do. But, you have to believe and trust that we will keep you both safe. I won't let this asshole take you from me, Dee. I finally have you back in my arms, and I'll be goddamned if anyone threatens what we have."

Her eyes close briefly and she takes a deep breath. I just continue to rub my hands lightly against her back. I would give anything to take this fear from her, but I can't. Isn't that the kicker? I would do anything for this woman, and I am completely powerless in this situation.

"I do, I promise. I know you and the guys will do everything in your power to keep anything bad from happening, but that doesn't change the fact that the threat is here, and we have no idea how to stop it."

I can hear the desperation in her tone. I shift our bodies so that we're laying on our sides facing each other.

"Listen to me; you've come so far, Dee. Not just with your personal demons, but Baby, you've finally let it all go. The pain, the fear, all of it is gone and you better believe that I will fight an army if it means I keep this look of peace in your eyes. You hear me? I refuse to ever let you feel powerless or afraid. As long as I'm here, you will never, ever, feel that darkness touch you again." I wipe the few tears that have fallen from her eyes and kiss her lightly. "Forever, Baby. You and me forever."

"Forever," she echoes with a wobbly smile.

She burrows as close as she can get, wraps her arms around my body, and tangles her feet with mine. Not once throughout the night does her hold let up. My girl knows exactly where she's meant to be, and exactly who will move heaven and fucking earth to make sure that not one hair on her head is harmed.

****

Frustrated doesn't even come close to describe how I'm feeling right now. It's been eight days since we all sat down at my house to put all the cards on the table. Eight long days with nothing. Not one fucking thing. The unsub hasn't sent another letter, hasn't called, no smoke signals… not a damn thing.

Dee's doing her best, but I can tell she is worried. I've been keeping a close eye on her. My worst fear is that she will start pulling into herself again. I know from experience that PTSD doesn't ever completely go away. Some people go their whole lives after treatment ends and don't have a setback, while others have triggers. So far, I haven't seen anything that leads me to believe that she is struggling. For now, I just have to wait and watch her. She's promised me that if she feels like things are getting dark again that she will immediately call Dr. Maxwell.

Even through all of this, she's staying strong, and fuck, that feels good. It's probably the only damn good thing that's come out of all this. I have my girl and she has herself back.

Sighing deeply, I toss my pen down on my desk and turn to the latest email from Maddox. Apparently, Adam's last call on his cell has been traced to a few towns over. He doesn't seem to think we should be concerned yet, but I know he feels the heat of the flames getting closer. We're trained to trust our instincts. We didn't spend years overseas fighting an invisible army not to have a fine tuned gut. Trouble is coming, and just like overseas, we have no idea from which direction things are going to blow.

The ringing of my phone wakes me up from my thoughts. Caller ID shows 'Greg Calling' and that earns another frustrated groan. He's been calling for the last few days, wondering if he can swing by to talk to Dee. I've been trying to put him off, because with everything else swirling around us, I need him to focus. No matter what, when he and Dee have their talk, he's going to feel that, and he's going to feel it hard.

"Beck," I bark.

"You doing okay, Brother?"

"About as good as I can be doing. Ready to pull my hair out if we don't start getting answers soon. How is it possible for one motherfucker to be a complete ghost? And this Adam shit? He's not even careful, and we still can't fucking find him. We're trained goddamn Marines and two idiots are besting us. I don't even think frustrated comes close to how pissed I am." Fuck, that felt good to get off my chest. I haven't wanted to pile all of that on Dee. She knows I'm worried, but I don't want her to take my shit on top of her own fears.

"I understand. These guys will screw up, and when they do, we'll be there." He sounds just as pissed as I am so at least I know I'm not alone here.

"Anything new on your end?"

"Not a thing. Maddox stayed at the office all night monitoring the computers. Unfortunately, that asswipe turns his phone off when he's done making a call. Whatever kind of idiot he might be, he at least knows his shit when it comes to tracking."

"That's what I'm afraid of, Greg. He could be on my doorstep, and we wouldn't fucking know." I need to punch something. Pound the shit out of anything to get rid of all this stress and anger.

"You've got eyes on the place, and a security system that would make the White House look like child's play. Try to take a breath for a minute."

"Not that easy, Greg, not even close to being that easy. One day. That's all that we have left until she's supposed to meet some impossible deadline. And now I

239

have her going stir crazy." I know she isn't used to being stuck inside without being able to leave.

"Why don't you bring her down to the office? I know it isn't the spa, but at least it gets her out of the house, and we can still keep an eye on things here." The hopeful sound to his voice has me narrowing my eyes. I hate questioning his motives, but I know exactly why he wants me to bring her there.

"Don't play me for a fool, Greg. I know you want to talk to her, and I'm not trying to stand in the way of that, but are you sure you really need to do this now? In the middle of all this bullshit, you want to open this can of worms?"

"I need to know, Brother. It's killing me not knowing, and thinking the worst. If anything, knowing will be better than the thoughts that have been rolling around in my head. Melissa thinks the same thing as you. That I need to wait until this is over, but fuck me, I just can't."

"Yeah, I hear you, but this shit… Greg, make sure you really want to know because it can't be unknown. I know you, and I know how you feel about the females in your life. I'm not even going to lie to you. When Dee told me everything, I felt that hard enough that the earth shook. That's my woman, my life, so I felt that, and I still feel that. I know she's like a sister to you, and it doesn't matter if there isn't a relationship between you two like the one I have with her. That shit will hurt." I spit the last few words out, gripping the phone so tightly I'm sure it will snap. "Hell, I lived most of it right by her side, and *I* didn't even know the half of it."

240

"Right. That doesn't change things for me. I need to know, Beck. I've already heard it from Axel. Izzy was in tears for almost three full days. You don't think I get that this shit is heavy? I *know,* and that's what keeps running through my head. One of the most important people in my life was in pain for years, and I couldn't see shit. I have to know."

We don't talk after that. I can feel my neck getting tight in frustration, and I growl in the phone. Fuck!

"It's not just about you, Greg. I don't want this to set her back," I say quietly.

"What?" he whispers, his voice deadly calm. "Set her back from what?"

I realize my mistake right when the words come out. If I had any hope of calling him off before, now it is gone. He's going to know with those words that it is probably as bad as he has imagined.

"I'm coming over. You want to sit in on this talk, that's fine, but I'm on my way."

When I hear the phone disconnect, I slam the receiver down, and push back from my desk with enough force to cause my chair to crash down. Fuck me. Looks like I need to go let Dee know that a storm's coming.

CHAPTER 24
Dee

I need out of this house, and not being able to just go whenever I want is probably the only reason that I'm so antsy to leave. At this point, I don't even care where the hell I go. I just want to see something other than the walls of Beck's home. Chelcie is handling this a whole hell of a lot better than I am. Either that or she's just hiding it better. I think her toes have been painted and repainted about fifty times. I've tried to get her to tell me what's going on with her and Coop, but she just evades the question. If I didn't think something was going on before, I definitely do now.

This morning has been exceptionally boring. We have all the work done for the next week it seems. When all that you have is time, it's amazing the stuff that gets finished. I've contacted a real estate agent that I know back in North Carolina, and told him that I want it sold. Gone. I don't want to ever see that building again. So far, there haven't been any issues with my clients. They know that I will still be handling their business; it just won't be from the same state.

The policyholder that Adam had screwed with wasn't too happy when I explained the situation. Luckily, since it had only been a few hundred dollars, they agreed to take a settlement in order to not press charges.

Regardless of how many times I explain the situation, I know there will never be a chance of getting business from them or anyone close to them in the future.

For the first time in almost ten years, the job I love is becoming something I hate.

I have just finished emailing the agent handling the sale of Roberts Insurance, NC. Things are looking good for a quick sale. I didn't expect to get a bite within the first week of putting the listing up, but so far, there are two companies with heavy interest. Thank God.

"Dee?"

I smile when Beck's voice carries out of the house onto the deck where I'm relaxing with Chelcie. I shut my laptop and look over at her.

"I'll be right back. Do you need anything?"

She looks up from her own computer for a second, shakes her head, and returns her attention to whatever she's working on.

Walking through the double doors and back into the living room, I make my way towards where I hear his heavy steps echoing from the front of the house. I round the corner into the foyer and almost collide with Beck. "Whoa there, Big Boy, where's the fire?" The smile on my lips slips away when I notice the look in his eyes. "What is it?" I whisper.

He doesn't answer right away. He pulls me into his arms and just holds me. My anxiety is climbing. It really could be anything as long as we have some sick fuck out there watching our every move. "Beck, please, talk to me."

"Greg's on his way. I tried. I really did. I know you aren't ready to have this talk, but he wouldn't take no for an answer. I'll sit with you if you need me to, but I think he needs to know what really went on." His eyes are pleading with me to understand, and I get what he's saying. Until Greg knows everything, it won't be out of the way and in the past.

"Okay." Wrapping my arms around him, I let his comforting scent and strong body ease some of the tension from me. "I know you would sit there with me, and that means the world, but we both know you don't want to reopen that wound. We've moved past it, and I don't *want* to see that pain in your eyes again. I need to do this on my own."

"Are you sure?"

His arms pull me in tighter and I smile against his chest. What did I do to deserve this man?

"Yeah, Baby, I'm sure." I pull back and look up into his loving eyes. "It's something I need to do. I need to stop leaning on you for my strength." He offers me a small smile and an understanding nod. "I love you. Thank you for understanding."

"I love you, too." His lips press against my forehead and I close my eyes relishing his touch. "I don't like leaving you when I know you might need me, but I get it. How about I take Chelcie down to the office? I'm sure she would love to visit with Sway, get out of the house, and have his crazy ass pamper her. It's almost lunchtime anyway, so someone can chill next door with her while Sway does his thing."

"That sounds perfect. I'm going to go change out of my pajamas. Come find me before you head out?"

244

He gives me another soft kiss, but lingers when my tongue dances across his lips, asking for access. When we finally break apart, he pulls me in for another tight hug before taking off through the house calling for Chelcie.

With a deep breath, I head up the stairs to get ready for Greg's arrival.

****

Beck had come to tell me that Greg is here before heading out with an excited Chelcie. Regardless of the reasons for them leaving the house, I'm happy that she will be able to breathe some fresh air. Maybe when I finish this heart-to-heart, I can talk Greg into letting me leave, too. I might as well take advantage of these overgrown apes offering their protection.

Walking down the stairs and through Beck's large house makes me feel like I'm walking the length of ten football fields. Knowing that Greg's waiting, and that the conversation with him isn't going to be a nice, happy one, makes the walk even more daunting. I hear him puttering around the kitchen when I reach the hallway leading into the living room. I take a deep breath and come out of my hidden sanctuary. His head snaps around when he hears my footsteps against the hardwood floor. I can feel the distance between us in the energy floating through the rooms.

"Hey." I smile weakly as I walk around the thick leather chair that Beck and I love to cuddle in, and run my fingertips along the back, hoping to ground myself to something that Beck's touched. It might sound stupid, but just that little touch makes me feel like he's right here with me.

Greg doesn't speak. He just stands behind the little half-walled, breakfast bar that separates the kitchen and the living room. His blue eyes, which normally hold nothing but kindness and love, are clouded with worry. God, I hate this. I wish he could have just remained oblivious to all of this shit.

"You want to go sit outside? It's a nice afternoon." I try to smile again, but he still just stands there looking at me. "Can you please say something?"

He breaks eye contact and looks off to the side, just staring into space. I know he's thinking, because he runs his hands through his hair a few times, drops his head, and holds the back of his neck, just shaking his head lightly.

"Please."

His head pops up and the pain behind his eyes squeezes my heart. Between Izzy and Greg, I think I always knew he would handle things the worst. Even though we didn't even know each other when the majority of this shit went down, it doesn't matter to him. I'm his family, and if anything happens to his family, he feels it like it's his own pain.

He takes a few more minutes before walking towards me. His eyes never leave mine until I'm forced to look away when his chest crashes into my face. His arms wrap around me in a vice like grip. He just stands here, holding me as if he's afraid that if he lets go, I'll fly away. I give him this, sliding my arms around his thick torso and holding him just as tight. His heart races against my ear, and his breathing is coming in rapid pants. My heart breaks a little, knowing that there is no way to explain this without hurting him more.

"I'm sorry," I mumble against his chest.

"Are you kidding? What the hell do you have to be sorry for?" He pulls back, and my arms fall from his body and hang lamely by my sides. His warm grip against my biceps keeps me standing when I see the emotion in his face.

"I didn't mean to hurt you. We've always been able to tell each other everything, but this... This was just something that I didn't know what to do with. It's taken me a lot to get to this point, Greg. You had so much going on this last year that, even if I had been ready to talk, there was no way that I could have thrown this on you. Not with everything that was going on with Melissa and Cohen."

Things got a little crazy for a few months when Greg almost lost his son because of a crazy grandparent. Not to mention, the drama he went through with that whore he used to sleep with. Now that Melissa is almost six months pregnant with their twins, and they are all finally happy, things are definitely in a better place for me to let him in. He has someone to help him ease his mind from this.

"God, Dee. You know I would do anything to help you. You've been my family for years. When family needs you, for whatever reason, you're there. Don't you realize how much the people in your life love you?" He looks so confused. Damn, this is not going to be good.

"Come on, let's go sit down."

He lets my arms go and follows behind me. I walk back around Beck's chair, once again trailing my hands across the soft leather. I close my eyes and picture his handsome face, smiling and full of love. I let my body fill with his love and open my eyes with a new determination.

I sit down on the couch and pat the cushion next to me. Greg smiles and shakes his head with my action. I've seen him do that a million times with Cohen, so he knows it's my poor attempt at throwing some lightness into this darkness that's swirling around us.

"I'm just going to start at the beginning and as hard as this is going to sound... just please, let me finish before you say anything."

He nods his head and I take a deep breath before I start telling my story.

He doesn't move once as I begin speaking. I start with my childhood and work my way up through high school. His eyes get hard a few times, mainly whenever I mention my father. I pause for a second before I tell him about Brandon breaking into my office. I know he will be able to handle that part, but it's going to be a stretch thinking that he'll be able to control his anger when he finds out just how bad it got. My eyes have been watching my fingers play with a string hanging from my shirt, while I try to figure out how to tell him the rest.

"Dee?" I look up and see his puzzled gaze. The question in his eyes and the understanding nod show me that he realizes that this is part of the bad I've been keeping from him. "Go on, please."

I open my mouth a few times before I get the words out. I keep my eyes glued to his as I tell him about the first attack Brandon made against me, the rape, and the fear that kept me from saving Izzy before she was finally able to free herself. I rush to get each word out, because with each continuing second, I watch a little part of one of my best friends break apart and splinter into a million pieces.

"I don't think I ever dealt with it. At least not like a normal person would. I pushed it under the rug and continued to live my life the only way I knew how at the time." I pause and look away from his angry eyes for a second, trying to calm my nerves. "When he hurt Izzy, that time at the condo we had, I think that was the start. Beck noticed and didn't let me cave in, but even he couldn't save me from myself. We had the most amazing week together before it all blew up and the lights went out in my life." His eyes narrow in question, but he doesn't interrupt me.

"It was a few weeks after Izzy got hurt. I had been pushing him away and doing my best to keep him in a nice little box so that he wouldn't work his way into my heart, but Beck worked his way in." I smile remembering those early days. "We didn't even have a chance to tell anyone. Funny how that works. Everyone thought that we'd been playing these bedroom games for the last two years, but in reality, he's held my heart the whole time." I shake my head. I still can't believe that Beck was the only one who ever noticed my pain. Well, Beck and Maddox, but Mad never let on that he has been silently watching my private struggle.

"I wasn't even upset that you guys didn't notice, you know?" I whisper the words, but he jerks when I finish talking. I swing my eyes back to his face and flinch when I see his eyes and lips pressed tight. I have to look away to get the rest out. Part of me wants to scream at him, but I know whatever angry words I might say, he doesn't deserve them and knowing him, he's beating himself up worse than I ever could. It's no one's fault but my own that I shut down and didn't know how to process the pain. I wore the masks I needed to wear and I locked them out. I was my own worst enemy.

"After you got shot and all of the stuff with Brandon finally ended, something inside of me shut down. I didn't know how to deal with everything. The memories of what he had done to me and to Izzy. I couldn't see past the fear he had brought back when I was tied and at his merciless hands. Seeing Izzy's life so close to being taken, and you, Jesus, Greg, watching you almost die. I shut down. The depression wasn't even a match against the rest of the battles raging inside of me. Beck was there every step of the way for months until I finally succeeded in pushing him away." I keep my eyes locked with his as I finish my story. I tell him about the times Beck saved my life, the therapy I've been in for the PTSD, and everything in between. When the first tear falls from his eyes, I almost have to stop talking, but somehow, I manage to get to the end.

When the last word leaves my mouth, he takes a great shuddering breath. He stands from the couch and walks over to the window overlooking the backyard. I can see his reflection against the glass. His eyes are closed tight, and I watch him struggle with his control. Right when I'm about to open my mouth and beg him to say something, anything, his eyes open and he turns, just staring at me. His eyes are full of unshed tears, and his Adam's apple is bobbing with the force of his emotions. He opens his arms, and I move quickly from my spot on the couch. It's only a few steps, but when his arms come around and close tight around my body. I let out a sob. He buries his head in the crook of my neck, and I can feel the wetness of his tears against my shoulder. His big powerful body is shaking with the enormity of his grief. We stand here for the longest time, just offering each other the strength needed. I know he needs to let all of it sink in, and if we have to stand here for hours, then so be it.

By the time he pulls back, my own tears have wet the fabric of his shirt. His eyes are dry but bloodshot, and the sadness in his gaze causes my own tears to come rushing back.

"I'm sorry." I repeat my earlier words. He shakes his head and offers me a small smile.

"The way I see it, you have nothing to be sorry for, Dee. As much as it tears me apart to know you were fighting all of that and didn't tell anyone, I look at you now on the other side of all that pain, and I couldn't be more proud. Beck's your rock and, Babe, even if I hadn't been so foolishly blind I'm pretty sure that he's the only one that would have ever been able to help pull you back up. God, it's eating me up to know what you've been living with." He shakes his head, clearly still trying to calm the emotions that I've brought forth.

"I don't blame you. I don't want you to think that, even once, during all of this time, that I blamed you for not seeing. I didn't *want* you to see. I hid and put the happiness on to the extreme. You can't beat yourself up when I did my best to make sure that you couldn't see. That's on me, Greg." I can tell he doesn't agree with me, but he doesn't argue.

"Don't keep things from me anymore, Dee. Family doesn't do that shit." His eyes lose a little of the sadness, and his tone gets sharp.

I silently let some of the worry seep from my body when I realize the worst is over.

"I won't, I promise."

"Are you doing okay… with everything that's happening right now? You aren't struggling or anything?"

I know what he's asking. He wants to know if I'm sinking and need a life vest.

"Yeah, Greg. I'm really doing okay. I'm worried, but I think that's pretty normal. I've called Dr. Maxwell a few times since I've been back from the hospital. She's helped me stay on track, and to be honest, I don't feel the hooks of my old fears at all. I'm stronger now. Between all of my coping techniques and everything that is John

Beckett, I'm pretty close to normal. I still have my moments, but most of the time, those are a few nightmares that keep me up, and even those are coming less frequently."

"And Beck? You two are good?"

"We're amazing." The conviction behind those words has Greg's smile coming out, and for the first time since he got here, the smile I return isn't forced, and it washes all of the pain from my body like a waterfall. The thought of Beck and all the love we share is enough to heal even the deepest of my wounds.

"Thank you for telling me. I know that wasn't easy, and I'm not going to lie to you, it hurts like hell, but I'm glad that you let me in." He takes a deep breath and looks me hard in the eyes. "If you ever keep shit like that from me again, I'm going to let Melissa kick your ass for me."

We both laugh, and just like that the mood is lifted, and even though the pain lingers in his eyes, I know that everything is going to be okay.

CHAPTER 25
Beck

I'm about two seconds from climbing the walls of my office. I have been here for almost two hours and haven't heard a word from Greg or Dee. Axel and Coop have been giving me my space and I'm thankful for it. Axel came in when I first got here, and I almost took his head off with one of the books I threw at him.

Coop doesn't even bother. He takes one look at me and keeps walking past my office until I hear the door close to his own. Emmy is the only one I've been able to talk to and even that's been with a bark to my tone.

Maddox takes one for the team and spends the next two hours next door with Chelcie. Sway doesn't pick on Maddox as much as he does the rest of us, and even when he does, Maddox doesn't seem too bothered by it.

The knock on my door pulls me from my own head, and I look up to meet Coop's hesitant eyes.

"I've got to run out for about an hour. We've got another stalk and snap case. Another rich homemaker who is convinced her husband is sleeping with the secretary." He laughs and shakes his head. "This is exactly why my ass won't ever let a chick get her hooks in me. I would end up being a case on your desk to come stalk and snap."

"You know, the best thing that's ever happened to me is having Dee return my love, so I won't ever see where you're coming from there." Leave it to Coop to lighten the lead ball in my gut. *Where the hell are Dee and Greg?*

"I'll take your word for that one, Brother. You know I respect you assholes and your relationships, but that shit just isn't for me. I'm not the kind of guy worth some chick's trouble. Too many mommy issues."

"We all have our own issues to bear, Coop. You'll get your happiness one day." I frown when I see the serious look he's putting out.

"Don't hold your breath there. Anyway, you need anything while I'm out?"

I shake my head, but before I can answer, my phone rings. I wave him off and swipe the phone to answer, letting the tension fall from my shoulders when I hear Dee's voice come over the line.

"Hey! Guess what?"

She sounds happy, so at least I can stop picturing her hiding in the closet in a ball.

"What's that?"

"I'm finally leaving the house! And before you start telling me a million reasons why I shouldn't leave, you don't have to worry. Greg's with me. We're going to swing by and grab some take out before we come to you. Will you ask everyone if they want anything?"

I can't help but smile when her tone hits my ears. There isn't even a sliver of the sadness that I have been expecting. I know that the talk they had wasn't easy, but I also know that Dee isn't the same person she was a few months ago. She's proven today just how far she's come. My girl is strong and she did it all on her own.

"Yeah, Baby, give me a second."

She hums her agreement and I place her on hold long enough to go ask Axel and Emmy what they want.

"You there?"

"Yup!"

My heart expands a little more with every word she speaks. Yeah, she's got this.

"You're going to have to call either Maddox or Chelcie. She's been next door for about a couple of hours now with Maddox standing guard. Coop ran out to meet with a new client, but whatever you get him will be fine." I finish up telling her what Axel and Emmy want before reminding her to grab her handgun and to keep it in her purse with her at all times. With her assurance and the knowledge that I know Greg will protect her, we hang up and I start my new stream of worries.

I wouldn't be as calm as I am knowing that she's left the safety of my house if I didn't know she has protection. I might not be there, but Greg can handle anything that pops up, and the fact that she's got her concealed doesn't hurt.

That was one of the first things we did when we returned home from North Carolina. After she was well enough, I went out and bought her a Glock of her own, and then we went to get her permit to carry concealed. She hasn't had the chance to fire it yet, but she knows how to use it, and just knowing that she's got some way of protecting herself makes me breathe a little easier.

The thirty minutes it takes for her to walk into my office seems like forever. I have been close to pacing the room when she comes breezing in. I stand here next to my office window and take a moment to drink her in before I am able to move. She's wearing a black tank top and a pair of white shorts that cover just enough to make her decent. Her long, bronzed legs seem to go on forever, and of course, she's got on a pair of white and black, polka dot heels. The things those shoes of hers do to my body should be illegal.

"Snap out of it there, handsome. You'll have to wait to act out all those dirty thoughts flying around in your head until we get home. Lunch is served." She walks her sexy ass over to my desk and starts emptying the contents of her bag. I let out a painful groan when she bends over to pick up a pack of soy sauce that fell from the bag. *Goddamn, that ass!* She laughs and tosses my fork at me before sitting down and starting to eat without me.

It takes me a few seconds before I can will my dick to calm down, and then I walk over towards her. I bend down and kiss her deeply before pulling my chair closer to her. We eat in a comfortable silence, both of us just happy enough to be together right now. I know why I have been so anxious; I needed to see for myself that she was really okay. Even if she doesn't speak the words, I know that she's here because after that talk with Greg she needed me, and damn if that doesn't feel fucking great.

It really brings it all home, just how far we've come. Before she would keep shutting me out and would never allow me to think that she needed me. Now... now she doesn't even have to think about it. She needed me, so she came and got me.

"Where's Greg?" It's driving me nuts not knowing how things went, but I don't want to push her to talk about it unless she wants to. Mainly, I just want to make sure that she really is okay.

"He's eating in the conference room with Axel. I brought Maddox, Chelcie, and Sway their food before I took the little happy trail of joy to get in here. I swear, I don't know why you guys let Sway leave that on the sidewalks."

She laughs and I shake my head, remembering when Sway spent two whole days painting the sidewalk in front of the business strip gold... with glitter speckled all over the place. We all gave him a hard time about it, but he's got a point. There isn't anyone around that can walk on that ridiculous paint without a smile.

"Anyway, dropped Emmy's off with her, but she was on the phone when I came in, so I'll go catch up when we finish our little lunch date." She turns back to her food, takes a few bites before closing up what's left, and walking over to the fridge in my office to save the rest.

I toss the empty containers from my meal in the trashcan and pull her into my lap when she walks back over to take her chair. She giggles and wraps her arms around my neck.

"Hey," she whispers against my lips.

"Hey." I almost don't get the word out before her lips crush against mine. She takes my mouth in a rough kiss that shows me just how desperate she had been to get here. I answer every move she makes. Our tongues dance together, and it doesn't take long before her kiss starts to turn more heated.

I pull back and give her a minute. Her eyes are still closed and her breath comes in quick bursts against my face. She takes a few beats before her lips curl into a beautiful smile. It feels like I've been handed the whole world in my hands when she gives me that smile. It's the one I've been craving for so long. There's nothing fake or forced about it. When she opens her eyes, the blinding joy that is like a blazing fire inside her, spills out. I give her a smile in return, and let the rest of the stress and worry from the day just pour off of me.

She lays her head against my shoulder and shifts so she's more comfortable in my lap. I keep one arm around her back to support her body but take her small hands and wrap mine around them, rubbing her silky skin with my fingers.

"Things went well today."

I nod my head and give her the space she needs to keep talking.

"He took it about as hard as I thought he would but in the end you're right. He needed to know, and I feel so much... more free." She laughs and the sound wraps around me. I close my eyes and savor this moment between us.

"He's going to be okay. I know this isn't something that he'll just snap and be over, but he has Melissa and Cohen to help him get through it." She leans up, pulls her hands free, and frames my face. Her thumbs rub the stubble of my day's worth of beard a few times before she brings her mouth to mine, giving me a small kiss before pulling away. "And I have you."

She smiles, and right there I can see it. She's moved on and is finally letting every, single, last one of those things that has been hurting her go. Like a sea of balloons being released into the sky, you can almost physically see her letting it all go.

"Always."

If possible, her smile gets even bigger before she lays her head back down and pushes her arms around my chest. With our hearts beating together, and a peace like I haven't known in a long time settling around us, I just enjoy this moment.

Greg walks by my office door, and I turn my head to see what he needs. He nods his head and gives me a look that confirms what Dee just said. He's okay, but he's going to need a little while before he can move on from what he now knows isn't what he thought. He stands there for a few minutes and keeps his eyes on Dee's back. I can't tell what's running through his mind, but then he silently looks back up and offers me one hell of a look. He's got his approval, acceptance, and happiness that Dee is in good hands. That right there is the look of the man who has accepted responsibility for Dee as if she were his own blood relation, letting go and allowing me to take over that honor.

Harper Sloan

CHAPTER 26
Dee

After lunch with Beck, I spend some time with Emmy while we wait on Chelcie to finish up with Sway. According to Maddox's last grunt filled, one-word response, phone call, she is happily being 'fluffed like a fucking bird'. I start laughing so hard that I almost drop the phone when he tells me that Sway has already tried to sit on his lap twice. Those guys can play all they want, but they secretly love the attention that Sway is not shy about throwing at them.

"We need to get Sway a man. Not just any man, but we need someone that could stand up next to these C.S. boys and belong. Certified, grade-A, hunk material."

Emmy looks up from where she's entering some notes from an earlier meeting the guys had and drops her jaw.

"You aren't seriously thinking about playing matchmaker, right?"

"Why not? It shouldn't be that hard to find him someone. I bet if we checked Craig's List right now, there would be a million men looking for companionship!"

Emmy snorts. "Yeah, maybe if you were in the market to start pimping. You can't pick him a man off Craig's List… That's just dirty."

"Okay then, Ms. I Know Everything, where would you like to find him a man?" I cross my arms and huff.

"Uh, how about, I don't. I have enough trouble with my own dates, let alone picking up someone else's." She turns her attention back to the computer, effectively cutting me off.

Whatever. I turn around from the front desk and take in their lobby. I was shocked when Greg told me that the guys did all their own decorating. The lobby is pretty dark, but still welcoming. Emmy's desk is the center of attention when you walk in the door, literally, the first thing you can see. Then of course, there is the Corps Security logo in huge black letters behind her head. The walls are a dark gray, and on either side of Emmy are two thick black couches. Both sitting areas have a gray coffee table with various piles of crap magazines on them. We had finally talked the guys into adding some red accents around the place to at least make it look a little happier and less 'my wife is cheating, will you catch her' gloomy.

I walk over to the left of her desk, pick up the most recent People magazine, and start flipping the pages.

"Emmy, we've got to take an important call in the conference room, so hold all the other calls, and when Coop comes back, tell him to get in here." Beck's voice draws my attention away from the magazine. He walks over and gives me a brief kiss. "You okay up here for a second? We're just right down the hall."

I smile up at him and reach out to rub the frown from his brow. "I'm fine. Emmy and I were just discussing the benefits of getting into the pimping trade, so just go along, and let us work our magic."

He walks away with a smile and all traces of his frown gone.

"You are nuts," Emmy says from her desk, punctuating each word with a hard snap of the keyboard.

"But you love me!" We both laugh, but before she can go back to her work, I ask her the one question I know she hates to be asked. "So, how are things with Maddox?"

She loses the small smile on her face and stops what she's doing.

"Things aren't anything and they won't be anything. That man is impossible."

"You're giving up?" I really never expected her to hold on to her flame for him this long, but I had been hoping that he would at least let her in when he realized how awesome she is.

"It's for the best, Dee."

Before I can reply, Coop comes dancing in the door, running his fingers through his shaggy blond hair. We both start laughing when we notice the gold glitter falling from his locks.

"This isn't funny! I swear Sway has some kind of tracker on my truck. Ever since Greg told him I was some glitter fairy, he finds the need to come shower that shit all over me."

I can't hold back the laughter. I have to walk over to the desk and hold on so I don't fall over, and squeeze my legs together so I won't pee in my pants like a little kid.

I'm so busy laughing that I miss the second the mood shifts from light and laughing to deathly serious. I'm wiping the tears from my eyes when I notice something out of the corner of my eye. I take in Emmy's stark white face and bugged-out eyes, before looking over at where Coop is standing. He's frozen with his hand still in his hair, but his attention isn't on the glitter anymore. I have never, not once in the two years that I've known him, seen him look like this. Playful and joking Coop has been replaced with someone that would give Maddox a run for his money. He looks absolutely lethal.

"Dee, get your ass behind the desk. Now." Coop's voice sounds the same, only much harder. I try to move, but the second I shift, the figure standing in the doorway turns his attention back towards me. I don't even need to focus on him to tell that he's pointing a gun right at the side of my head. The sickening click of him releasing the safety is all I needed to hear.

"If you even think about movin' a fucking inch, I'll put a goddamn bullet through your head."

You would think that when you hear the voice of someone you know has clearly gone in-fucking-sane that he would at least sound demonic, but no, Adam sounds just like the same southern frat boy I hired not too long ago.

"Adam, put the gun down and let the girls go. Let's me and you sit down and talk." I beg. I try to swallow the lump of fear that's crawling up my throat, but my mouth is bone-dry. I sneak a glance at Emmy to see that her face is impossibly pale, and she has tears streaming down her face.

Shit! Okay. Think Dee... I can feel the claws of my own personal hell trying to latch on and pull me under, back into that darkness that I've finally overcome, but I'll be damned! There is no way in hell that I'm going to finally move past that to find my own happiness, then have some motherfucking cokehead take it away from me.

"I have nothin' to say to you! All of yous assfucks have been in my business. You don't think I know yous been lookin' for me?! NO! I ain't lettin' you take me to him!" He sounds high as a kite. Surely, I can make it behind the desk and grab my purse. I made sure that my Glock was loaded before I put it in my purse earlier. All I need to do is get a little closer.

"DON'T FUCKIN' MOVE, BITCH!" His maniacal screams cause me to jump, and I reach out to grab the desk again to help keep me from falling.

"Please, Adam." I beg. I just need to buy a little time to get behind the desk. Fuck! Why haven't the guys come out! Surely they... Oh, God! They're in the conference room. The conference room isn't just in the back of the building, but it's also completely sound proof! My heart sinks when I realize that, unless Maddox comes back, there isn't anyone to help us.

"No! No! NO!" My mind flashes back to when Brandon held Izzy and me hostage. He was the same kind of crazy, bashing his head with the gun, and pulling frantically at his hair. The only difference is that Adam looks completely insane, while Brandon was able to hide his under his perfect exterior.

The gun never wavers when he starts rocking back and forth, muttering under his breath. His beady eyes look over every single inch of the lobby, pausing to leer at Emmy behind the desk before a sick smile curls his lips. "Who is this little thing? You sure do look a lot like that bitch Chelcie. Where is that little shit?" His bloodshot eyes swing back towards me, and I flinch when I see his vacant expression.

"She isn't here, Adam. She's back in North Carolina." I hold my hands up, and hope that by showing him I'm not a threat, he will drop the weapon and give us enough time to take control. I can see Coop shift just slightly, and I know he's trying to get to his gun. He's the only one out of the group of Corps men that keeps his gun in a shoulder harness, and there isn't a way he can get to it without drawing more attention. "Adam," I start, trying to make sure he's looking at me. "Why didn't you just tell me you needed help? I would have helped you." I keep my tone calm and hopefully void of the terror that is washing through my body.

"You ain't foolin' me, Dee! I know what kinda sneaky bitch you are." His laugh comes out completely possessed. "You couldn't just keep your nose outta my business. Noooo, you had to come in and fuck everything up!" I back up a step when he turns his attention back to Coop. "Stop fuckin' movin'!" he screams, coming closer to Coop by a step. It's like a nightmare square we're forming. Emmy is behind the desk and I'm next to it. Coop is standing in front of Emmy with Adam at the doorway pointing the gun right at him.

"Adam, please let them go. It's me that you have issues with; these people are just innocent bystanders. Okay? I'll go with you, and we can go get the money and take care of everything." He laughs again, and I know that he isn't going to be reasoned with.

I just need one more inch, and my purse is right there on the floor. I take a step back, hook my purse strap with my heel, and try to bring my leg up slowly where he can't see it. Luckily, we're at an angle where he can't see the bottom part of my body since he's moved closer to Coop.

"Adam, you don't want to do anything stupid. Let me have the gun, and we can go in the back and figure this out. You want some protection against this guy? We can do that. Come on, Adam, let me have the gun." Coop moves just a step closer, and I use the distraction to grab the strap and pull my purse up. My gun is in my hands before he even has a second to notice I've moved. The heavy weight feels like the only lifeline I have right now.

"Oh, really? I don't wanna do anything stupid? Yous idiots can't protect me from D. He will find me, and since I'm already a dead man walkin', there ain't shit to stop me from, oh, I don't know, taking blondie's head off first."

It's as if the world starts only working in slow motion. Adam turns and points his gun right at Emmy's head. She gasps but doesn't even move. Absolute terror washes over her body and she goes statue still. I scream and go to raise my gun, but before I even have it halfway up from my hip, I hear the deafening sound of the bullet leaving the chamber. And then the slow motion, horror show keeps rolling. I watch with helpless, stone-cold dread as Coop flings his body to the side. His large frame jolts when he takes the bullet meant for Emmy's head.

"YOU MOTHERFUCKER!" I scream and finish raising my gun. He just laughs, and before I can pop the safety and shoot, I hear another shot echo around the room. A burning like nothing I have ever felt in my life sears through my left shoulder, but I don't even falter. This sick bastard just shot my friend, and I'll be damned if anyone else here takes a bullet. It seems to take forever, but really, it's only been seconds since Coop hit the floor, before I take a deep breath and fire my own weapon. When the recoil rocks me back, I lock my knees and keep my eyes trained on the sick fuck that just took *my* bullet between his fucking eyes.

I drop the gun, and with a sob, I rush towards where Coop's body is lying motionless on the black tile floor. My ears hurt from the screams that are echoing throughout the office, and it takes me a second to realize that they are coming from my own mouth. When I reach his side, I slip and fall, crashing to the floor next to him. "COOP! Oh, God... Zeke Cooper, open your eyes, please! HELP! SOMEONE HELP US!" He opens his eyes for a second, but they slip closed just as I'm pulling his heavy body into my arms. I search his body, but when I see the dark red hole right in the middle of his stomach, I know this isn't good.

"EMMY! Come on, Em, help me."

She doesn't even move.

"COOP, wake up, Babe! Please, God..." My sobs start to echo around me. I lean back, pull my tank top over my body, and press it tight against his stomach. I don't know if this is going to help, but I'm not going to stop short of trying everything.

I know they had to have heard the shots next door. There is no damn way they didn't. "MADDOX! God, PLEASE..." I sob, begging for the only person that can be any help now. Unless the guys in the back open that door, there is no way they can hear anything happening, but I keep trying.

"Coop, please... stay with me, Coop!" I keep pressure against his wound, but when the blood starts coming through my shirt and coating my hands, I start to panic.

"FUCK!" I'm not even sure how I hear Maddox scream over my sobbing, but he is immediately by my side. He pulls his shirt off and puts it on top of my hand. "Hold. Don't fucking move."

He bends down and speaks in Coop's ear. Coop's eyes open and he tries to nod his head, but his eyes widen before a sickening wet groan comes up his throat. I watch in horror as he coughs once and a massive amount of blood comes pouring out of his mouth. I try to shift my body so that I can offer him something, anything, but my legs slip and my body almost slides, crashing down when I lose my traction. I look down and notice the amount of blood that I'm kneeling in.

"Maddox!"

I call him to come help me, but he's looking at Emmy as he barks orders into the phone. She still hasn't moved from her spot behind the desk, tears still pouring down her face, and her small body shaking with so many violent waves, I know she's about two seconds away from going into shock. Shit.

I see a flash of hot pink and long blond hair rush past me and down the hallway to the back of the building. I look up for a second to see Chelcie with her arms wrapped tightly around her belly, just shaking her head back and forth.

It doesn't take long before Beck, Greg, and Axel come rushing down the hallway followed by a frantic, crying Sway. They don't waste any time springing into action. I don't move from my position, and continue pressing the two soaked shirts against his solid abdomen. Maddox finishes telling the 911 operator the rest of the details before slinging the phone across the room where it crashes against the wall.

"I've got it. Go get Em." Greg's rough voice, thick with emotion, tells Maddox when he moves to come back to Coop. He looks torn for a second between the man that is like his brother, and the woman that he's been fighting his feelings for. With a heavy sob, he picks himself off the floor and rushes over to where she is sitting. She doesn't move, but he picks her up from the chair and quickly carries her over to one of the couches. "Chelcie, find me a jacket, blanket, some fucking thing now!" His tone snaps her attention from Coop, and she rushes back through the office.

I bring my focus back to the men surrounding Coop and take in each one of their faces. They hold so much pain and grief. This is what the face of hopelessness looks like.

"No, no, no! Coop, Coop, you stay with us. Do you hear me?" I sob and scream. Beg for him to be okay. When the paramedics rush in and tell me to move out of the way, I refuse at first. I'm keeping him alive. How can they think of asking me to move! It takes both Beck and Greg to pull me off of his body. When they finally roll him into the back of their rig, I collapse and let out every single scream and ounce of agony left in my body as Beck holds me tight. Axel leaves with Coop, Maddox leaves in the second ambulance with Emmy, and when they come to tell me I need to be checked out, I fight them tooth and nail. Beck finally tells them that they will have to look me over while I sit in his arms.

I look around the room while I hold onto Beck with everything left in my body and take in the grief stricken faces of those that are left. Greg is standing off to the side talking with one of the cops. Another one is talking to Sway over by the couches. Chelcie, having just finished giving her statement, comes to stand next to where Beck is rocking me on the floor.

I remember hearing Beck tell the officers that they would have to follow us over to the hospital before they would get the rest of our statements. Greg finishes up and helps Beck stand from the floor so that he can keep his arms around me. I don't realize until we are on the way to the hospital that the reason he couldn't stand on his own is because we had been sitting in the middle of the slippery, dark red, pool of blood that Coop's body had left behind.

CHAPTER 27
Beck

Three hours.

Three painful hours.

That's how long we've been sitting here waiting for the closed door to finally open. Waiting for answers and praying for a miracle. When I look at the faces of the people around me, I know that we all know how grim this looks.

We arrived at the hospital to find Axel in the waiting room. Maddox hasn't left Emmy's side since he carried her into the ambulance back at the office. He's currently sitting in one of the stiff waiting room chairs with her small body curled in his arms. Dee moves her head off my chest long enough to give her statement to the police. Listening to her play back the events that lead us to where we are right now does nothing to ease the gut-burning dread that is eating away inside me.

Coop was shot right under our fucking noses, and because we had been stuck on some stupid, fucking conference call with some stupid, fucking city official that wanted us to check on his wife, we hadn't been there.

Right now, Coop is fighting for his life, and I can't help but think this is our fault. The only reason we shut that door is because we couldn't let the girls hear the city official on the phone. Eight minutes later, we have Sway throwing the door open screaming for us to get to the front.

Eight minutes is all it took for our backs to be turned long enough, and the unthinkable happen. Right. Under. Our. Noses.

I can't even let my mind think about how close I came to losing Dee again. Every single time my mind tries to go down that path, I feel as if my heart is being torn from my chest. I shift her and pull her still form closer to my chest. I need to feel that she is alive and right here with me.

I see Chelcie shift, her arms still wrapped around her stomach, and her pale face still dripping with the occasional tear.

"Chelcie?" I wait for her to look at me before continuing. "Are you okay?"

She jumps slightly before her body stills and her tears pick up.

Shit. I don't want to upset her more. "Chelc?"

She just looks at me. With her eyes vacant and her head slowly shakes back and forth. I sigh and shift one of my arms from Dee's body. I feel her wiggle closer to make up for the loss of my arm before settling in again. I motion for Chelcie to come over. She doesn't waste a second rushing across the room and dropping into the chair next to us. I wrap my arm around her shoulder and pull her into my chest. She wraps her arm around both Dee and me, and lets out the emotions she's obviously been holding in tight. Dee reaches out and hugs her, offering her some of the strength she has left. We sit here like this for what feels like forever before the door opens.

We all stiffen, waiting to see who will be walking through that door.

I've settled back in my seat when Izzy and Melissa come in. Izzy rushes right into Axel's arms. He drops his face into her neck, and I watch his shoulders shake. He's held it in, and I have no idea how. The only thing keeping me from breaking down is knowing that I need to stay strong for Dee right now. Melissa walks as fast as her belly will allow, and Greg meets her halfway. Like Axel, he holds his wife close, and they just stand there. None of us knows what else to do but keep praying and try our hardest to keep our shit together.

Chelcie pulls away after another thirty minutes of crying and settles back against her chair. I keep my arm around her shoulder, hoping that what little comfort I can offer helps whatever she's fighting.

Dee lifts off my chest and turns her red-rimmed eyes my way. I try to give her a smile, but she just shakes her head. "Don't think you have to act a certain way for me, Beck. Let me be *your* rock. Let me be there for you because, Baby, I know you're hurting right now, and I'm here."

Her words rock me straight down to the floor. I've been so worried that if I let my grief show, it might trigger something in her. For about two seconds, I think about how fucking proud I am that in the middle of tragedy, my Dee is back and stronger than ever. Those two seconds end, and all of the fear, pain, and distress I've been feeling come rushing to the surface. She notices my break, winds her arms around my neck, and pulls me into her body. I give myself a few minutes to let it out before I take a few deep, calming breaths and pull back. She gives me a wobbly smile and a small kiss against my lips.

"Someone needs to call Ash," Greg rumbles from where he and Melissa have taken a seat across from us.

I look over where Chelcie has stiffened again before looking back at Greg. "Yeah. You want me to do it?"

He shakes his head at me before kissing Melissa, rubbing her belly, and taking off to the corner of the room so he can have some privacy to make one hell of a hard call.

I keep my eyes on Greg the whole time he's on the phone. His body language is telling me enough. Ash is flipping out, and Greg is doing his best to stay calm. Five minutes later, he closes the phone and turns back to the room. I'm sure that my eyes are just as wet as his are right now.

"Ash is luckily about forty-five minutes outside of Atlanta. My guess is that door will be experiencing one hell of a tornado in about fifteen minutes, though."

I nod and we all settle back in. Chelcie lets out a sob before rushing from her chair and into the connecting bathroom.

"What's that about?" I whisper to Dee.

"I'm not sure. She's been acting really weird ever since her and Coop… yeah, it's just been weird."

I don't say anything, because I'm not exactly sure what to make of this now. I know for a fact that Coop hasn't hooked back up with Chelcie. Last time I talked to him, he told me that it was just that once and even Chelcie had agreed that it shouldn't happen again. Either way, I can't worry about that shit right now.

Twenty minutes is all it takes for the door to slam against the wall, and a six-foot-five inch carbon copy of Zeke Cooper to rush into the room. Asher Cooper, Zeke's older brother by ten months, and the only family he has left. I feel Dee gasp when she realizes just who Ash is.

"Holy shit," she whispers.

"Any news?" His voice, deeper and grittier than Coop's, booms through the room. He's not addressing anyone in particular; he's just as desperate as we are for some answers.

"Nothing yet." Maddox breaks his silence to answer him.

"Ash." Axel gets up and pulls him in for a hug. They have a few words before Asher pulls away, and looks over the room before his eyes settle on me. I've always been closer with Coop than the other guys have, so I know before he starts walking that he's headed to me.

Asher walks over and sits next to me in the seat that Chelcie vacated. "Please tell me what happened, Beck. I got just enough to stop my fucking heart before I jumped in the truck and headed this way."

I give him a run down on what happened, pausing to let Dee fill in the blanks that I didn't know, and watch as the hope Asher had when he walked in the door disappears.

"Don't fucking bullshit me, Beck. How bad is it?" His eyes, darker than Coop's light blue, are begging me to tell him it's just something minor.

"It's bad, Ash. It's real bad."

He nods his head and leans back. I watch him pull it together and harden his heart, preparing for the worst.

Not even a minute later, Chelcie finally comes out of the bathroom, and she just stands there staring at Asher as if she's just seen a ghost. All of the color, or what little is left, drains from her face, and a shaky hand slaps against her mouth.

"What the fuck?" Asher grunts next to me.

"Chelc?" Dee's soft voice snaps her out of the shocked daze she's in, and her eyes bounce between Dee and Asher.

"Who… who are you?" she asks, with a hint of fear in her voice.

"Asher Cooper, who are you?"

She doesn't even answer. I can hear her gag before she runs back into the bathroom where the sounds of her heaving come through the door.

"I've got it," Dee whispers and climbs out of my lap for the first time since we arrived over five hours ago.

I stretch my legs while she shuts herself in the bathroom with Chelcie. Not much that I can do about chick problems when the chick isn't mine.

It takes Dee a while to get Chelcie out of the bathroom. She looks horrible and keeps sneaking glances at Asher. Dee takes one look into my eyes, and I know instantly that whatever the hell is going on with Chelcie is a lot bigger than a girl hung up on an ex-lover. She settles Chelcie into a chair on the other side of me and climbs back into my lap. Before she puts her head back down, she just looks into my eyes. I see what she's saying. We'll talk later, and I need to be prepared for this one. I nod my head and give her a kiss before she lays her head back down.

Dee's back in my arms and we sit here, continuing to wait. I've been staring at the white bandage peeking out of the sleeve of the shirt she threw on before leaving the office. My mind can't wrap around the fact that if it had just been a few inches in the other direction, she wouldn't be sitting with me. I close my eyes when the images of her bleeding out on the floor become too much. As it is, I don't think I will ever forget the picture of Coop lying there, Dee covered in more blood than the floor, working desperately to stop the blood flowing from his body.

I open my eyes when the images become too much, and loosen my tight hold on Dee when I hear her soft grunt. Shit. It takes every fiber in my body to turn the thoughts in my head back into the hopeful prayers that I've been repeating since we left the office.

****

Another two hours pass before the doctor finally comes to find us. His face is void of emotion when he addresses the room and asks for Zachariah Cooper's family. Asher stands and walks over to the doctor with his back straight and his head high. The doctor speaks in low tones, but when Asher's body starts heaving, and his head shakes rapidly, my heart sinks. I look over at the rest of my brothers as the realization of what news has just been delivered sinks in. Ash lets out a noise so painful, that if my heart hadn't already split in two, it surely would have then. Dee slides off my lap without a word, and I stand, walking over to where the doctor is still speaking.

"…did everything we could but there was just too much damage."

And just like that, Ash's legs lose the power to hold him up, and I grab on as he unleashes his grief. I look over his head and meet Dee's eyes. Her tears are coming fast and fierce, but she gives me a weak smile so that I know she is holding it together. There isn't a single person in this room that hasn't been touched by Coop in one way or another. None of us is able to hold in the pain that we are feeling, knowing that he didn't make it.

Zachariah 'Zeke' Cooper died a hero. He was one of my best friends, my brother, and he died saving the life of not only my woman but Emmy as well.

CHAPTER 28
Dee

Coop's been gone for four days now.

Four days since I sat in the hospital and watched the strongest men I know break down.

And it's been four days since Chelcie told me what's been going on with her.

Pregnant. She's pregnant, and Coop will never know that he's going to be a father. That one time they shared may have been mutually no-strings, but now he's gone, and there isn't anything we can do to change that. I know she's having a hard time with things. She and Coop might not have had any feelings for each other, but that doesn't change the fact that there is a baby coming into this world that will never know his or her father. I think the hardest part for her right now is knowing that she never had a chance to even tell him.

I take a deep breath and continue to apply my make-up. Beck's already dressed in his Dress Blues, and if it was for any other occasion, I might be able to appreciate how good looking he is. I've chosen a simple form-fitting black dress. The short cropped sleeves cover enough of my nasty healing wound from where the bullet grazed my arm. I grab a pair of black, four-inch heels before walking down the stairs and meeting Beck in the kitchen. I watch his back as he moves about fixing a cup of coffee. He's holding his body tight, and I know that today is costing him emotionally.

After fixing his cup, he turns, picks up his white Barracks Cover, and leans back against the counter, just looking at his hat. I walk over and take his face in my hands. I don't give him words. Right now, he doesn't need them. I pull his head down and place a soft kiss against his lips. When I drop back down on my heels, I keep my palms against his cheeks. His eyes are closed, but a single tear spills from the corner and rolls onto my fingers. My heart is breaking for him right now, and I have no idea how to take some of the pain away.

"I love you." I remind him, just as I have every single night for the last four days.

"And I love you." His voice is thick with emotion, but he looks like he's holding it together a little better than he was two minutes ago.

Chelcie comes down about ten minutes later dressed in a black dress similar to mine. She looks a little better than she did yesterday, and I have to take that as a mark on the positive side of things. She gives me a small smile before sitting down to wait until the limo gets here to take us to the funeral home. Since Izzy and Melissa are sharing a sitter for the kids, we're going to be the last stop before heading out.

Deep breath in. Stay strong. I keep repeating those five words over and over. For the most part, I'm holding it together better than I ever expected. The night we got home from the hospital, I had to put a call in to Dr. Maxwell's private cell. After explaining what happened, she was more than happy to help me with my issues over the phone. It took about an hour, but when I hung up the phone with her, I realized that I just lived through something terrible and wasn't shutting down. I knew what I needed to do without having someone remind me. I saw myself being pulled in by those dark thoughts and fears, and made the call that I needed to make. We discussed the warning signs that I should look for, but she seemed pretty positive that I was holding myself together the best way I could.

She also stressed that I let Beck know that if he needs to talk, her door would be open for him. We talked about it last night, and he agreed that he would go speak with her. Watching him suffer in his grief, and knowing that he was blaming himself for what happened had me worried. I never thought I would see the day when I would be able to repay all of the things he's done for me in the past. Or I should say start to repay him.

****

The service for Coop was one of the most emotional things I had ever experienced. All of the boys wore their Dress Blues, and they looked breathtaking. I wasn't even shocked to see Asher sitting front and center in a uniform of his own. All of the guys took their seats next to Asher, and all five of Coop's 'brothers' sat stoically. They didn't flinch when the rifles went off, not a twitch in their faces when the bugle started playing, and when Asher was presented with the flag that had been draped over Coop's casket, they each kept their faces forward and eyes on Coop.

They didn't move until the last person had walked away from the gravesite. It wasn't until Izzy grabbed my hand to draw my attention across the graveyard that I watched those strong men crack a little.

I hadn't seen Sway since *that day*. I knew that he had watched the kids for Izzy and Melissa when they came to the hospital, and that he closed the salon for the last two days out of respect for Coop.

Watching Sway walk across the grass, weaving to avoid stepping on any markers is almost too much. Gone is his normal flamboyant garb, and in its place is a perfectly tailored black suit. His trademark blonde wig is gone, and his normal hair which I have never seen before is buzzed close to his scalp. There is nothing about this version of Sway that I have ever seen before.

He did this for Coop.

I know he waited for the service to end and the crowd to clear before he paid his respects. Melissa reaches over and takes my other hand, and we sit here waiting to see what happens next. From where we are, we have the perfect view of the scene playing out. All five of the men watch as Sway walks up to the casket and sets a single mason jar on top. It has a beautiful red, white, and blue ribbon tied around the top, and when my eyes take in the contents, a sob bubbles out before I can stop it. He presses his hand against the wood next to the gold, glitter filled jar and dips his head. He takes a few minutes before he pats the top twice and stands back.

At this point, all of us are sobbing uncontrollably, but what is most shocking to me is that all five of the men across the way have finally cracked. Obviously, Coop had filled his brother in at some point about the whole glitter prank because even his eyes are shining despite the small smile playing his lips. These big, strong, proud men aren't even trying to stop the tears that are falling as they look at Sway with small smiles.

Sway dips his head before he walks back off in the direction he came. His shoulders are bent and his soft cries trail behind him. He makes his way to his car and drives off. There isn't a single dry eye left as we all take in the beautiful glass jar full of the simmering of happiness.

CHAPTER 29
Dee

It's been two weeks since we said goodbye to Coop. Some days are harder than others are, but things are slowly starting to pick back up to normal. Asher has taken up the other guest room at Beck's, and between him and Chelcie, things are a bit awkward. She hasn't told anyone other than me about the baby, and I respect her wishes that I keep it to myself but that doesn't mean I feel good about it. Asher should know that there is a part of his brother that will live on, and for better or worse, Chelcie needs to let him in her life so that her child will know a part of their father.

Beck has been to speak with Dr. Maxwell three times now, and I can tell it's really helping. We've spent almost every night lying awake in each other's arms just talking. I feel closer to him than I ever have before. He's been here for me when I wake up in a cold sweat when the events of *that day* play out in my dreams. His soft words and warm embrace are the only things that I want when those dark moments come back. There are times when I catch him staring off into space, and I know those are the times when he's thinking about Coop.

No one really knows how to completely move forward from this. Whenever the group is all together, there's always that moment when someone checks the door, waiting for Coop to come barging through with some hilarious comment. We can't stop wishing that we could just see his blue eyes twinkling with humor one more time.

Grief is such a bastard.

Asher's decided to stick around for a while. I know he's taking his brother's death the hardest out of all of us. There have been a few nights when he's come home, drunk out of his mind, and stumbled into his room. The sound of his agony echoing through the walls is overwhelming, and I have no idea how to ease his pain. One thing's for sure, he's not healing, and at this point, I'm not sure he wants to.

Today, we're moving Chelcie into my apartment. The one thing that Coop's death has driven home is that tomorrow is never promised, and there should never be an excuse to not live your life to the fullest. No regrets and no fear of the unknown. So today, Chelcie will start a new chapter of her life in Georgia, and I will start mine with the man I love.

"Are you sure you don't want to stay another night, Chelc? You know you're always welcome here."

She smiles weakly but continues to pack up the last of her clothes. She doesn't have much, just the two suitcases of clothes she brought down, and a box of things that she didn't want to leave behind.

"No, I need to be alone right now. I need to figure out where I go from here."

"Are you okay? I know we've talked about it, but how are you dealing with all of this?" I sit down on the bed and still her hands when she goes to pack some more.

I know she's just trying to avoid this conversation that we need to have.

"I love that you're worried about me, Dee, but I'm really okay. I just wish I would've had a chance to tell him, you know? We didn't have that kind of relationship, but that doesn't change the fact that he would have been a great father." She sits down next to me and fidgets with the shirt in her hands. "I'll make sure that our child knows who their father was and that he died a hero... every day, Dee."

I have to choke back the emotions that threaten to sneak past the lump in my throat. God, I miss him.

"I think you need to talk to Asher. He's spiraling out of control over this, and he needs something to hold on to. Something that will keep him pushing forward. This little baby will be a part of his brother, his nephew or niece. He needs to know that there is something positive."

She doesn't speak for a while, and right when I'm ready to just give up on my newest round of 'convince Chelcie', she shifts on the bed. "I will. Let me get settled in the apartment, and then I'll have him over one night. I think it's something that needs to be done away from everyone else."

We continue to pack the rest of the clothes and head out. Asher's door is shut tight, but I know he's in there. He came in around four this morning and hasn't come out since. I checked on him around breakfast time but he was passed out. His room had the unpleasant stench of stale smoke, booze, and cheap sex. I pulled his shoes off and covered him with a blanket before leaving his room.

Beck is waiting outside for us when we finally come down. He takes my breath away every time I see him. Plain and simple, he is perfect. He's wearing cargo shorts and a USMC tee shirt. His University of Georgia ball cap has his eyes shaded, but I know he's looking right at me. I walk over to Chelcie's car and throw the bag that I'm carrying in the trunk. She doesn't waste time with hellos or goodbyes, just drops her bag in, jumps in the driver's seat, and takes off.

"Where are you headed, Handsome?"

His crooked smile has my panties on fire.

"Nowhere. Waiting on Maddox. Apparently some shit went down with Emmy last night." He drops his eyes, but not before I see how worried he is.

Truth is, we've all been worried about her. She hasn't spoken to anyone, and not for our lack of trying. She spent the whole time at the hospital in Maddox's arms but when we went to leave, she crawled out of his lap and walked over to Melissa. She and Melissa have always been the closest out of us girls, but I'm still surprised she left Maddox. Even at Coop's funeral, she didn't speak to anyone. She stood next to Melissa and never took her eyes from the casket.

"What's going on? Please don't keep it from me because you think I can't handle it. Me and you now, Beck. I need you just as much as you need me, so don't lock me out because you're worried about how I'll handle things. I'm stronger today because of *you,* so let me help you when you need me."

He doesn't say anything for a beat but lets out a rushed breath, looking away before turning back to me. "She's gone. He went over to check on her and she was gone. It looks like she left in a hurry, but she did take the time to leave a note. He didn't tell me the details about what she said, but he's on his way over so we can figure out what to do next."

"What?" The whole time he was talking, my mind kept wondering and twirling about what he was really saying. Emmy is gone? There's no way. She wouldn't leave her family.

"This is why I didn't want to say anything. I know you're going to get upset about this, Dee. Just trust us to take care of everything, okay?" He takes me in his arms, and I breathe in his woodsy scent and try not to panic, thinking about Emmy out there alone and scared.

"You have to find her, Beck. You just have to."

"We will. I promise you, we will find her."

I smile weakly and go to leave when his voice stops me short of my car. "Hey, let me get Ash and let him go with you? I would feel a lot better about you running around town if you had him with you. I would go myself, but this needs to be handled."

Chelcie is going to flip when I show up with Asher, but I just nod my head and wait for him to run up to wake the bear. Ten minutes later, a frowning Beck and a pissed off Asher come walking out. He doesn't say a single word on the fifteen-minute ride to the apartment;

hell, I'm pretty sure he passed out the second I started driving.

****

After leaving Beck, I make my way over to the apartment to help Chelcie get unpacked. It doesn't take long to get her settled in, and in reality, I'm not sure she even really needed me there. All of the furniture is staying and we have already moved all of my clothing and personal items over to Beck's, my new home. Ash throws himself on the couch the second we walked in the door. Chelcie looks horrified that he's here, but when his light snoring starts echoing around the room, she calms down.

Chelc being tired makes it easy to just do as little as possible, but we still manage to get a few hours of work in before we call it quits for the day.

Before I leave the spare bedroom that I've had set up as an office, I turn and address the giant elephant that's currently passed out on the couch. "Think about what I said, okay?" I give her a quick hug, hoping that she will at least think about it. I just know that deep down, Asher needs this. I don't know him well enough to know for sure, but I know for me, knowing that Coop is still around in anyway helps the pain.

"I promise I'll think about it. Will you... will you let me know how he's doing? Just keep me updated?" She doesn't meet my eyes, which isn't like her at all.

"Sure thing and you call if you need anything. Maddox is just a few floors up, so if you get freaked or anything, just call him. I know he comes across all broody and moody, but he's one of the best to have by your side."

I can tell she isn't in the mood for me to stick around, so after a quick goodbye, I shake Ash awake, and we head out. Even though I didn't live here that long, it's still hard to leave the one place that I've thought of as my sanctuary. I wave at the doorman and head out to my car, grabbing my phone to call Beck before I head home.

Home.

My home with Beck.

As in, my house that I share with the man I love.

I've got the biggest smile on my face when he picks up. Asher just drops into the passenger seat and leans his head against the window. Still silent.

"Hey," He growls into the phone.

I shiver when I hear his voice. There really is no way to describe how that man sets me on fire.

"Hey, you. I'm leaving the apartment now. I'm going to stop by the store before I head home. I figured I would make that stuffed chicken that you love so much for dinner tonight, and I have a few things to pick up anyway. Is there anything you want me to grab?"

"No, Wildcat. All I need is you."

"Is Maddox still over?"

"Actually, we're not there. He needed me to check something on the computers at the office, so I ran down here real quick. I should be right behind you after I finish with all of this." He sounds so stressed. With everything he's been dealing with, I'm not surprised. Not only losing Coop, but now, Emmy. Work, worrying about me, and not knowing who the hell attacked me is eating him hard. We haven't heard anything since I shot Adam. For all we know, that asshole is done with us, but Beck won't let it go.

"Emmy?" I ask, because really there isn't any need to say anything else. He knows I'm going to worry about her. That's why he didn't want me to know.

"Yeah, Emmy… I'll fill you in later, but according to her letter, she's not coming back. She's going to stay with a friend or some shit in Florida. There's more, but I'll tell you when I get home."

There's that word again. *Home.* God, that feels good.

"Promise me that you'll tell me, Beck. I need to know what's going on, or I'll never stop worrying about her."

"I know. I didn't mean to keep it from you earlier. I just worry about you, Dee. You can't blame me there. With all this shit swirling around, I just need to protect you. I can't explain it any better than that. I need to protect you, even if it's from your own mind."

How can I be upset when he puts it like that?

"I understand, I do, but I'm a lot stronger than you think. I love you for wanting to make sure that I'm okay.

294

Just don't shut me out. If things start to get too much, I promise to let you know."

"Yeah, you sure are. Fuck, I'm so proud of you." I can hear the smile in his voice, and it matches the one on my face.

I never thought it would feel so good to let *me* be free from all the webs I was trapped in. Being loved by John Beckett is the best feeling in the world.

We finish up our call, and I pull out of the parking garage. With a smile on my face, I hurry to finish my errands so I can get home and into my man's arms.

CHAPTER 30
Dee

"Ash?" I'm half-tempted to leave his ass sitting in my car. Hell, I've been sitting here for the last ten minutes attempting to get him up. If it weren't for the awkward angle that his head has fallen, I would just leave his ass here. Well, that and I'm pretty sure he still smells like a bar and sex. Not a pleasant combination when you're stuck in a car together.

"ASHER!"

There... I see a twitch this time.

"Seriously!" I sigh in frustration, "Asher James Cooper, wake the hell up and get out of my car!"

He peeks one dark blue eye open and just glares at me.

"Please?" I whine. His lips twitch slightly, and I let out the breath I'm holding. For the first time in two weeks, his lips have tipped up from the frown that has taken up a permanent residence on his handsome face.

"Next time, you don't have to scream so loud." He opens the door and unfolds his large body from my car. I expect him to just start trudging up the path to the front door, but he turns and walks to the trunk. He stands there for a few minutes, looking around. Even in his hangover and grief, he still seems to be keeping alert. Or at least he's trying to.

I shake my head and climb out, walk around the car, and reach to pull the groceries from the trunk. Asher's large paw crosses in front of me, and just scoops the massive amounts of groceries up. I watch him walk into the house, and I hear the sounds of him deactivating the alarm before I realize he has left me one bag and the milk. Seriously? That man was passed out two seconds ago, and now, he's heaving my massive amounts of groceries like it's nothing.

Not even attempting to understand how the hell he's managing, I start to walk up the path. Even with the small load that he left for me to carry, I still have my arms full between my purse, briefcase, and groceries. My phone starts ringing in my back pocket as I walk over the threshold and into the house.

Maybe if I hadn't have been so distracted listening to *Love Sex Magic*, the ringtone Beck set for when he calls, I might have noticed how still the house is.

I don't even have two feet inside the house when I stop dead; everything I am carrying falls to the floor. I feel the milk explode and splash against my legs, but I can't move. I just stand here, looking into the ice cold eyes of the man who beat me, and then left me for dead.

I should be worried about myself right now, but the only thing I can think of is Asher. He came in before me! He should be right here. Even knowing he isn't anywhere near fighting form, he should be right here!

Oh, God, please, let him be okay!

"Hello, Denise. It was so sweet of you to leave the bodyguard detail to just the drunk for once. You, my dear, are a hard woman to get alone these days." He laughs, but he sounds so mechanical, like he isn't used to ever laughing so he doesn't know how to make it believable.

I just stand there gaping at him, struggling to battle the talons of fear trying to sink into my skin, and keeping me frozen in place. When he moves to take a step towards me, I finally snap out of my daze.

No, just fucking no! I'm so sick of everyone trying to take my happiness from me. This is going to end now, no matter what!

"Oh, little Dee, I had so hoped you would behave like the last time we were together."

I jump when he moves to grab me again and when he slips on the milk spilt all over the floor, I take off through the foyer and down the hall. I look in the doorways that I pass before hitting the living room. No Asher in sight. It isn't until I skid into the kitchen that I see him on the floor in front of the fridge. I use the second it takes to make sure his chest is rising to rip my heels off and move behind the breakfast bar. I stand there with both my heels in my hand and wait, staring at the hallway that I can hear him coming down.

"Dee! Where did you go, little girl?"

Goddammit, even his voice is terrifying.

"You had to be a stupid cunt about this, didn't you?" He walks into the kitchen, and I stand in front of Asher's prone form, guarding him with all I had time to grab… my four-inch heels. I chance a look at the knife block, but it's too far for me to reach without having this fucknut get to me.

"What do you want?! I don't have your money, you sick fuck! Adam is gone, so what?!" I'm spitting mad, and thankfully the fear I first felt is gone. I'm not letting him win. I hear Asher groan, but I don't look down. It's only going to take a second of me taking my focus off of this guy before I lose my advantage.

He stands before me with his face hard and his hands clenched. Once again, he's dressed in all black, but this time, he's not hiding his face. It's quite shocking how handsome he is. His skin is tan, hair thick and black, and those eyes... his eyes are not what you see in a man you would approach at the bar. Instead, his eyes reflect the soul of the devil. I shiver just thinking about all the evil swimming in those pale blue depths.

He starts to step closer to me, but before he can complete the move, I scream and chuck one of my shoes at him, nailing him right in the middle of his forehead. If I weren't so worried about his reaction, I would laugh at the picture it made. My bright yellow shoe sails across the room, the heel hits his head, and snaps off from the rest of the shoe with the force of my throw.

"You bitch! If I didn't think it would cause more trouble than it's worth, I would snap your fucking neck in two for that shit." He wipes the blood running down into his eyes away before narrowing them at me. "Consider that your last warning. Don't fuck with me."

I laugh. Really... don't fuck with him? Not only have his own hands hurt me, but because of the shit he threw into my lap, we lost Coop. I plan on fucking with him hard.

His eyes narrow even further, and he goes to take another step, but I fling my other shoe at him. He ducks easily, but before I can move, he lunges and grabs me by my waist. I try to fight, but his strength makes it impossible. I'm just not strong enough, no matter how much I struggle. He swings me around until my back is pressed against his hard chest. I start panting when I realize he has the control now.

"You little bitch," he growls, and I close my eyes tight, trying to keep my body from shutting down. "I'm going to say what I came to tell you, and then I'm going to have some fun. No one makes me fucking bleed without paying the price."

I try to get free, but he still has his arms wrapped tightly around my body, pinning my arms to my sides so that I couldn't get an inch if I wanted to. I attempt to kick my legs, but he backs his body against the wall for support and folds one of his legs over both of mine.

Fuck!

"Listen closely, and make sure you actually hear what I have to say. My employer is very pleased that you took care of the whole Adam situation, saved us the trouble of putting a bullet through his head. Unfortunately, that still leaves the unsettled debt, but he's willing to take the fact that you so kindly sacrificed one of your own in place of a monetary payment. Such a shame about your little friend, but the blood he spilled is good enough for my boss. One less person digging in his business. Now, here's your little warning. Call off your mutts before someone else gets hurt. I know you would hate to see your boyfriend with bullet holes through his body, hmm?"

His warm breath against my neck makes me gag. My skin crawls where he's caressing my neck. When he keeps talking about Coop, talking about his life as if it meant nothing, I want to kill him. If he wanted me to submit, he's going to be sadly mistaken. Every word out of his mouth fuels the rage burning inside of me.

"Do you understand, little bitch?" His hand tightens against my neck when I take too long to answer him, and for once, there is not an ounce of fear.

"Yes." I ground out the word, my chest heaving, and my mouth watering to fight.

"Perfect. Now, let's have some fun."

He lightens his hold; I have the brief flash of hope, until I feel his hand painfully cup my crotch. That's all it takes for my body to go rock solid and the fear to invade again. It's like Brandon all over again.

"Did the little bitch decide to stop playing so hard to get? Going to take it like a good whore?" He brings his hand up and grips my waistband before giving a hard tug and tossing my body on the floor.

The biting pain of my head hitting something solid seems to clear the fear that has begun to fog my mind. I look up at this nameless man, and all the things I wish I had done to Brandon come rushing to the surface.

"NO! Not this time!" I rush to my feet and charge at him. My nails scratch and claw at his face. My feet, legs, knees, anything that can make purchase, slam into his body. He grunts and blocks what he can, but I have the benefit of catching him unexpectedly. He never thought I would fight, but I have too much to lose to lie down and let him win. "You motherfucking fucker!"

I start moving as quick and as powerfully as I can, slamming into him with every limb. By the time he finally manages to push me roughly off of him, I'm breathing heavy and covered in blood. His blood. I let a smile curve my lips up when I think about how good it feels to fight. I'm not just fighting for Asher's life and my own. No, I'm fighting for everything that this man and his *employer* have taken from us.

This is for Coop.

That's the last thing to filter through my rage before I pick myself up and throw my body against his again. He manages a few hits, but he has nothing against me now. I have too much to lose, and too much keeping me fighting. My violent fury is almost a living, breathing thing.

I push hard against his chest, kick up and slam my foot into his crotch, and watch with satisfaction when he crashes against the floor. Right when I'm about to kick again and collide with his head, I'm jerked back. I can't focus around the blood thirst. I want to kill that fucker with my own hands. Panting roughly, I finally place the scent that is surrounding me.

Beck.

My Beck is here.

"I've got you, Wildcat."

And just like that, I sag against him and the fight drains from my body.

CHAPTER 31
Beck

There are no words to describe how I feel when I walk up to my house and see the door wide open, Dee's stuff mixed with a pool of milk, and the sounds of a fight coming from inside my house. I pull my gun from the holster at my side and start to step over the mess at my front door.

For as long as I live, I will never forget rushing through my house and finding my wildcat fighting with everything that she has in her against a man almost twice her size. I don't even know what she's saying; it's all coming out in garbled, unrecognizable words. Before I can reach her, she brings her leg back and slams his crotch with one hell of a kick. She goes to kick him again, but I hook her by her waist and pull her to my body. The sense of relief I feel when her body is next to mine is unimaginable.

She is safe.

She is fighting.

And I'm going to kill this motherfucker!

"I've got you, Wildcat."

Her body relaxes against mine. The adrenaline, the fight, falls from her body.

"I've got you." I whisper again.

"Oh, God," she sobs. "Asher!" She pulls herself from my hold, and I watch her run behind the bar and drop to the floor. I don't have time to ask her if he's okay, because I see this motherfucker that was trying to hurt my woman start to stand.

"I don't fucking think so." I don't move my gun from his head when I call over my shoulder for Dee to call 911. "Who THE FUCK are you?"

He doesn't move a muscle. Nothing, but his eyes narrow.

"I won't ask you again. You came into my house, you touched MY woman, and I don't even know what the hell you did to my friend. It won't be hard to put a goddamn bullet through your fucking skull and work that in my favor, so do not fucking try me. Who. Are. You?"

His smile grows before he speaks "Nico Slater. Your woman is fucking delicious."

He licks his lips and I don't even have to think twice. I let off a round and smile when he is thrown back with the force of the bullet slamming into his shoulder.

"Don't fuck with me." I walk over to his withering body and stand over him, "Who do you work for?"

His lips press tightly and he looks away with a grimace.

"Answer me!"

He doesn't say a word so I bring my booted foot up and press against his bleeding shoulder. The howl he lets out in pain brings a smile to my face.

I lean down and press my gun against his forehead. "Who. Do. You. Work. For?" With each word I speak, I tap his head with the barrel of my gun. He might be a tough little shit, but there isn't anything more terrifying than having a loaded gun pointed at your head.

"Dominic Murphy."

The fuck he says?

"You're kidding?"

He shakes his head and groans when I press harder against his shoulder. Dom Murphy has been on our radar since we set up Corps Security. It's no secret that he has his hands in just about everything dirty that can be found in the South East. Especially Atlanta, but there has never been one single thread to connect him to anything. He's essentially a ghost with little pissants running the show for him while he sits back like a king.

"You might as well kill me. I'm as good as dead anyway."

"I wouldn't give you the satisfaction, you sick fuck." I pull my empty hand back and land a punch to his temple that has his eyes rolling back in his head. Out like a light.

Pushing my gun back into my holster, I stalk to where Dee is sitting on the floor with Asher's head in her lap. She's just running her hand through his hair and whispering softly to him. His eyes aren't open, but I can tell he's awake.

"One second, Baby." I rush out of the kitchen to the garage, grab the rope off one of the shelves, and making quick work getting back inside to tightly secure this fucker Nico. He doesn't even flinch when I throw his bound body against the wall.

Turning, I rush back to Dee's side. "Are you okay?" I check her over, making sure there isn't anything pressing.

"I'm fine. I'm fine."

She looks up, and when I meet her eyes, I realize that she's right. She's obviously shaken up, but there isn't anything else behind her eyes other than relief.

"I'm really okay, Beck. A little scared, a whole lot shaken up, but I wasn't going to let that asshole win."

"You did good, damn good. Fuck, Dee, I think you took ten years off my life when I came in and saw you going head-to-head with that guy!"

Asher makes a noise and opens his eyes. "Would you two shut up? My head hurts. I'm never drinking again."

It doesn't take long before the sounds of sirens start to echo through the air. Asher's already standing and threatening to kill Nico, who is still passed out against the wall.

"That asshole sucker punched me. Didn't even have the balls to take me out like a man. No! He just waited until I had my back turned and got me. Let me at him!"

At one point, I have to push him out of the room because he won't stop barking at the officers to turn around and let him finish what was started.

"Calm down, Ash. He doesn't deserve a quick death. Let him get his ass in prison and make some Big Dick Don happy to have a new little bitch."

His eyes heat, and the wickedness that is usually present is back with a blinding force. For the first time since Coop's death, I can see a little of the old Asher coming back. It's not going to be an easy battle, but he's going to be all right.

It takes a while to finish answering all the questions, but with Dee tucked to my side, unharmed, we settle in. The detectives don't even bat an eye when I explain why Nico has a bullet fired from my gun in his shoulder. However, when they find out that Dee is the reason he looks like he just got the shit beat out of him, there isn't a single person that doesn't smile at that.

Nico Slater has warrants out for his arrest in four surrounding states. He's a known drug dealer, a suspected enforcer, and wanted for the murders of numerous individuals. He's been a ghost to the authorities for the last three years, and there is no doubt in my mind that he will be going away for a long time.

When Dee repeats his message to the detective, the energy in the room goes electric. I don't have to look to know exactly why. I can hear Asher panting, his emotions almost too much to control. Luckily, we now have the name of the motherfucker who put all of this in motion, and if I know Asher Cooper as well as I think I do, there isn't going to be anything that can stop him from avenging his brother's death.

Six hours later, the house is empty of all emergency responders, the milk cleaned from the entryway, and all other messes are gone. The house once again looks like it did before the hellish afternoon. The only difference is that the heavy feeling of grief and heartache is starting to thin. Don't get me wrong. I miss Coop more and more every day, but knowing that we're one step closer to bringing those responsible down, makes that pain just slightly more bearable.

For once, Asher isn't passed out drunk, but he's locked in my office looking up everything he can on Dominic Murphy. I'm sure the day will come when we have to fight again, but for today, for once in the last few months, the good guys win.

After shutting the house down, I make my way upstairs with one thought in mind... taking my woman in my arms and reminding her just how much I love her. It's been a long damn road, but the woman waiting for me in *our* bedroom doesn't hold a single thread of those ropes that have been holding her back and tying her down. No, not my wildcat. She's back, and she's finally, fucking finally mine.

EPILOGUE
Dee

(One Month Later)

I had my last appointment with Dr. Maxwell today. It feels beyond liberating to know that I have not only hit rock bottom, but have also fought to overcome. Even with all the struggles along the way, I'm finally in control of my own happiness. No, I haven't just overcome... I'm flying higher than I ever thought possible. I've embraced the love I never thought existed, and I've conquered each and every roadblock that has held me back.

Things with Izzy and Greg didn't immediately go back to normal. They both held some guilt about everything that happened to me. I kept telling them that they shouldn't feel guilty about something they didn't know about. I didn't want them to know, so I played the part to make sure that they didn't.

Things lately have been perfect. We're back to the friendship that we had from day one.

Not everything is perfect, though. Chelcie has finally agreed to tell Asher. Since Asher started looking into Dominic Murphy, he's been channeling all of his pain over losing Coop into a new unhealthy obsession. We all want the people that are responsible for Coop's death to be dealt with, but Asher isn't able to do anything else. He eats, sleeps, and breathes vengeance, and I know

I'm not the only one that's worried about how he's coping with things. Or not coping. So, after a long talk with Chelcie she has decided that maybe if he knows about her pregnancy, he will be able to focus on the positive things left from Coop. It's a stretch, but at this point, it's all we have.

They've grown closer over the last few weeks. Since selling the North Carolina branch, I've had a lot of my time freed up. I have a few more people here, and taken a step back to a less active roll. Chelcie, having her time cut in half as well, has taken to helping Asher whenever possible. I've promised Beck that I won't stick my nose in their business, so I can only hope she knows what she's doing, and pray she doesn't get hurt in the end.

Coop being gone is something that we notice more and more every day. It's hard to fill the void that a personality as strong as his used to fill. I know for a fact, that as long as I live, there will never be another person like Zeke Cooper. The guys have had a photo of Coop in all his big grinning glory framed and it is one of the main focal points when you walk into Corps Security. It's pure Coop... big, smiling, and the twinkle of mischief shining from his beautiful blue eyes. Underneath the picture, a simple quote is engraved into the frame. 'Tomorrow is never a guarantee; live life to the fullest and never stop smiling.' He was taken from us before we were ready, but he lived his life unapologetically full, and I know somewhere up there, he's flirting with angels and watching over each one of us.

The only part of the last six weeks that's unsettled is Emmy. God, Emmy. She's hurting, and she's hurting bad, but she's also running. I remember Beck sitting me down after all that Nico garbage went down, and he explained to me why he wasn't home.

He said that Emmy had left a letter resigning from her position at Corps Security, effective immediately. She didn't leave details on where she was going, but did say that it was just too hard to stay, knowing that Coop was dead because he took a bullet meant for her. She didn't need to be here, but he did. The guilt and blame that she was carrying was unimaginable. Beck had gone to the office to send Maddox the location her GPS was picking up. Much to my shock, Maddox had placed a tracking device on her car almost a year ago, along with one in her purse, and he keeps her phone tracked. After explaining all of that to me, he dropped the bomb that Maddox was taking a leave of absence to 'get my girl and bring her home.' Yeah, I was beyond shocked that Maddox openly claimed Emmy. Between Coop's death and Emmy's running, something was awakened inside of Maddox. The last call Beck got from him was three nights ago, and he was no closer to getting her home.

My heart broke for Emmy, but I had a feeling that, regardless of what happens, they have a climb ahead of them. After what I saw at Cohen's party a few months ago, I have no doubt that the demons he's fighting are all-consuming. Even if he manages to get her home, there is a lot of healing needed. Not saying that Emmy isn't less important than Maddox, but something tells me that the scars he has are far deeper than anyone could imagine.

****

I pull into the parking lot of the complex where my office, Corps Security, and Sway's salon are all located. My door is a good four businesses down from the boys, but theirs sits right next to Sway's.

After Coop's funeral, I helped Sway extend the sidewalk of gold glitter, to extend all the way down to my door. I wanted a piece of that when I went to work. It's silly, gaudy, and sometimes obnoxious, but it's our thing. The other business owners love it, but then again, it's really hard not to love anything that Sway does.

I have just stepped out of the car when I notice Sway through the window of his salon. He's waving like he normally does, loudly. I laugh to myself and walk his way. By the time I get to the sidewalk, he's already thrown the door to the salon open and is bouncing on his purple four-inch heels in anticipation. I love this man.

"Dee! My sweet, beautiful Dee! When are you going to let me have at your marvelous shoe collection! I must have those two-toned Chanel knot-shaped pumps! Don't think I didn't notice them, you sneaky little devil! You went shopping without Sway, and oh, my little diva, that is just not okay!" He pauses, I'm sure for dramatic effect, before continuing. "And that outfit! Spin, spin!" He brings one of his large hands off his hips long enough to spin his finger in a circle. "You have the perfect outfit. Oh Darlin', it is to die for! I could just take a bite out of your booty. You must tell me your secrets."

He's right. I look damn good, but then again, I chose this outfit for my man today. I've got on one of my favorite dresses. The light pink color looks amazing against my tan, and the hemline hits mid-thigh, covering just enough leg that Beck won't flip his shit, but leaving the rest of my long legs bare. I know he has a weakness for my legs; he's never shy about reminding me... usually when they are wrapped around his waist. The bandage style dress is as skintight as possible without looking trashy, hugs my figure, and pushes my breasts up. The bust is a weave of black and pink lines that make my already generous chest look even bigger. Two straps hug my shoulders and wrap around the top of my biceps. I've finished the look with my five-inch black heels.

I laugh, and twirl until Sway stops moving his finger. He's got the biggest grin on his face. "You are something else! I know what you're up to. You're going to seduce that fine hunk of yours. Don't think I don't know this. Good Lord was he looking edible today. Walking sex, I'm telling you. That man is a walking, talking orgasm."

I throw my head back and laugh because he isn't wrong. Beck is *that* good-looking. "Sway, what did I tell you about fantasizing about my man?"

He cocks his hip to the side, tosses his blond hair over his shoulder, and rolls his eyes. "Then you should put a bag over his head." He pauses and seems to space out for a second. I don't even bother opening my mouth because I know he isn't done. "Better yet, you're going to need to start stuffing his clothes... making him look good and thick, so no one will look at him." He laughs before pulling me into a hug. I wrap my arms around his thick waist and hug him back.

"You're a mess, Sway, but I love you." I press my cheek against his silk blouse and enjoy the moment. Sway can be a bit much for anyone, but his heart is pure gold.

He pulls back and his face gets serious for a second. He looks both ways before motioning me to lean closer. "Have you seen him yet?"

"Have I seen who? Beck?" I honestly have no clue who he is talking about. I know Axel, Greg, and Beck are in today. Asher is at the house working from Beck's office, and Maddox is still… well, Maddox isn't here. I take a second to really look at Sway and notice the excitement written all over his face. Good Lord, he looks like he's about to pop.

He leans in, moves my long brown hair off my shoulder, and whispers in my ear, "The new one. Oh my gawd! My senses tell me there is *finally* hope for one of those boys. My team, Dee. Do you hear me? This one is all over team rainbow, I can tell!" By the time he finishes 'whispering', he might as well have just yelled that out loud.

I pull back and look at him. I had no idea there was a new guy. Last I heard from Beck, they were just going to hire a temp to take Emmy's spot until she came back.

"You've got me, Sway. I have no idea, but I guess I'll find out soon."

He doesn't even give me a chance. He opens the door to his Salon and yells to Brandy, the adorable pixie like receptionist, that he's going next door to ogle the hunks. She laughs, clearly used to this from Sway, and waves him off.

"Does this mean you're coming with me?"

He doesn't answer, laces our hands together, and all but pulls me to the door of Corps Security. The glass is tinted so we can't see in, but that doesn't stop Sway from vibrating his excitement.

"Would you calm down? You're going to jerk my arm right off my body."

He doesn't respond, but the second I open the door, he rushes in, pulling me with him.

I smile at Coop's portrait before my eyes sweep over to Emmy's desk. I've been so used to hearing her sweet voice over the years that the very masculine voice echoing through the room takes me off guard. When I look over and see just what has Sway in knots, I can almost understand his ridiculous behavior.

"See what I mean? Gorgeous." He doesn't even try to keep his voice down, and the object of his eyes looks right at him with a large smile.

What the hell am I watching right now? This man is most definitely gorgeous. His blond hair is perfectly styled, not a single piece out of place. His face is almost too perfect... high cheekbones, strong jaw, big smile and perfectly white teeth. I can't tell from where I'm standing, but his eyes almost look violet. His body is partially hidden by the desk, but from what I can tell, the rest is just as good as his face... strong shoulders, and trim, muscular chest.

And the best part, he hasn't even taken his eyes off Sway once. Hell, I might as well not even be in the room. Oh my God! I want to jump up and clap my hands like a mad person. I feel like I'm watching that matchmaker show play out right in front of me.

He finishes up his call, and places the receiver down lightly, and turns his eyes back to Sway with a smile. "Dilbert. It's great to see you again."

Dilbert?! There are only three people I know that call him that. His mother, Greg when he's annoyed, and Cohen... constantly.

"Davey."

I stand here with my jaw dropped and watch as Sway walks over to *Davey*. Neither one of them have stopped smiling. Who knows how long I'm here just taking it all in. When a warm arm wraps around me. I jump, but when Beck's delicious scent washes over me, I smile just as big as the two love birds at the front desk.

I turn, wrap my arms around his neck, and press my lips to his for a quick, but no less toe-curling kiss. When I fall back on my heels and look into his eyes, so full of love, my smile grows so large it hurts.

"Hey," I whisper against his lips.

"Hey, back." His smile is just as panty melting as it was the first time I saw him and I can't help but think how lucky I am that this perfect man never gave up on me.

"I've got a present for you."

His smile grows wicked and his eyes darken. He knows exactly what it means when I surprise him at work with a present.

I run my hands down the thick-corded muscles in his arm, and grab one of his hands, spinning on my heels I start to walk. I hear him groan and turn around to see his eyes on my ass. "Eyes up, John Beckett. You don't want to scare the children." I laugh and point over to Sway and Davey. They don't even notice us, but Beck narrows his eyes when he sees Sway.

"Sway! I told you to stop coming over here and getting your drool all over the counter! Let David do his job."

Sway laughs and waves him off, and Davey/David blushes. Oh wow, Sway so called it. I can't wait to see how that plays out.

Beck takes the lead and starts stomping down the hall. Whether he's impatient to get me in his office, or he's frustrated with Sway's normal antics, who cares? He's taking me where I want to be, and I could care less how fast I have to run to keep up with him.

When we walk into his office, he slams the door and clicks the lock with a loud pop. His body crushes against mine before I even have a chance to turn completely. His hands go right to my ass, and his fingers dig in. I open my mouth when I feel his tongue lick across my bottom lip, begging for access.

"God, I missed you," I moan against his lips before crushing my mouth back to his. Our tongues slide and curl together in a kiss so demanding our teeth knock together, and our breathing becomes rapid in seconds.

"Only been two hours…" He doesn't finish, just digs his fingers in deeper, and lifts me off the floor. I wrap my legs around his waist, run my hand up his neck until I can push my fingers through his soft hair, and palm his cheek with my other hand.

We continue to kiss until he puts my ass down on his desk, forcing my legs and arms to fall from his body when he steps back.

"Tease," I whine when he doesn't make a move to come back to me.

"Oh, hell, no. There is no way you're going to call me a tease when you come in here looking like that. Good God, Dee. I almost tore that dress from your body and took you right there in front of Sway and David." He adjusts his pants that are doing a poor job of hiding his large bulge.

"Well, aren't you lucky your willpower is stronger than mine." I jump off the desk, grab the package I need out of my purse, and push him back until he falls onto the couch against the wall. "Sit and shut up." I undo his belt, unbutton his slacks, and slowly pull the zipper down. When his rock-hard cock springs out, I raise my brow in question.

"With you around, do you really think I bother anymore with any unnecessary restrictions?"

His smartass tone dies when I wrap one of my hands around his thick length. I stroke him a few times, rubbing my thumb through the drop of come beaded at the top, enjoying the velvety softness of his dick. My mouth waters, and I can tell by the expression on his face that he is more than ready for my mouth.

I pull my hand away and want to laugh when he groans. When I bring the package from my purse into his line of sight, he tries to jump up. I push down on his hips and give him one wet lick across his swollen head. His head drops back and bangs against the wall. I rip open the package and tip a small amount in my mouth, enjoying the strawberry flavor and the sizzle against my tongue. I wait until he picks his head up and locks eyes with mine before I lower my mouth to his dick and open wide. I use my tongue and saliva to move the Pop Rocks around in my mouth, making sure that the soft pops bounce off his sensitive skin. The first one that sizzles and pops in my mouth causes his body to stiffen before his fingers push into my hair almost painfully. I pause, waiting to see if he's going to pull me off, but when his hips start to rock slightly, that's all the encouragement I need.

Slowly and carefully, I keep taking his dick in my mouth, pausing a few times to put more Pop Rocks in my mouth. With each sizzle and pop against his shaft, he moans loudly, and his fingers constrict in my hair.

"Fuck, Dee." He breathes. "God... damn..."

I bring my hand up and circle my fist around him, pumping in turn with my mouth. My tongue swirls around his thick head every time I bring my head up, and wraps it around his shaft with every slide down. I can tell he's getting closer, so I drop the candy on the floor, and bring my other hand up to caress his balls. He doesn't miss a beat. His hips rock with my mouth, and my hums of excitement dance with his grunts and groans.

"Dee, if you don't want me to come in your mouth, then back off. Now, Baby."

I take him deeper, until I have to relax my throat to pull him even deeper. I swallow with my lips open wide, and the tip of his dick as deep as I can get it. When he feels my throat close around him, he goes solid and breathes my name.

"Deeeee…"

I keep milking him until the last tremble quivers through his body, and then unlatch my mouth with a pop. I lean back, rest my ass on my heels, and smile up at his flushed face.

"Sorry, Baby, I didn't think to bring you lunch, but now that I got mine, I can run out and get you something." I smile as innocently as I can before he pushes his body off the couch and knocks me to the floor in a fit of laughter.

"You, my wildcat, are crazy. Where in the hell did you hear about that?"

I'm not sure if he even cares about my answer because he's too busy pushing my dress up my legs.

"No, Beck… that was for you."

His hands still and he looks at me clearly confused.

"You've been working hard, long hours, and I know you're stressed. I just wanted to do something to ease some of that tension you seem to be stuck with."

His forehead falls to mine, and his eyes close.

I run my hands through his hair and wait for him to control himself before lifting my lips, asking for him to let me up. He finally stands and tucks himself back in his pants.

"You better hurry out of that door before I change my mind. I don't like being the only one who gets something out of our lovemaking."

"You perfect man." I shake my head and cup his cheek. "I got plenty out of that, and tonight when you get home, you can return the favor." I lean up and press a soft kiss against his lips, fix my dress, and walk out the door.

Sway is still standing at the front desk when I walk out. I offer him a smile and wave, but he doesn't even turn his head. I just keep going and make my way to the car. I drive all the way home with a big smile on my face.

Beck

How the hell I made it through the rest of the day after Dee left was beyond me. When she walked out the door, I snatched up the package of candy she left on the floor and tucked them in my desk. Hey, you never know.

I make a mental note to find out whoever told her about that little trick so I can thank them. Holy shit, when the first pop bounced against my dick, I didn't know what to think, but that was without a doubt the best blowjob I had ever gotten. Fuck, I came so hard I'm pretty sure I blacked out for a second.

I manage to get about three hours of work done before I can't take it anymore. She had drained me dry, but I'm craving her body now. I say a quick goodbye to Axel and Greg before heading out to the front. I know that Sway left about thirty minutes after Dee did, so at least I won't have to drag him out so poor David can get some work done.

Not that it matters, because there's no way I'm standing in the way of that. David is a nice guy and clearly, he doesn't mind Sway's attention.

"See you later, David." I call over my shoulder. I hear him say something, but my mind is too focused on getting home.

When I pull in the driveway and notice that Asher's truck is gone, my anticipation jumps through the roof. A night alone with Dee? There isn't much that would make me happier.

I sit in my truck for a second and think back to the night before, and my dinner with Dee.

"Do you want to tell me why we had to come all the way into Atlanta? I figured we could just stay home tonight?"

I smiled and shook my head.

"Nope. As much as I love sharing our nights with Asher, I needed some time alone with my girl."

She smiled and took my hand as we walked into the restaurant.

We continued to make small talk and just enjoy each other. These were the times I cherished the most. For so long, we didn't have this, the connection and companionship. The all-consuming love was always there, but now that it's recognized and returned, just being with her made all the stress and worry from work fall from my shoulders.

After paying the check, she smiled and took a bite of her chocolate cake, making me smile when I thought back to the early days that we knew each other, and her ridiculous theory that chocolate was better than sex.

"I love you, you know that?"

She looked up from her plate and smiled.

"Yeah, I know that. And I love you."

Before she could take another bite, I took her fork from her hand and moved her plate out of the way, placing the box I'd had tucked into my jacket in its place.

"What's this? I didn't forget something, did I?" God, she was adorable when she crinkled her brows in confusion.

"Nope, you didn't forget anything. I picked this up about two weeks ago when Izzy came to the office."

Her confusion grew and I reached forward to rub my finger over the wrinkles between her brows.

She opened the long box, and I saw a smile form and the confusion vanished. "How did you know I wanted one of these?" She pulled the necklace out of the box and took a second to take it all in.

Izzy had come into the office almost a month ago, selling some silly locket things. She kept calling them living lockets or some weird shit like that, but when I started looking through it all, the idea popped in my head and I couldn't resist. It was just pure luck that Dee mentioned wanting one of these Origami Owl things.

I watched her face taking in all the charms that I ordered to go inside the locket. She moved the little key attachment I included and looked deeply at the locket. I sat back and ran the checklist over in my mind. The key attached to the necklace was to symbolize her holding the key to my heart, yeah about as corny as it got, but it's the truth. There were the two word charms: faith and love, which she shouldn't need any help figuring out. Then the house charm that represented her making her home with me. The high heel shoe because... well, it's Dee. My smile grew when I thought about the chocolate bar. I knew the exact moment when she hit the last charm in there, a little diamond ring. Her eyes shot up and locked with mine. I took note of her quivering lip and unshed tears before I stood up, and pushed my chair back, and knelt in front of her seat.

I gently tugged the necklace from her grip, brought it around her neck, and latched it. I ran my finger down the chain, around the locket, and flicked the key clipped to the top. When I looked up and met her eyes with a smile, she tried to return it. Pulling her left hand forward with one hand, I pushed the other into my pants pocket and brought the ring out. I'd been carrying this sucker around for the last six weeks, just waiting for the perfect time.

"Since the day I met you, I knew you would be someone worth fighting for. We've been through so much together, and it still feels like our love is brand new. There isn't anything in this world that would make me happier than making you my wife. Dee, Baby, will you marry me?"

Her tears spilled over and her beautiful smile shone through. Her head nodded and through her soft hiccups I heard the best words in the world.

"God, yes!"

I slid the ring on her finger and stood up, pulling her from her chair at the same time, and took her lips in a bruising kiss.

With the other patrons clapping in the background, I kissed my girl, and showed her just how much I love her with one single kiss.

When we finally came up for air, I framed her face in my hands and swiped the tears away with my thumbs. She just stood there, smiling the smile that never failed to bring me to my knees. The smile that was gone for so long, but every day since it'd been back, I thanked my lucky stars.

She thinks I saved her but the truth is, she saved me.

Her love gave me a purpose, a reason, and the strength to stand by her side and fight any war that is thrown our way.

With a smile on my face, I make my way into the house that I share with the woman I love, with every intention of dragging her up to our room and making her mine. All. Night. Long.

~The End~

The problems that Dee faced during the span on Axel, Cage, and her story in Beck are very real and can affect anyone.

For more information on mental illness and suicide prevention please visit: http://www.afsp.org

Acknowledgments:

(An unedited compilation of thank yous)

It's hard for me to even fathom that this is the THIRD book I've written. What an amazing ride. I've been blessed beyond my wildest dreams during this process, and I wouldn't even be here without the help of every single reader that decided to take a chance on my books.

First- Thank you to my family. My husband for dealing with the mess the house becomes when I jump head first into my book world. My kids who deal with mommy talking to herself constantly and not freaking out when I walk you to the bus wearing my sweats and having my hair all over the place.

To the bloggers, reviewers, and every reader that's picked up my books – THANK YOU. When I started 'Axel' I had no expectations, just dreams, and y'all have made them come true.

To my betas, Amber, Angela, Becky, Elle, Danielle, and Debi. I love y'all. It's true. You ladies are hands down the best team ever. You keep me going, tell me when I'm shit, and tell me when I rocked it. With love, of course! I couldn't even imagine what it would be like to write a book without you ladies!

Katie Mac – Don't hate me for not letting you edit these, but come on… you need some surprises! You've opened your arms and welcomed me and my words. I love you hard and your support and love keeps me going when I feel like throwing in the towel. You're the rock behind me and I can't wait to see what the future holds for us.

Brenda- My formatting queen, blog tour master and friend... we've been through some crazy turns together and sitting back now we can laugh at all the crazy that we've been through together. Thank you for everything, and I mean everything, you have done for me.

Meli- Where do I even start with you, girlfriend? It was by chance that we met and you best believe I'm thankful for that day we first messaged each other. Not only do you bend over backwards to make sure I'm happy with everything that you create for me, but you doing it with so much love and care! Even if I pass out too early and leave you in an emotional book mess... I still love you! LOL! I can't wait for future books and the beauty you create.

Toski- Girlfriend, you rock! Thank you so much for taking a few comments and getting me exactly what I wanted! Everyone should have a Toski in their life.

My three musketeers. Angela, Katie and Kelly. I don't know how you girls put up with my crazy. My round the clock messages, talks about zombies, and half naked men pictures. Well, okay, I know how you deal with the men pictures. You girls help keep me calm when I start freaking out and have no issues telling me when I'm acting stupid. True friends that I am so thankful for each day.

To Chelcie- I love you... hardcore, Babe! Thank you for EVERYTHING. You are an incredible friend that I thank God for daily.

To every other single person that I've had the pleasure of meeting and chatting with. The authors that have opened their arms and welcomed me into this world and still love me when I freak out like a fan-crazed idiot.

When it comes down to it... this is for the readers and I LOVE YOU ALL.

CPSIA information can be obtained at www.ICGtesting.com
Printed in the USA
LVOW01s1431100715

445774LV00002B/291/P